A SLICE
OF MURDER

A totally gripping British crime mystery

BRIAN BATTISON

Detective Jim Ashworth Book 8

Originally published as
Mirror Image

Revised edition 2021
Joffe Books, London
www.joffebooks.com

First published by Constable in Great Britain in 1998
as *Mirror Image*

Cover art by Nick Castle

ISBN: 978-1-78931-900-2

To Patty,
for breakfast at Asda, midnight in the rain,
and for being there when it really mattered.

PROLOGUE

The lake was covered with thick grey ice, and warning signs were positioned at intervals around its perimeter. But its glassy surface looked so very tempting, and while parents' backs were turned many a child would place a tentative foot on its forbidden edge.

One small girl, bolder than most, cast furtive glances all around as she edged excitedly towards its centre, all warnings unheeded. She slipped and slithered, joyous giggles bubbling in her throat, and saw too late a network of cracks, like delicate lace, forming at her feet. The ice parted with a dull crunch, and her shriek of surprise caused all who heard to stop dead.

Perhaps a dozen strollers rushed to the lake, but they could only stand helpless at its edge, waiting for the child to reappear from the frozen depths, *willing* her to reappear. But she did not, and the telling silence swiftly galvanised one man into action.

Jerry Arnold, a jobbing builder, a jack-of-all-trades hired by the council to trim back overhanging trees surrounding the lake, now grabbed his steel ladder and extended it to its full length.

'Somebody give me a hand . . . quick,' he screamed in panic. Others crowded around, waiting for orders. 'Okay, now I'm gonna lodge the end of the ladder on to that small island and get across,' he said, his frantic breath fogging the air, 'but I'll need somebody to follow me out and take the girl when I get her.' He started to crawl along the ladder. 'Well, come on, somebody, she's been under there a full minute.'

When, behind him, the ladder dipped and vibrated with the weight of another, Jerry propelled himself forward, his darting eyes alert. The ice crackled and crunched beneath his bulk but it held, and then the hole into which the girl had vanished loomed before him. Jerry glanced left and right but there was no sign of her; he peered into the murky water but could see nothing. He uttered a tiny whimper of despair. And then there was movement on the edge of his vision. He shouted to the man behind that he had found her. She was about a yard away, floundering beneath the ice, weakly beating its underside with her tiny palms.

Desperation brought with it an amazing strength which allowed Jerry to break up the ice — inches thick in places — with each strike of his massive fists. Soon, freezing water lapped beneath him and the child surfaced for a moment, spluttering and choking, only to sink again. He made a grab for her anorak and prepared to heave her up, but the dead weight of her water-logged clothing threatened to pull him into the lake.

Thinking quickly, Jerry slid sideways off the ladder until cold water soaked through the shoulder of his donkey jacket. Then, grabbing a rung and holding on tightly he pulled again, grunting with exertion while the girl struggled and fought within his grasp. She was on the surface, her eyes wide with terror.

'Keep still and you'll be okay,' he said, hurriedly. 'Just keep still and then I can get you onto the ladder and you'll be safe. Okay?'

Her struggles ceased, her expression blank with shock. As quickly as he could, Jerry manoeuvred her onto the make-shift bridge and worked her towards the waiting man.

'Hurry up and get her dried off,' he shouted. 'Get her wrapped in something warm.'

Jerry rested for a moment, pulling in breath; and an ambulance siren could be heard coming closer when he finally started to move towards the bank. His progress was slow, hindered by the numbness that had stolen all feeling from his fingertips.

Then a sudden trembling overtook him and he had to pause. He could so easily have fallen in, become trapped under the ice, his lungs filling with water as he battled to break through it. A light sweat glistened on his forehead and his trembling became a violent ague. He closed his eyes, tried to block out the tormenting images.

And when he opened them again he was looking down at a dead woman. Her face was tinged with blue, her green eyes bulged, and Jerry was too scared even to cry out. He could only stare with ever-increasing revulsion at her long blonde hair that billowed in the undercurrent as the body slowly drifted away.

CHAPTER 1

The face of pathologist Alex Ferguson broke into a welcoming smile as he watched Chief Inspector Jim Ashworth of Bridgetown CID stomp around the lake. The DCI was closely followed by Detective Sergeant Holly Bedford.

'Morning, Jim . . . Holly,' Ferguson called out.

Ashworth responded with a disgruntled, 'Alex.' He had been called away from his *Sunday Telegraph* and the aroma of roasting beef. He was not pleased.

'What have we got?' he growled.

The pathologist sobered. 'Female body. Probably in her thirties.' He jerked a thumb towards a small tent that now housed the corpse. 'She's been strangled, but that's all I can tell you at the moment.'

Holly glanced around the immediate area which had been sealed off with police tape. And she hid a grimace when Ferguson pulled back the flap of the tent and said, 'Take a look.' She stood with Ashworth on the threshold while the pathologist stooped by the body.

'She's almost fully clothed,' he said. 'Only her pants are missing. Can't answer any of the usual questions yet, such as when she was murdered . . .' He glanced up at Ashworth.

'But murdered she was, Jim, unless she waded out into the lake and strangled herself.'

Ashworth stared into the dead woman's face. It was hard to imagine how she might have looked in life; the hands of her killer and the inhospitable water had, between them, destroyed her uniqueness. That face would once have smiled, would once have creased into a look of anger or sadness; but now it resembled a block of marble, the features crudely etched. His stomach lurched and in his mind's eye Ashworth could see his roast beef and Yorkshire pudding being speedily confined to the pedal bin.

'Will you be able to give us time of death after the post-mortem?' he asked.

'I'll be able to make a guess at it, but no more than that.' Ferguson straightened up. 'I can tell you one thing, though — she wasn't killed before the freeze-up. No signs of decomposition, you see. Being under that ice was like being in a freezer. April's a funny time of year for a big freeze-up — don't you think?' he finished in a conversational tone.

'Yes.' Ashworth averted his eyes. 'Let us know the results as soon as you can, then, Alex.' He turned to leave.

'There is one quite interesting feature,' Ferguson said. 'Take a look at this.'

'If I must.' Ashworth crouched down, his expression indicating that he, at least, found little interesting about a dead body. Disturbing, yes, but interesting, never.

'There . . . on the forehead. Do you see it?' Ferguson was pointing to a slight colourless groove that punctured the skin. 'See? It goes right down the nose and over the mouth and chin.'

Ashworth studied the mark which was hardly visible on the pale translucent face. 'Could it have been made by an object the body may have come into contact with while in the water?'

The pathologist was quick to shake his head. 'Definitely not. It's too precise for one thing. See? It goes under the chin and down the neck. And, from the glance I've taken, it continues down the centre of the body to the pubis. And don't be fooled by the appearance; it's not a deep cut, but it would show up very clearly if the body hadn't been immersed in water for some time.'

Ashworth scratched his head and frowned thoughtfully. 'Are you telling me that someone strangled her, stripped her, then cut her from the forehead to the middle and put her clothes back on?'

'No, I don't think so, Jim. The blouse was probably open, and the skirt was as likely as not around her ankles with the missing pants.'

Holly made a face. 'Rather you than me, love, in this weather,' she muttered wryly.

'And there, Jim, lies your first clue,' Ferguson said with a flourish. 'I believe our friend is, or rather *was*, a lady of the night . . . a prostitute.'

Ashworth's frown deepened. 'How do you work that out?'

'Well, look at her clothes, for a start, Jim. With the sort of weather we've been having, who in their right minds would dress like that?'

Ashworth's gaze skimmed over the woman's short leather skirt, her pink halter top. 'Yes,' he said, 'I think you might be right, there.'

'But why would anybody want to do that?' Holly asked. 'The cutting, I mean.'

'Ah,' Ferguson said. 'That's the part of the detective work *you're* paid to do. I'll get the post-mortem started as soon as I can.'

The officers said their goodbyes and wandered towards the ambulance where Jerry Arnold was sitting huddled beneath a thick blanket, a steaming hot drink in his hand.

'Mr Arnold?' Ashworth said.

The man gave a dull nod.

'You're to be thanked for your quick thinking, sir. But for you, we could have two corpses on our hands. I've no doubt you'll be hailed a hero by the local press.'

'Thank you,' he said, smiling briefly.

'We will need to speak to you again,' Ashworth went on, 'so I suggest you give your address to one of my officers and then get off home before you catch *your* death.'

They threaded their way through patrol cars and uniformed officers *en route* to the lake, both lost in their thoughts. Finally, Ashworth said, 'Thanks for turning out, Holly.'

She smiled. She had worked with the indomitable chief inspector for a number of years and was still not used to his old-fashioned courtesy. He would open doors and pull out chairs, and yet had the knack of making a woman feel both feminine *and* equal.

'I had no choice, guv, it's my job.'

'I know, but I do appreciate it. You could have made some excuse.'

'And miss a good body?' She flashed him a grin and dug her hands deep into the pockets of her quilted coat.

As if on cue the body bag was carried from the tent by two mortuary attendants who took it to their waiting vehicle. Ashworth stood with Holly by the lake, both of them watching its slow progress.

'So, guv, we have a girl who's been murdered and marked in some kind of — what? — ritual?'

'By some sort of madman.' He cast a moody glance across the water. 'If Alex is right, and she is a prostitute, it's going to be a devil of a case to solve without any forensic evidence.' He sighed heavily. 'I just hope it's not going to be the second unsolved murder on our files.'

'We solved the other one, guv, you know we did. It's not our fault that a few good citizens of Bridgetown decided to change their stories or failed to testify at the trial. *That's* why the five pieces of scum were acquitted.' She gave him a friendly nudge with her elbow. 'It's not your fault, guv.'

Holly was referring to the murder of Clive Allan, an horrific incident that had attracted nationwide news coverage. Mr Allan, a paraplegic, was travelling in his motorised wheelchair along Bridgetown's main high street one dark winter's afternoon when he became the target of a robbery. Five youths descended upon him, and when Mr Allan attempted to put up a fight they responded with a torrent of kicks and punches. So savage was the beating that Mr Allan suffered a ruptured liver at the scene and all attempts to revive him failed.

The police had had a watertight case against the youths. But then the witness intimidation had begun, and by the time of the trial all had either changed their stories or refused to appear for the prosecution.

A slight sneer distorted Ashworth's face as he recalled the scenes when the youths were acquitted. From within the dock they had jeered and mocked the victim's distraught family, and had merely laughed when rebuked by the judge. Ashworth had taken that personally.

He turned now to Holly, his expression one of defeat. 'That murder's still unsolved on our files, though, isn't it? And will remain so until there's a conviction, which there is not now going to be.'

CHAPTER 2

It was Ashworth's view that ninety per cent of weekday television programmes were utter rubbish, with the weekend offerings only marginally better. Therefore, that evening, he found himself with plenty of time to brood as he fixed his gaze on the flickering screen and allowed his thoughts to wander. As from today his troubled mind had two subjects on which to rest: the Clive Allan murder, and now the body in the lake.

Why would anyone inflict upon their victim a shallow cut from scalp to groin? What could it possibly mean? Already he was convinced that it did mean something, that it was the key to the whole puzzle. If he could find out why it had been done, then catching the murderer might be an altogether simpler prospect. He shifted about in his comfortable armchair.

'You all right, dear?' his wife asked.

'Yes, Sarah,' he grunted.

She gave him a kindly smile. 'Has your stomach settled down since this morning?'

Ashworth glanced up, a sudden thought brightening his features. 'A little, yes, although a glass of malt might be just what's needed to calm it properly. Fancy a sherry?'

Sarah's smile became a grin in the time it took her husband to cross to the drinks cabinet, with Peanuts, their Jack Russell terrier, at his heels. His cure for almost all ailments was one or three measures of malt whisky — and where was the harm in that? Although Sarah Ashworth led a full and active life involving work with the Women's Institute, the Samaritans and various other charities, she doted on her husband, catered for his every need with a zeal that would drive a rampant feminist to distraction.

The bond of love between them was still very strong, and neither had any reason to doubt the other. And yet as Ashworth poured the drinks Sarah found herself pondering, not for the first time, on the unfairness with which the two sexes aged. For some years now her face and figure had borne witness to her advancing years, but the same could not be said for her husband. He was more attractive now, his rugged face more handsome, than in their courting days. Sarah knew that women were still attracted to him. And who could blame them? He was six foot two, thirteen stone, and super fit, thanks to a combination of exercise and a sensible diet. His black hair was greying, it was true, but those silver streaks enhanced rather than detracted from his fine looks.

'Why would anybody do that to someone they'd just murdered?' Ashworth murmured, slicing through Sarah's thoughts.

She picked up the *Sunday Telegraph* and studied the crossword she had been struggling with for most of the day. 'Symbolic?' she suggested. 'Cutting someone in two?'

Ashworth nodded his agreement. 'And it's the symbolic part that bothers me.'

'Perhaps it means something only in the eyes of the murderer.' Sarah accepted a glass of dry sherry and, while Ashworth returned to his seat, she wrote 'Two halves of a whole' beside the crossword and scrutinised it as she would a cryptic clue. 'The news should be on in a minute,' she said, absently.

'Thank the Lord for that,' Ashworth muttered.

* * *

Holly Bedford disliked viewing dead bodies as much as her guv'nor did, but once away from the scene she was able to put the disagreeable duty to the back of her mind. Besides, as she slipped into her bra and pants in the bedroom of her modest semi-detached she had other problems to contend with.

Her main one was lying beneath the lace-trimmed quilt strewn across her crumpled double bed. He was Donald Quinn, a thirty-five-year-old solicitor whom Holly had first met at the Clive Allan murder trial; Quinn had been acting for the defence. Their affair, brought about by the solicitor's almost constant showering upon Holly of gifts and compliments, was but four weeks old and already she was tiring of him.

Holly's libido was perfectly healthy, and it pushed her from one sexual encounter to the next with astonishing speed. She deliberately shunned emotional attachment, however. Having lost her husband, Jason, to leukaemia at the tender age of twenty-three, she was still not ready to lay herself bare to the pleasures and the possible pain of a one-to-one commitment. Recently, though, Donald Quinn had started hinting that his interest in her went beyond sex — hence the problem. The time to say goodbye was fast approaching.

He was smoking a cigarette, his contented gaze centred on her shapely body. 'We were good tonight, I thought.'

Feeling that she had made enough appreciative noises over the last hour, Holly merely nodded. 'Do you want a drink before you go?'

Quinn stretched lazily. 'I was hoping to stay the night.'

Holly smoothed down her pencil-slim black skirt, her back towards him. 'Sorry . . . neighbours,' she said. 'I don't want them thinking I'm a slag.'

'I'm sure they don't.' He was suddenly pensive. 'There's nobody else in your life, is there, Holly?'

She shot him an exasperated look. 'Don't let's go through all that again, Donald . . . please. Okay, I've had a lot of boyfriends — but, so what? I'm a free agent.'

'Trouble is. I get so jealous when I think of you with someone else. I was . . . well . . . I was hoping we could make a go of things.'

'Donald . . .'

Holly sat on the edge of the bed and her spirits sank when she saw his puppy-dog eyes gazing at her with such loving devotion. She was eager to get rid of him, desperate to have the house to herself. Perhaps the final goodbye could wait for another day. Why start an argument now that could last well into the night?

She smiled. 'We'll have that drink, shall we, Donald? I'll pour them while you get dressed.'

* * *

By day he stood in the high street, a large man dressed from head to toe in black. He read aloud from the Bible, promised all that hell and damnation would be theirs unless they repented their wicked sins.

Most of those mingling on the pavements ignored him, while others were wary of meeting the gaze of that ranting giant; but the impression he gave to all of them was one of darkness, of blackness. His plain black suit, its weave bald and shiny at the knees and elbows; his wide-rimmed black hat atop black hair which hung in greasy rats'-tails before merging with a thick bush of black beard.

He stood in the high street yelling the words of the Bible into the milling crowds. But by night he stalked the back streets of Bridgetown where flesh was on sale in seedy public houses and on every street corner. Although tempted, he resisted, most of the time, the urge to buy a girl for five minutes of carnal lust. He merely looked, praying while he did so for God to make him strong, to make him worthy of His love.

Time and again, night after night, the red-light district would pull him back, to long legs beneath tiny skirts, to large breasts beneath skimpy tops. Sometimes the temptation was too strong and he would succumb, but even as he took his pleasure he hated himself and the woman providing it. Tonight was one of those times. After three weeks of abstinence the fire in his loins was raging out of control and he sank once again into the deep pit of sin.

Afterwards he prayed for forgiveness. All the way back to his small basement flat he mouthed silent litanies with a fevered passion, head bent, eyes cast to the ground, unworthy before God. He needed to get off the streets, to hide himself away, and he hastened down the steps to his front door on trembling legs, his key held aloft.

He crept stealthily along the dark passage, hardly daring to breathe for fear of giving himself away. At last he reached his bedroom and was turning the door handle when a shrill cry came from a room on his left.

'Boris? Is that you?'

He took in a long breath and opened the door to that room. A low-wattage bulb lit its interior, created shadows where there should have been none. Its dim glow was hardly bright enough to illuminate the old man lying prone in the antiquated wooden bed. His wizened face was whiter than the pillow on which he rested, his long grey hair and his raised beard were brittle and lacklustre. But his small blue eyes shone in the half-light like polished jewels. And those eyes missed nothing.

'You have been among the whores,' he accused, his Russian accent strong.

'Only to spread the word of our Lord—'

'Liar . . . liar. *Liar*,' the old man shrieked. 'My son is a *liar*—'

'I do not lie, father. Do not call me that name.'

'You do not like it?' The eyes glistened. 'What about *murderer*? Is that a name you do not like? You murdered your mother and your brother. And soon you will murder me. Do you think I don't *know* that, Boris? Do you think I don't know that?'

CHAPTER 3

At some time during the night the bitter freeze relinquished its hold on the Midlands, and by breakfast a thaw had set in with temperatures close to ten degrees centigrade. Fast-melting snow and ice led to a waterlogged road network which, in turn, brought the usual spate of accidents, keeping the uniformed division busy until well after their usual coffee breaks. As a result, tempers at the police station were more than a little frayed.

Chief Inspector Ashworth, tucked away in the CID office, was unaware, however. He had been given Alex Ferguson's post-mortem report on the body in the lake and was now seated at his desk, studying its details with an eagle eye. Every so often he would pause and stare up at the ceiling, lost in thought. And it was during one such interval that Holly came bustling in. She was sharing a joke with a civilian worker called Mark Hartland.

Mark had been brought in a month ago to help deal with the mounting piles of paperwork, leaving the detectives free to fight crime. That was Superintendent Newton's intention, anyway. But as Ashworth viewed the pair through narrowed eyes, listened to their animated whispers, he wondered whether Mark might turn out to be more of a hindrance than a help.

The chief inspector gave a stern cough and tapped the report against his desk in a warning manner. The pair sobered immediately. Mark grabbed a handful of filing and Holly was settling at her desk when the final member of CID breezed in and sat at his computer. Detective Constable Josh Abraham was tall and handsome with steely grey eyes — the very type Holly lusted after, but his homosexuality kept him safely out of her grasp.

Ashworth was about to start the morning's briefing when Police Constable Bobby Adams appeared in the doorway. Bobby had done a short stint in CID, and the fresh-faced officer had been hoping for a recall ever since.

'Ah, good. Come in, Bobby,' Ashworth said. 'I need to have a word with you about Operation Sting.'

Bobby perched on the edge of Holly's desk and gave her a wink. Ashworth held up Ferguson's report. 'First of all, though, give me all that you've got on the dead woman in the lake.'

'It's not much, guv,' Josh said, flicking through his notebook for the relevant page. 'She was known as Natalie — whether that's her real name, I don't know. She *was* a prostitute, and the local girls say she was either from Coventry or Birmingham — she started working Bridgetown when the West Midlands police set up a war on kerb crawlers. She commuted and kept very much to herself, never mentioned her family, never talked about anything much, apparently. Everybody I spoke to seemed to like her well enough. She did have a running dispute with one of the girls, though; it started when Natalie inadvertently muscled in on her patch.'

'Did you get the girl's name?'

'No, guv, nobody would say, and as they were cooperating so well I thought it best not to push too hard.'

'Fair enough,' Ashworth said, scribbling on his blotter. 'It's something we can look into later.'

'She worked the pubs mostly,' Josh went on. 'And she was an open-air girl, but if the weather got too cold it was a back-of-a-car job.'

'And when she was killed it would definitely have been a car job,' Ashworth mused. 'Anything else?'

'Yes, guv, I've left the best till last. More than one of them hinted that Natalie was frightened of Lee Swanson. Again, they refused to elaborate, but I got the impression he had something to do with the feud between Natalie and the other girl — just a feeling I've got, guv, nothing concrete to go on.'

'Isn't it amazing how that young man's name keeps cropping up?' Ashworth said, making another note. 'Holly, what did you come up with?'

She had been despatched with Josh to gain the confidence of the call girls. It had been hoped that they would more readily talk to a female officer, especially one with Holly's down-to-earth approach.

'I think the girls were on the level, guv; if they'd known anything, they would've said. God knows they've got enough to cope with — sexual diseases, the normal drunken violence, pimps . . . If they knew anything about that nutter, I'm sure they'd cough.'

Ashworth sat back and tapped the report. 'Alex Ferguson can't pin-point the time of death. It could have been any time in the last few weeks. The freezing temperatures had kept the body on ice, so to speak. Cause of death was strangulation, and she was dead when she went into the water.' His gaze dropped to the typed pages. 'Alex has been most helpful, as usual, by suggesting that the body probably went into the lake at the start of the freeze-up — any later than that and the killer would have had to break the ice to get her in there.' He glanced up. 'Now, the cut on the body was made by a small, very thin blade. Alex has put "possibly" and then in brackets "definitely" a Stanley knife.' He spread his hands. 'So, what have we got?'

'This is probably a bit far-fetched, guv,' Holly said, 'but a lot of serial killers mark their victims, don't they? It's like leaving their calling card at the scene.'

Ashworth balked at the suggestion. 'With only one body, Holly, we're hardly talking about a serial killer. I'd say it's more likely to be an angry pimp.'

'Can I say something?' Bobby cut in. He blushed. 'Sorry, guv, this is none of my business.'

Holly and Josh shared an amused look, and even Ashworth had to hide a smile. It was commonly known at Bridgetown nick that Bobby was a wealth of knowledge, addicted as he was to postal courses on any subject; and he was forever studying at the reference library, too. Ashworth never joined in the ribbing that went on. He had spotted Bobby's potential from the start, had encouraged and nurtured it, had enjoyed watching it bloom. Although Bobby undoubtedly deserved his nickname, The Professor, Ashworth would never have dreamed of using it.

'Carry on, Bobby, let's hear what you've got to say.'

The constable glanced around shyly. 'It's just that, well, this "angry pimp" idea . . . If that was the case, why cut her like that, when she's already dead? If he'd wanted to underline a warning to his other girls, I reckon the slashing would have been more violent.'

'And what are your thoughts on it, then?'

'How about a nutter who's likely to kill again if we don't catch him?'

Ashworth grinned. 'That's just another way of saying "serial killer", surely?'

'But, guv, I've been reading up on the subject—'

'I know about serial killers myself, Bobby — possibly more than you've gleaned from your books — and it's not a road I'm willing to travel along until more than one body's turned up.' Ashworth rapped his ballpoint pen on the desk. 'Josh, you'd better check for murders of this type in other parts of the country, just to be on the safe side.'

'Already done it, guv.'

The chief inspector fixed him with a look of mock suspicion. 'If you're after my job, Detective Constable Abraham, you can forget it — I'll not be leaving for a while yet.'

'Right, guv,' Josh said, grinning. 'Anyway, I found out that two prostitutes have been murdered in the Reading area, but the incidents aren't linked. Swansea police are currently searching for a hooded bloke who's killed two blonde women and hacked off a handful of their hair to keep as a souvenir. And the body of a West Indian woman was found in a river in Yorkshire, but the husband's already on remand for the murder. No other bodies have been marked like ours anywhere in the UK.'

'Back to you, then, Bobby,' Ashworth said. 'Still think we've got a serial killer on the loose?'

Bobby's smile was one of good-humoured defeat. 'Point taken, guv. And what you said about the pimp is a possibility.'

Ashworth swivelled his gaze. 'Holly, what do you think?'

'You could be right, I suppose.' She sounded doubtful. 'And if that was the case I don't think the girls would talk about it. Some of the city girls coming in are hard cases, they think they've seen it all, and they wouldn't take kindly to being pushed about by country bumpkin pimps.' A frown added to her doubtful look. 'But, guv, we haven't got any really bad boys in that department.'

'There are some up and coming . . . I'm sure of it.' He pushed the report aside. 'Oh, and, Holly, see if you can get the name of that girl our victim fell out with.' He straightened up. 'Well, thank you all for that. It's opened up a few possibilities, if nothing else. By the way, Bobby, I'm recalling you to CID.'

'Oh, thanks, guv.' He grinned widely, and Holly gave his shoulder a congratulatory pat.

'You're to work on Operation Sting initially, but this time I'm hoping to make it permanent. With our increasing workload, we could do with another body.' Ashworth retrieved a bulletin sheet from his desk drawer. 'Now, about Operation Sting — it's on Friday morning, at five a.m. Superintendent Newton will be briefing both uniformed and ourselves before we set off.'

A collective groan sounded at the mention of Newton's name. Ashworth allowed himself a laugh, and then held up a hand.

'I do hope that display of displeasure was directed at the early start rather than at our commanding officer.' He turned

18

in his seat and pointed at a large map of Bridgetown pinned to the wall. 'As you all know, our target is the council estate . . . here. We'll be going into four houses. I'll be leading team number one; Holly, you'll take team two, Josh, team three, and Bobby, you'll have team four. You all know the drill — we knock to announce ourselves and then go in there fast and hard before they have time to wash any illegal substances down the toilet.' He gazed at their faces, Holly's in particular. 'Do not use more force than is necessary but then, I don't have to tell you that . . . do I, Holly?' She shook her head, grinning. 'We're looking for stolen property, drugs, and anything that could be described as an offensive weapon.'

'Excuse me, sir . . .' Mark Hartland stood before Ashworth's desk, his arms laden with files. 'I'll just take this lot down to the collator's office. Be about five minutes.'

'Good man.'

Ashworth stared grimly at the notes on his blotter. He knew someone who was very fond of carrying and using a Stanley knife. And, come Friday morning, he would be the first to go through his front door.

CHAPTER 4

Friday morning had hardly dawned when the police van carrying Ashworth and six uniformed officers pulled into Kirkstone Crescent. Muddy spray splashed out from under its wheels as the van cornered sharply and the officers inside prepared to spring the trap.

'Okay, lads, this is it,' Ashworth said. 'Don't forget, we go in fast and hard.'

They piled out of the back doors the moment the van came to a silent halt outside number six. Their shoes splashed through deep puddles, and a light but persistent rain beat against their faces as they ran. Ashworth was the first to reach the front gate, and in one fluent movement he lifted the latch and went through. Moments later, his large fist was banging on the front door.

'Open up — police,' he called. Seconds passed and he called again.

'Sir, the light's just gone on in the front bedroom,' PC Gordon Bennett shouted from the gate.

'Right, we're going in.'

Ashworth motioned to the officer carrying the battering ram and ordered him to smash the lock. One swinging blow was enough to send the door flying inwards and then the hall was alive with blue uniforms. Ashworth took the stairs two at a time and strode briskly along the landing towards the front bedroom, its door slightly ajar.

With the lightest of shoves the door swung open, its hinges creaking, and the stink of tobacco billowed out. Ashworth was unable to keep the look of disgust from his face as he stared at Lee Swanson. The nineteen-year-old was sitting up in bed, a cigarette dangling from his sneering lips.

'That's gonna cost you a new front door,' he said.

'We meet again, Mr Swanson,' Ashworth said, just about managing to keep his voice steady. 'You know why we're here.'

''Cause you're a prat.' Muscles rippled on Swanson's lean torso as he reached for the ashtray. 'There's people on this estate that don't like you . . . Chief Inspector, sir.'

Ashworth's eyes narrowed. He knew this to be true. Swanson was the leader of the gang that had murdered Clive Allan. True to form, after the acquittal proceedings the dead man's relatives and friends had turned on the police, had blamed them for mishandling the case. Those same relatives and friends lived on the council estate.

Swanson's eyes sparkled with devilment. 'They blame you for poncin' around and lettin' killers get away.'

'We got the killers,' Ashworth told him.

'Pity the jury didn't agree with you, don't you think?'

They locked eyes. 'I'll have you, son.' Ashworth spat the words, his voice low.

The youth responded with a mocking grin. 'Not for that, you won't. I've been acquitted. You can't do me again for it.'

'I'll get you for something,' Ashworth promised.

Swanson took a drag on the cigarette and studied the chief inspector through the smoke haze. 'You'll never get anybody on this estate to testify against me in court. They wouldn't dare.'

'Do you still carry a Stanley knife?' Ashworth asked, deliberately changing the subject.

'Sometimes. If I've got some carpet to lay.' He stubbed out the cigarette. 'That's what they're used for, Stanley knives.'

Ashworth crossed to the bedside table and stared at the collection of possessions taken from Swanson's pockets the night before. There was a leather wallet, some loose change, cigarettes and disposable lighter . . . and a black-handled Stanley knife.

'You've also slashed a couple of people with them, haven't you, Lee? I've studied your record — it makes interesting reading.'

Swanson yawned. 'That was before I reformed.'

'A prostitute's turned up dead with knife marks on her. Do you know anything about it?'

'You got any proof that says I do?' A cocksure grin spread across his face.

'I did hear that you and your gang of thugs were protecting some of the girls,' Ashworth fired back. 'What can you tell me about that?'

Swanson glanced towards the open door. He did not want their conversation to be overheard. 'Okay, I've got a couple of cousins on the game, if you must know. They got fed up with the arseholes at the dole office always pesterin' them into getting jobs, so they started sellin' it.'

'And you make sure they're not interfered with? You make sure no one tries to steal their patch?'

'Yeh . . . yeh, something like that. See, some of the girls get a bit above themselves and somebody has to put them right.'

Ashworth gave a hollow laugh. 'So you slap them about a bit? Cut them? Perhaps even make an example of one of them?'

'I wouldn't dream of doin' such a thing,' Swanson said, smiling.

'We've been told, Mr Swanson, that the dead girl was frightened of you, and I've been trying to guess why that was. Perhaps she tried to work a little too close to your cousins.

Perhaps you had to "put her right" with your Stanley knife. Only you went too far . . . just like you did with Clive Allan.'

'Tell you what, Mr Ashworth, get the girls spreading these lies about me to make statements, and then you can charge me. Yeh?' He grinned.

There was the sound of heavy boots on the stairs and seconds later Police Constable John Moore appeared in the doorway.

'A word, sir.'

With one last withering look at Swanson, Ashworth headed for the landing. 'Yes, John, what have you got?'

'No drugs, sir, but we've found three video recorders and two satellite dishes in the front room.'

Ashworth returned to the bedroom. 'Those video recorders and satellite dishes in your front room — where did they come from, Lee?'

'Bought them,' Swanson replied, completely unfazed. 'I'm thinkin' about goin' into business.'

'You'll have a receipt, then?'

'No, sorry. Lost it, didn't I?'

Ashworth motioned for PC Moore. 'Do in here, John.' Then, to Swanson, 'On your feet, son, and get dressed. You're nicked. I'll read you your rights.'

'Don't bother,' he said, clambering from the bed. 'I know them backwards and inside out. Anyway, I rang my brief while you was knockin' on the door and he'll be at the nick, waitin'.'

PC Moore was rummaging in the wardrobe. He turned to Ashworth, his expression hopeful. 'Sir, there's a tracksuit in here with a lot of mud on it.'

'Well, well.' Ashworth approached the wardrobe with eager strides and carefully picked up first the purple trousers and then the top. Large mud stains had dried at the knees and the elbows, and more mud was embedded in the neck-to-waist zip fastening. 'Now, if that matches the lake . . .' he mused.

'Then you'll know I've been there. You're so clever, Mr Ashworth, you never cease to amaze me.'

Ignoring the taunts, Ashworth said, 'I'll be taking that suit and the Stanley knife for forensic examination.'

'Just make sure I get a receipt,' Swanson said, pulling a sweater over his head. 'I don't want you lot nickin' anything.'

PC Moore quickly continued his search of the room, but nothing else was found.

'Right, take him away,' Ashworth ordered, heavily.

'Hands off me.' Swanson warned Moore. 'Touch me and I'll deck you.'

'Please do,' Ashworth said, smiling. 'Then we can have you for assaulting a police officer and resisting arrest, and that'll suit me fine.'

Swanson's anger simmered and he allowed himself to be handcuffed and led from the room. 'You're gonna have to buy me a new front door, *and* I want an apology,' was his parting shot.

Ashworth stared out of the window. The dark sky was fast becoming a dismal grey over in the east, and beneath the stark glow of street lamps small knots of onlookers were gathering across the road. Why did police activity hold such a fascination? Given a choice he would be tucked up in a warm bed at that ungodly hour, not freezing to death in the hope of seeing . . . what?

Ashworth shook his head wearily. There was something about Lee Swanson that made his blood run cold. The lad was a cut above the average villain-in-the-making. He was cool, intelligent; he possessed a vicious streak that would stop at nothing. Inside that shaven head was a calculating brain that left no stone unturned in his quest to commit crimes and go unpunished.

Lee Swanson would be a difficult individual to get behind bars, but Ashworth planned to do just that.

CHAPTER 5

On the morning of 25 May, Ashworth was at his desk, his head in his hands, wave upon wave of bitter frustration sweeping over him. He had moments earlier received a report that the video recorders and satellite dishes taken from Lee Swanson's house remained unclaimed and could not be identified as stolen. Whereas the property taken from all other addresses in the raid had been returned to the rightful owners, all of whom lived in areas of Bridgetown other than the council estate. So, of the five arrested during Operation Sting, only four had been charged with burglary.

Ashworth reasoned that Swanson had netted his haul from break-ins on the council estate where his own brand of intimidation would prevent a single soul from claiming the recorders or dishes as their property. Yet again, the youth's violent methods had kept him beyond their reach, and they now had the irksome task of returning the items to number six Kirkstone Crescent together with a written apology *and* remuneration for a new front door.

And to make matters worse, Forensic could find no links with the lake from samples of mud taken from Swanson's tracksuit. Nor were there any traces of human cells to be lifted from the Stanley knife. No carpet fibres, either. The blade, and its handle, had been wiped clean — a questionable act, but hardly illegal. In a fit of pique, Ashworth flung the two reports across the office.

'Detachment, guv.'

He glanced up sharply to find Holly positioned in front of his desk. 'It's difficult,' he grunted. 'Don't forget, I had Clive Allan's whole family turn on me — out of sheer frustration, I admit — and all but blame me for his death. And Swanson's still running rings around me.'

Holly stooped to pick up the reports. 'I think you're helping him, guv. You're going at him like a bull at a gate.'

Ashworth bristled. 'I don't think anyone could ever accuse me of that.'

She suppressed a smile. 'Perhaps I meant to say you're trying too hard. Think about it,' she said, holding out the forensic report. 'If that piece of lowlife had anything to do with the murder, do you think he'd leave that tracksuit and the Stanley knife lying about for you to find?'

Ashworth let out a long, desolate breath. 'I'm letting him make a fool of me — is that what you're saying?'

'Not yet, but you're heading in that direction.' She perched on the edge of his desk. 'Listen, guv, every copper in the force is after him. Don't worry, we'll get him for something.'

He managed a chuckle. 'I see what you mean about staying detached.'

'Thanks for the birthday card,' Holly said, in an attempt to lighten the mood.

Ashworth had some vague recollection of putting fifty pence into a kitty for the large card which now stood on Holly's desk. 'Happy birthday,' he said, warmly.

'You're coming to the Bull and Butcher tonight, I hope?'

'Of course.' He tried to sound enthusiastic, but he was not inspired by the thought of sitting in a pub drinking non-alcoholic lager when he could be sipping single malt at home.

* * *

26

The lounge bar at the Bull and Butcher was crowded with officers from the Bridgetown police force. The majority were there to toast Holly's health, but there were more than a few who were hoping that her reputation had not been exaggerated and she would therefore become receptive to their advances after downing a few drinks.

Holly was holding court in the centre of a scrum of uniformed constables, parrying sexual innuendoes and fruity suggestions and, as far as Ashworth could see, thoroughly enjoying herself.

The chief inspector had opted for the relative quiet of a corner table where he sat discussing the England football team with Josh, Bobby and Mark. But his peace was to be short-lived for Holly was soon weaving an erratic course towards him.

'You'll never guess,' she said, giggling. 'Gordon Bennett's just propositioned me. Honestly, two gin and tonics and they think I'm anybody's.'

Josh flexed his jaw and got to his feet. 'That's not on, Hol. I'd better have a word with him.'

She gave him an uncertain grin. 'He was only joking, Josh—'

'Sorry, but I'm not having you treated like that . . .' A betraying smile was starting to show. 'Everybody knows it takes at least three gins. He's selling you short.'

'You sod, Abraham.' She laughed, aimed a playful slap at his arm. 'You bloody sod.'

'My round, I think,' Ashworth said. He took their orders and shouldered his way through to the bar.

Holly drained her glass and placed it loudly on the table. 'Why don't you lot come and join in?'

'It's the guv'nor,' Josh said. 'We can't just leave him sitting here.'

'You lot go,' Bobby said. 'I'll stay with him. There's something I want to discuss, anyway.'

Holly was on the verge of comparing the party to a wake, but she bit her tongue as Ashworth was on his way back, the tray of drinks held high. He was passing them around when she said, 'We're going to circulate, guv,' and grabbed hold of Josh and Mark.

'Well, it looks like it's just you and me now, Bobby,' Ashworth said, sitting down. 'You don't have to stay, you know. To be honest, I'm waiting for an opportunity to melt away.' He glanced around the bar. 'Conversation at these gatherings always seems to be limited to sex.'

Bobby grinned. 'I know, guv. Actually, I wanted to talk to you.'

'Nothing on the love front for you at the moment, then?' Ashworth took a sip of his alcohol-free lager, and grimaced. 'My God, how they get away with selling this stuff . . .'

'I've taken a few girls out, but I'm in no hurry to settle down, I've got plenty of time.' He laughed. 'My mum says I'm studious — a bit like saying a plain girl's got a nice personality.'

'Nothing wrong with being studious, Bobby. Get yourself a good career-plan and then you can start thinking about marriage and kids.' He pushed his glass to one side. 'So, what do you want to talk to me about? Not sex, I hope?'

'Actually, I did want to talk about bodies . . . The one in the lake, to be precise.'

'Ah, I guessed you'd be giving that some thought. All right, then, what have you come up with?'

Bobby paused for effect, and then stated boldly, 'Prostitutes are promiscuous.'

'That's a real revelation,' Ashworth said, drily. 'You're coming on in leaps and bounds, son.'

'No, I mean . . .' He was blushing again. 'What I'm saying is, the murderer could have something against promiscuous women, rather than the thought of money changing hands for sex.'

'Bobby,' Ashworth huffed, 'I'll have nothing to do with the theory about serial killers — I've already told you. When you go off at a tangent like that, it's easy to miss the obvious. And the obvious in this case is that Lee Swanson is responsible for the killing. We've just got to find some way of proving it . . . some way that he can't wriggle out of.'

'But why would he mark the body like that, guv? I'm sure it means something.'

'But do you know *what* it means?'

The constable nodded excitedly. 'I think I do, guv. I've been going through my books and—'

'Bobby—'

'No, listen for a minute. I think that the killer feels he's being pulled in two different directions. Maybe he couldn't get at the person he really wanted, so he marked the body to gain some sort of relief. It happens, guv.'

'I know it happens. I've been there. I've seen it. Bobby, I've probably seen things that aren't in your books. But we've got to stick to the facts, and one of the facts is that we've only got the one body.' Ashworth took another sip of lager; it was no better than the first. 'We need to look no further than Lee Swanson. Believe me.'

A loud cheer went up. Ashworth glanced across to the bar where Holly was balanced awkwardly on the counter, pretending to be a go-go dancer. He let out an impatient breath.

'Bobby, do you mind if I make myself scarce? I feel like a fish out of water among this lot.'

''Course not, guv.' He nodded towards the bar. 'I'd better get over there and make sure Holly doesn't break her neck. Oh, and thanks for the chat.'

* * *

Holly was hardly three sheets to the wind by the time they left the pub, but she was definitely two and a bit. Mark Hartland, who had stopped at one pint, took her arm and guided her towards his car. She protested continually but allowed him to drive her home.

'Are you going to be all right?' he asked, pulling up outside her house.

'Yes, of course I am.' With head spinning, she fumbled for the catch of the seat belt.

He grinned. 'Here, let me do it.'

Mark leant across to unfasten the catch, their hands touched, and a strong mutual attraction flared to the surface. Their eyes met, their lips brushed, and when he felt no resistance Mark kissed her. Holly's arms went around his neck and she began to respond, but suddenly she pulled back.

'No, Mark, we've got to stop this, now,' she said, utterly breathless.

'Oh, God, Holly . . .' He fell back in his seat. 'You lead me on, and then—'

'Look, I don't need it — okay? You're a married man, Mark.'

He sighed loudly. 'Yes, a very unhappy married man.'

Holly snorted. 'You'll be telling me next your wife doesn't understand you.'

'Okay, I know it sounds like a corny line, but it happens to be true.'

She save him a sad smile. 'I couldn't care less whether it's true or not. I can't get involved with anybody at the moment, I'm still trying to wriggle out of the last one. And I definitely don't want to get tangled up with a married man. I've been there, Mark, and it's not a situation I want to revisit.'

'Well, you've made yourself very plain,' he said, moodily. 'I'll see you in the morning, then.'

'Yes.' She touched her forehead and winced. 'And I'll probably be nursing a king-sized hangover. Anyway, thanks for the lift.'

'My pleasure,' was his gruff reply.

Holly watched the car pull away. And as she followed its progress along the street she in turn was being observed. A car was parked just fifty yards away, near enough for the man inside to have witnessed their fiery kiss. He closed his eyes, his entire body trembling with suppressed rage, his jealousy hot and piercing like a knife turning in the pit of his stomach. After a moment he forced his eyes open. Holly was still watching the car's tail lights in the distance.

'You bitch,' he spat into the dark. 'I could kill you for this.'

CHAPTER 6

At ten thirty the following morning, a fax came through from the West Midlands police confirming the identity of the body in the lake. Ashworth stared hard at the printed report.

The dead girl's name was Julie Stevens, and she was born on 12 June 1962. No address could be found, so it was assumed she had been staying at a squat. Her criminal history comprised fourteen convictions for soliciting, and three for shoplifting. Her claims for Income Support, for which she gave a false address, had stopped eight months ago, so she could have started work in Bridgetown around that time.

As no photographs of the girl were available, a Polaroid shot had been taken of the face while the body lay on the pathologist's slab. It was a macabre image, but was better than nothing. Hundreds of copies were made, of which half were sent to the West Midlands police.

Those copies, according to the report, had been circulated around local hostels, given to all *Big Issue* vendors, shown to as many of the homeless as could be found, and featured on posters in the local towns and cities. It was hoped that friends or relatives of Julie might see the picture and help the police with their investigation. Not one person came forward.

'Doesn't tell us much,' Holly said.

'No, it doesn't,' Ashworth agreed. 'The trouble is, we don't even know she originated from the West Midlands; her family could be anywhere. The homeless are never that eager to help us, and her ex-clients were hardly likely to come forward, were they?'

'Where do we go next, guv?'

'We need the name of that girl, Holly. If we can prove she's Swanson's cousin, it'll bring the link between him and Julie Stevens that much closer.'

'I'm trying, guv, honestly, but the girls have just clammed up.'

'Well, we'll keep going over what we have got. We'll keep knocking at the door until it opens.'

* * *

Boris ambled slowly along the high street. He liked the warmth of the sun on his face, and yet it had a strange effect on him, made him hunger for the normal things in life. It would feel so good to shave off his beard, to cut off his hair, to wear modern clothes, to have a woman of his own to love . . . normality.

He had lived for so long in his father's shadow, steeped in guilt, forever reminded that his soul was beyond redemption. Only occasionally did such alien thoughts push to the forefront of his mind, but push they did, and with them came a longing that Boris found hard to bear.

If only his father would die. If only his father's spirit would rise up to join those of his mother and brother. Then Boris could escape, could learn to live.

Those notions made him stop in his tracks. Fire and brimstone would surely rain down on him that very minute; burn him up with a heat that was hotter than hell. But, no. The sun continued to warm his face. The crowds continued to mill.

Boris clutched his Bible tightly and went on his way. Escape was impossible, in any case. In the old country he had killed his mother and his brother. Even here in Bridgetown he had sinned. But he must block such thoughts from his mind. He must read from the Lord's book.

Boris stopped in front of a newsagent's shop, still ten minutes' walk away from his usual haunt. With trembling hands he opened the Bible and began to read from the Book of Isaiah. One or two people stopped on the narrow pavement to watch that strange man, that novelty, reading from the Scriptures. They shook their heads, exchanged curious looks, wondered what could have happened to make the man behave so strangely.

It was then that Lee Swanson and his gang tumbled out of Woolworths. They spotted Boris straight away and started to jeer and shout obscenities. Boris was used to such reactions and merely glanced up before continuing his impromptu reading.

But then he did a double-take. He had spotted a woman, an ordinary woman in her thirties. She was watching him intently, her expression open and kind. Her hair was golden and it hung across her shoulders in an old-fashioned style. In her hand was a wicker shopping bag. Boris had suffered enough himself to notice the tiny pain lines surrounding her eyes, her mouth.

But those lines vanished when she smiled at him. Such a radiant smile. It lit up her face and made Boris lose his place in the text. While he was searching through the paragraphs the strident voice of PC Moore rang out.

'All right, folks, move along, please. You're blocking the pavement.' The group melted away. Swanson and his cronies were the last to move, and they sauntered off noisily enunciating their dislike for the police. PC Moore glared after them.

'Move along, Boris,' he said, kindly. 'You know better than this.'

'I'm spreading the Lord's word, Constable.'

'Yes, I know.' Moore sighed. 'And don't let's go into how He was persecuted as well, like you usually do. Just move along and don't use the main road. Okay?'

Boris slammed the Bible shut. 'I will move, Constable, but you will suffer for this in the afterlife.'

'If you don't shift your arse, Boris, my sergeant's gonna make me suffer in this life. And, at the moment, that's more important. Come on,' he said, jollying him along, 'we try to be decent with you. Go to the park, or the market — any place where you're not blocking the pavement.'

The giant of a man sloped off, but he had not moved more than twenty yards when he saw the woman again. This time she was boldly approaching and gazing at him with interest.

'You read very well.' She nodded towards the Bible. 'Your accent . . . it's Russian, isn't it?'

'It is.' He swallowed loudly, his confusion rising. 'Russia . . . that is my home country, although I left it twenty years ago.'

The woman frowned. 'But surely at that time you wouldn't be allowed to practise Christianity?'

He nodded. 'You are right. It was driven underground, but my father never lost his faith. And, twenty years ago, we escaped.'

The woman opened her mouth to speak, but then thought better of it. 'Well . . . I'd better go.' That smile came again. 'I'll probably see you around.'

Boris gave a shrug. 'Perhaps.'

'I hope so,' she replied.

* * *

Mark caught up with Holly in the police station car park at around 5.30. p.m.

'Holly, I'm sorry,' he said, pulling her round to face him. 'I was way out of order last night, and I've been acting like a real shit all day.'

'Let's forget it, Mark.' They continued to the cars. 'Anyway, I'd rather not have an atmosphere in the office, to be honest. I'm sure the guv'nor picked up on it.'

'Me, neither.' They stopped by Holly's Micra. 'So, shall we just forget it ever happened?'

'It's a deal.' She put her key in the lock and then gave him an enquiring look. 'Just tell me one thing . . . When you said you didn't get on with your wife, was that just a line?'

'No.' He pulled a face. 'At the moment she's staying with her mother in Oxford. She spends a lot of time there, mainly because we can't stand the sight of each other.'

Holly thought about those words during the drive home. She hoped he wasn't a liar. But what if he was . . . She was determined not to get involved with him.

Pulling into her narrow driveway, Holly's thoughts turned to strong black coffee with a welcome cigarette, and then a long hot bath that would wash away the remnants of her hangover.

She was locking the car door when her neighbour, Mrs Perry, appeared at the top of the drive. She was holding an enormous bouquet of flowers.

'I took these in for you this morning,' she said. 'My, you do have a lot of admirers.'

'Thanks, Mrs Perry.' Holly took the flowers and glanced at the card. She saw the name 'Don' and her skin crawled.

'Look, Mrs Perry, this might sound a bit weird, but . . . Well, if any more flowers turn up, will you refuse to take delivery of them?'

The woman appeared puzzled. 'If you like. I thought I was doing you a favour.'

'Oh, you were and I appreciate it,' Holly quickly assured her. 'But I don't want any more flowers from this guy, so if the florist can't deliver them he might just get the idea.'

The minute her front door was shut Holly threw the flowers across the hall. 'Just piss off, Don, it's finished.' She fumbled in her shoulder bag for cigarettes and lighter. 'Christ, sometimes I wish I'd become a nun.'

* * *

Helen Palmer had been working the streets for almost four years and her attitude to life, along with her face, had hardened considerably during that time.

The seedier side of Bridgetown was a collection of alleyways and narrow roads that came to life at the first hint of darkness. That area went back centuries and had once been the main thoroughfare. Now the bright lights of the distant high street were merely a glow in the sky as Helen waited on a poorly lit corner, knowing that any man looking for action would pass along there, sooner or later.

During the day it was possible to believe that summer was waiting around the corner, but dusk brought with it fast-dropping temperatures and even frost on the high ground. Helen shivered; her scant mini-skirt and thin silk blouse afforded her little protection against the damp swirling mist that was bringing visibility to a minimum.

And then she saw him. He was across the road, standing stock still and watching her, a tall man dressed in dark clothing. The quiver running along her spine had nothing to do with the cold. Helen's breath quickened. What had happened to that other girl was always at the forefront of her mind.

The moment passed, however. Helen took in a long breath and approached the man. When you worked the streets, you took your chances.

CHAPTER 7

Ashworth parked his Scorpio at the end of the mews cottages and walked with reluctant steps towards number twelve. Outside the house last year's hanging basket was still suspended from its bracket, the compost now carpeted with the tiny green leaves of chickweed.

He took in a deep breath and pressed the bell. A moment passed, and then the door was pulled ajar by Mildred Allan, a thin, washed-out woman of fifty-five. Her eyes flashed anger when she saw him, but her tone remained polite.

'Hello, Chief. John's not in, at the moment.'

'It doesn't matter,' Ashworth replied, gently. 'I've only called round to see how you both are.'

'You'd better come in.' She pulled the door wide. 'And as for how we are . . . we're no better than the last time you asked.'

The warmth of the hall should have been welcoming, but the coolness of his reception made it pass unnoticed.

'Mrs Allan,' Ashworth began, hesitantly, 'I really will do everything in my power to help you and your husband.'

In the living room she turned on him. 'Can you bring Clive back?'

Ashworth stared at the dark blue Wilton carpet, desperately searching for words.

'No,' she said. 'You couldn't even bring his murderers to justice.'

Ashworth looked up then, dared to meet her gaze. 'We tried our best. You know as well as I do that the witnesses were intimidated. Those two sent to prison for contempt of court still refused to testify, so what could we do? Like I said, we tried our best.'

Mildred seemed to relent, her expression softened. She eased herself into one of the armchairs. 'I'm sure you did,' she said, 'but it makes me so angry to think . . .' She shook her head, her fists clenched.

'I know it's difficult,' Ashworth ventured. 'But it's you and your husband you have to think about now.'

She turned tired eyes towards him. 'I don't blame the police anymore, Chief Inspector. I know what you're saying is true. But it's John I'm worried about. I think he's ill. Not physically, but ill in his mind.' A hand went to her temple. 'When he's at home he just sits in the chair, staring in front of him. And he goes out a lot, just wanders about . . .' She gave him a sharp glance. 'And before you ask, I give him as much support as I possibly can.'

'I'm sure you do,' Ashworth said, ill at ease. 'You know, your GP could help suggest some form of treatment.'

There was a bitter edge to her laugh. 'Is that what you think we need? Treatment? Well, you just tell me what treatment can make you feel better after you've watched your son's coffin being lowered into the ground, and then you have to watch the worthless yobs who murdered him walk about free.'

Ashworth kept quiet. He didn't have an answer.

* * *

'I'm after straight sex,' the man said. 'But first I want you tied to the bed . . . hands bound tight.'

Nothing could shock Helen Palmer, but there was plenty that could make her uneasy. Although bondage cost extra she had decided, since the body had turned up in the lake, that it would be better to keep a toe on the floor and an eye on the door, and if the punters didn't like it, too bad. She needed money, not hassle.

'No, that's out,' she said, firmly. 'I go into that with some of my regulars, but never on the first time.'

'All right.' His breath fogged the night air. 'How much?'

Helen's brain worked faster than a calculator, listing all the things that 'straight' might involve. 'Fifty quid.'

'Forty.'

'Forty-five,' she came back. 'I'm worth it, I can tell you that much. And it'd be at my flat, not in some crappy room.'

He nodded. 'Lead the way, then.'

* * *

Ashworth was not easily intimidated. In fact, standing as he was in the lounge of the Allans' cottage, almost filling the small space, it was difficult to imagine the man even having an attack of nerves. But his heart did skip a beat when sounds drifted in from the hall: the turn of a key in the lock, the front door slamming shut.

Mildred turned her tormented gaze towards him. 'Here's John, now,' she said, wringing her hands.

The door to the lounge opened and John Allan stood on the threshold, shrugging off his overcoat. His dark eyes narrowed at the sight of the chief inspector.

'Oh, it's you again, is it?' was all he said.

Ashworth was shocked by the man's appearance. In the space of a few weeks his usually ruddy cheeks had lost their flesh, lending his face a skull-like appearance; and his large frame was now withered, his clothes hanging in folds. Gone was the bombastic manner, too. Now he was quiet, subdued, unwilling to meet Ashworth's eyes.

John Allan shuffled towards the gas fire and bent to warm his hands. 'You've brought us some news, have you, about what you're going to do about our Clive's murder?' he said, without looking up.

'You know there's nothing more that can be done about it.' By now Ashworth had made such a study of the carpet he felt he knew every detail of its pattern. He took a step towards the man. 'I came by to see how you both were.'

'That's very good of you.' His words were heavy with sarcasm and, sinking into an armchair close to the hearth, he allowed his hostile gaze to finally settle on the chief inspector.

'I worked all my life, you know, before this little lot. Picked up my wage packet with all the stoppages taken out. Never been in trouble with the police . . .'

Ashworth had heard it all before, but resisted the urge to sigh. 'I've made it plain, Mr Allan, there's nothing we can do to Lee Swanson with regard to . . .' He hesitated.

'Our son's murder?' Allan spat. 'Is that what you're finding difficult to say? Well, it's not good enough.' His voice had risen a pitch, and over by the door Mildred brought her hands to her face. 'They don't work, these bloody kids, they take drugs, they *kill* people, but they're above the law.' He leant forward, the movement aggressive. 'You want to know how I feel, Mr Ashworth? I feel like I've been torn apart, ripped in two . . . that's how I feel. Now, just bugger off and don't bother us again.'

Mildred showed him out. At the door her eyes were focused on his shirt collar, as if she was too embarrassed or perhaps too full of contempt to look him in the face.

A dejected Ashworth wandered back along the mews. He felt no resentment towards the Allans. He had called on them in his own time, had been standing in that comfortable little room for well over an hour with no invitation to sit, had been treated with not so much as a hint of courtesy, but none of that mattered. His chief concern was for the couple: they were suffering so much. If only he could get Lee Swanson for something, put him away for a long time, perhaps then the Allans might rest a little easier.

He opened the door to his car and looked up at the heavens. 'Can't you think of something?' he asked the Almighty.

* * *

At 9 p.m. the telephone rang in Holly's hall. She had enjoyed a long soak in the bath and was about to relax with a gin and tonic. Praying that it wasn't the station, she lifted the receiver.

'Holly, it's Don.'

She mouthed a swift count to ten. 'What do you want?'

'I want to see you, of course. Holly, I've never felt like this about any other woman. I—'

'Donald, it's finished between us — can't you get that into your thick skull?'

'You don't mean that—'

'Do you want me to say it again, Don? Christ . . . In any case, you don't really feel anything for me. I was your first girlfriend since your divorce, that's all. You'll find somebody else.'

'Will I? My wife got fed up with me, and now you have.' His voice oozed self-pity.

'Look, Donald, I told you at the start I didn't want anything permanent. I was upfront about everything.'

'I want to see you, Holly,' he almost cried. 'I want us to talk it through properly. I can get you to change your mind, I know I can.'

Holly had tried to put him down lightly, had tried to blanket his fall, but now she realised that had only made matters worse. The time had come to be firm.

'We've got nothing to talk about. It's over . . . done. I want you to leave me alone, Donald — do you understand? I want you out of my life.'

The line went dead. Holly stood there looking at the receiver and worrying. What if he did something stupid? At first meeting, Donald Quinn came across as self-confident, arrogant, the type of man who would love them and leave them. But Holly had soon learnt the truth. When his defences were down, along with his trousers, Quinn was utterly ineffectual, forever questioning her motives, a quivering mass of insecurities. Should she call him back? No, why should she? He was a grown man. He would just have to sort himself out; she wasn't his nanny.

Muttering oaths, Holly returned to the lounge and poured herself a large gin. She was topping it up with tonic when the telephone rang.

'Oh, God, if it's him again, I'll bloody kill him.' In the hall she snapped up the receiver. 'Hello!'

There was a moment's silence. 'Have I called at a bad time?' It was Mark Hartland.

'Mark, oh God, I'm sorry, I thought you were somebody else.'

'Don't ever try to make a living as a psychic.' His easy laugh drifted down the line and Holly found herself giggling like a teenager.

'Listen,' he said, 'I've been thinking about what you said in the car park . . . You know, about whether I really was unhappy with my wife. I kept thinking, I wonder why she asked me that . . .'

'Well . . .' she said, lamely. 'It . . . it just slipped out.'

'That's what I thought.' He was playing with her, and Holly loved it. 'As I stand here with my hand on my heart — you'll have to trust me on that — I can honestly say that, yes, I am unhappy with her and, yes, she really does spend long periods at her mother's.'

'Where's all this leading, Mark?' Holly held her breath.

He laughed 'I might be heading for another put-down, but I was wondering whether we might go out sometime — just for a meal, no strings attached.'

'Okay,' she said, grinning. 'I think I'd like that.'

'How about tomorrow? I'll pick you up at eight.'

'Great. Oh, but, Mark, you won't mention this in the office . . .'

'Not if you don't want me to. Right, then, see you tomorrow. Goodnight, Holly.'

'Goodnight, Mark.' Holly dropped the receiver back in its cradle and hugged herself. So much for her determination not to get involved.

* * *

Mark was smiling when he replaced the receiver. He was perched on the end of his bed. The light was on, the curtains were open, and he was totally unaware that curious eyes were watching him.

In the house opposite Elaine Marsden was standing well back in her darkened front bedroom, her sullen mouth drawn into a straight line, her gimlet eyes registering his every movement. She craned her neck when Mark opened a wardrobe that covered the whole of one wall.

'Yes, I thought as much,' she muttered to herself. 'Just as I'd expected.'

She dared to move closer to the window, but then Mark pulled across his curtains and Elaine's sour look worsened. She stomped downstairs and hurried into the living room.

'He was on the phone just now, Bill.'

Her husband let out a long breath and kept his eyes on the television screen. England were playing Brazil; he'd been looking forward to the match for weeks and nobody was going to spoil it, not even Elaine with her boring bloody tittle-tattle.

'Perhaps he was talking to his wife,' was Bill's curt reply.

'He's done her in, don't you worry about that.'

She paced across to the sideboard and stood thinking for a while. Bill stroked the last few strands of greying hair across his bald head and gasped at the late tackle on England's centre forward. Elaine's mouth puckered with displeasure.

'I said he's done her in, Bill,' she repeated loudly. 'The rows they had . . . You could hear every word, even over here. Shouting and screaming . . . and the language, well . . .'

'A good row clears the air,' Bill said. He suddenly moved to the edge of his seat. 'Kick it man . . . Bloody hell, an open goal and he missed it.'

'And the rows were always about other women,' Elaine went on, ignoring his outburst.

Bill let out another long breath. Any hope of watching the football in peace was out until they'd been through this, yet again.

'We didn't hear any such thing, my love.'

'Mrs Irons, next door to them, did. And what do you think? She reckons he goes with prostitutes.'

'Gossip and tittle-tattle, that's what that is — I've told you before. He seems a nice enough bloke to me.'

'Huh, that's what they said about Crippen.' Elaine positioned herself in front of the television, arms folded below her non-existent bosom. 'And why did he dig the garden over? Eh?'

Bill, usually a placid man, felt his temper rising. 'It's the spring, my love. Everybody digs their gardens in the spring.'

'She's under there, I reckon. Under the patio, would be my guess.'

'Then why's he digging the garden up?' Bill queried with a fair degree of logic.

Elaine frowned. 'I don't know, but I'll tell you one thing, I was watching just now and he opened the wardrobe. And guess what? All her clothes are still inside. You don't go away and leave your clothes, Bill.'

'She's gone to stay with her mother — he's told you. She wouldn't take all her clothes to her mother's now, would she?'

But Elaine refused to be swayed. 'She's been gone four weeks. Mrs Irons was saying maybe we should report it to the police.'

'You can't do that. You'll get into trouble.'

'Why?' she retorted. 'They're always saying on that *Crime Busters* thing on the telly you should report anything suspicious.'

'But there's nothing suspicious to report,' Bill countered, wearily.

'I can't talk to you, Bill — never could. You can't see the nose on your face. Always take the easy way out, that's your motto.' She strutted towards the door. 'My mother warned me not to marry you. You weren't good enough, that's what she said.'

'I wish you'd bloody well listened to her,' he muttered, then settled back to enjoy the match.

CHAPTER 8

Boris came awake early next morning. Cold and damp had invaded the flat and he lay in bed shivering beneath his coarse shabby blankets. He kept his eyes shut tight, for to open them would show a willingness to face the day. If he could only stay in the dubious sanctuary of his bed, well away from his father's sharp tongue, well away from the women put on every street corner to tempt him.

Boris had never known a mother's love and had always associated women with pain and guilt. Almost all of the bad things in his life had happened because of women. Even the few he had liked over the years — kindly schoolteachers, devout church members — had been capable of whipping his guilt to fever pitch, filling him with an almost insane desire to grab them by the throat and squeeze . . . and squeeze. Those feelings were only fleeting, however, vanishing almost as soon as they had surfaced. But they frightened him, nonetheless.

Boris threw the blankets aside and climbed from the bed. Daylight filtered through the window and picked out the rippling muscles of his huge body as he stretched. He padded along to the bathroom and washed himself with ice cold water (another daily penance) and then, with one eye on the closed door, he trimmed his beard for the third day running. It was getting shorter and shorter, but so far his father had failed to notice.

As soon as he was dressed Boris knocked on his father's door and entered without waiting for a reply. No conversation passed between them as he helped the old man from the bed. His father's legs were emaciated, hardly capable of supporting his meagre weight; beneath his thick nightshirt the skin on his torso hung in deep folds. But he was a proud man who refused to use a bedpan, choosing instead to stagger on his son's arm and reach the lavatory fighting for breath.

With those early morning ablutions done, with his father back in bed, Boris prepared breakfast. He set the bowl of steaming porridge on his father's lap and handed him a spoon.

'I'll be back at mid-day to make your next meal.'

'You have the Lord's work to do.' The words were uttered on a feeble breath, and they brought with them a spasm of coughing that racked the old man's slight frame. Boris rushed forward to retrieve the porridge dish before it could topple from the bed.

'I wish you would let the council help you, father. The Social Services would send a woman to look after you.'

'I'll have none of the whores of Babylon to look after me,' his father hissed. 'Go, do the Lord's work, warn of the dangers of sinning.'

* * *

Ashworth's brow was furrowed as he prepared to finish that morning's briefing. He glanced around the small CID office, his gaze taking in his team, their chairs in a semicircle before his desk. With the ever-increasing workload he could envisage detectives from other areas being drafted in to help with crimes of a serious nature. And that he did not want. Better to step up their enquiries and get results before the crisis point was reached.

'Right, last but not least . . .' Ashworth stopped to glower at Mark whose erratic typing skills were fetching tiresome beeps from the computer. 'I don't have to remind you that we still have an unsolved murder on our books. Now, Alex Ferguson, at my request, took another look at the body. I wanted to know if any of the marks or bruises he'd attributed to underwater obstacles hitting it might in fact have been made by the killer. And he came up with something very interesting.' He reached behind him and selected a report from his desk. 'It seems there are marks on the right ankle which might, just might, have been caused by a person grabbing the ankle and applying considerable pressure.'

'Hardly a breakthrough, guv,' Josh said.

'No, but it's something.' Ashworth pointed his forefinger. 'And while the case is still open we'll be looking for even the smallest detail.'

Holly gave a loud sigh. 'Every way we turn, guv, we're hitting a brick wall. And in the meantime we've got organised car theft, we've got drug trafficking, we've got burglaries . . . What I'm trying to say is, we've got our clear-up rate to think about.'

Ashworth banged a fist on the desk. 'I'm well aware of that, Holly, but I want this murder cleared up. And while we're at it — still no luck in finding that girl? The prostitutes still clamming up, are they?'

She fixed him with a sullen stare. 'I left a—'

'Isn't it a fact, Holly, that the majority of Swanson's family live on the council estate? Not a very large area, I'd say. Can't you possibly get your two brain cells working on finding his cousins' house?'

Holly sprang to her feet and glowered at him. 'Guv, you want this case cleared up by us arresting Swanson for the murder. You've closed your mind to any other possibility. Say it wasn't Swanson. Say it was somebody just passing through Bridgetown. Say it was a local man you'd hardly give a second glance in the street . . .'

Mark's computer had stopped chattering, and so sudden was the silence that all heads turned to look at him. He was staring into space, his fingers resting lightly on the keys. That momentary pause went some way to calming the atmosphere.

'I think what Holly's getting at—' Bobby began.

'I can speak for myself, Bobby, thank you.' She snatched up a report from her desk and thrust it at the chief inspector. 'Using my two brain cells, guv, I finally traced Swanson's cousins. They denied being on the game or having any knowledge of the murdered woman. Short of beating the information out of them with a rubber hose, I can't do any more.' She paused, her breathing ragged. 'You've no idea how much fear Swanson generates on that estate. And until we find somebody with the bottle to go against him, we'll get nowhere.'

'I know only too well the extent of that lad's hold on the estate,' Ashworth said, before quietly adding, 'You should have told me before that you'd found the girl, Holly.'

'If you'd have let me get a word in edgeways, guv, I could've told you I'd left a copy of my report on your desk.'

With a frown Ashworth searched through the piles of papers before him. Finally he moved to one side a set of files brought up from the collator's office. The string holding them together suddenly came apart and files and papers were strewn everywhere. The incident did little to brighten Ashworth's mood; nor did the fact that the files had been placed on top of Holly's report.

'Mark,' he bellowed. 'Never, ever, cover up things on my desk. If you can't find room, then use the floor.'

'Yes, sir. Sorry, sir,' Mark stammered.

'Holly, I owe you an apology,' Ashworth said. 'I shouldn't have laid into you like that.'

She sank back into her seat. 'It's okay, guv; it makes a change to be on the receiving end.' She grinned. 'I'm usually laying into you — remember?'

'That you are, and too often for my liking,' he said, returning her grin. 'But, I'm sorry, I shouldn't have questioned your intelligence like that.'

'You were well out of order there, guv,' Josh said. 'She's got at least four brain cells, maybe even five.'

'Yes, thanks a lot, Abraham,' Holly said, pulling a face.

Ashworth looked again at the report. 'Maybe I am concentrating too much on Swanson being the killer. I just feel that if we can get proof that the girl on bad terms with Julie Stevens was his cousin, it'll open up a whole new line of enquiry. And that's what we need most of all, at the moment — a line of enquiry. Anyway, let's keep an open mind.' His brown eyes raked over them. 'But let's make sure we *keep* it on our minds.'

Chairs were hastily returned to their original positions and, while the officers prepared for the day's business, Mark surreptitiously signalled to Holly who collected her coat and crossed to his desk.

'How do you spell "judicial"?' he whispered. 'It's gone completely out of my mind.' She told him the spelling. 'I felt such a prat when you all looked at me. Does your mind ever go blank like that?'

'Every time I look at you, sweetheart,' she replied with a wink.

* * *

Boris could not face reading from the Bible. Not today. His faith was still strong, but the ache in his heart was stronger. The heavy book felt cumbersome in his hand, and the faded gold lettering on its cover seemed to berate him for his indolence. With his gaze cast aside Boris slid the book into the pocket of his jacket, a small act which did little to assuage his guilt.

He decided to go to the park and once there wandered aimlessly around its perimeter. After a time he sat on a bench facing the cricket pitches. A large conifer hedge protected the spot from an eager breeze, making it a pleasant sun trap, a perfect place for whiling away the hours. Boris had been sitting motionless, his head lowered, for almost fifteen minutes, when he felt a presence.

'Hello, again.'

The voice startled him, made him glance up. It was the woman from the crowd; the woman who had spoken so kindly the previous day. Puzzled, Boris mumbled hello in return and took a moment to study her silken hair, her smiling face with those compassionate brown eyes. Many years ago Boris had been shown a faded photograph of his mother and, even today, her features were firmly etched in his mind's eye. The woman now standing before him reminded Boris of his mother.

'Can I join you?' she asked, already sitting down.

'Of course,' he replied. 'As you see, I do not have a queue of people waiting to speak with me.'

The woman's smile stretched into a grin. With her eyes still on his face she took a large pack of sandwiches from her bag and motioned for him to take one.

'So, what's your name?' she asked.

'Boris. Boris Cywinski,' he replied, his huge hand grasping the top sandwich.

'Phew, that's a mouthful. Your name, I mean, not . . .' She nodded towards his full mouth.

The ham on white bread was delicious, and even as he ate his mouth watered in anticipation of the next bite.

'I'm not very good at talking to people,' Boris stammered, still eyeing the food.

'Well, you could start by asking me my name.' She held out her sandwiches again. 'Go on, take two. Anyway, I'll save you the trouble — I'm Megan Rowntree.'

Boris did indeed take. 'That is a nice name.' He hesitated. 'Why are you taking an interest in me, Megan Rowntree?'

'You're very blunt. But you're right, I am interested in you. You see, I know a little bit about you, and you're not quite what you seem.'

'Don't I frighten you?' he asked haltingly.

'Goodness me, no.' Megan tilted back her head and laughed, the sunshine catching her golden hair, making it shimmer. Boris stared on in awe. 'I do sense that you're troubled, though, and I'd like to help.'

A sudden warmth spread in his chest. That a woman as fine as she should feel driven to help him — it was beyond belief. He had wished his father dead; he had hankered after things that would compromise his faith; he had failed for one day to share the Bible's truths. And instead of destroying him in the bowels of hell the blessed Lord had seen fit to reward him with a golden-haired angel.

'Who are you?' Boris asked gently. 'Where are you from?'

'I work for the council,' Megan said.

'The council? So, you're not . . .'

She saw the stricken look that darkened his eyes for a mere moment. 'What, Boris . . . what?'

He shook his head. 'Nothing.'

'You asked for help with your father — remember?'

Boris glared at her accusingly. 'You've tricked me.'

'Plied you with ham sandwiches, you mean? Maybe, but I haven't tricked you.' She edged closer. 'I've seen your file, Boris, I know everything. I know of your father's condition, how well you care for him, the state of your flat . . .' She willed him to meet her gaze. 'Your father should be in a home, Boris, and you should be rehoused — that flat isn't fit to live in. And you — what about you? You're an intelligent, educated man, but you're wasting your life. Do you realise what's going to happen to you? Sooner or later you'll become ill, mentally ill; the sheer burden of your life will affect your mind.'

Boris knew she was right. In fact, sometimes he feared that the balance of his mind had already gone. He turned to her. 'Do you really want to help me?'

'Yes, I do. I'm a social worker and I'll do anything I can to help you.'

Boris smiled. 'You must be a true Christian, Megan Rowntree.'

'I try to be. I can't work miracles, Boris, but sometimes just talking about your problems, confronting them, can make you see them for what they really are.' She got to her feet. 'Let's go for a walk by the lake and talk some more.'

His head came up sharply. 'No, no, not the lake. I don't like the water.'

Megan noticed that his hands were trembling, saw that some of the colour had left his face. 'All right, it was only a suggestion.' She delved into her handbag and took out a card. 'Here's my office address and telephone number. I want you to come and see me.'

Boris took the white card and studied the small black lettering. 'Thank you,' he said.

Megan backed away. 'You promise you'll come?'

He nodded and watched her stride off. She had left the remaining sandwiches on the seat beside him, but Boris was more interested in the card. He put it to his nostrils and inhaled her perfume . . . the sweet delicate scent of womanhood.

CHAPTER 9

Holly had splashed out on a new dress for her date with Mark. It was black, with a lace bodice, an A-line skirt, and was halfway between prim and sexy. It was on a hanger behind the door and Holly was finishing off her make-up when the telephone on her bedside table started to buzz.

She dived for the receiver. 'Hello?'

'Holly, it's Mark. I'm sorry, but I'm going to have to cry off our dinner date. I think I'm coming down with flu. I keep shivering and I feel absolutely awful.'

'Oh, I am sorry, Mark.' She tried to keep the disappointment from her voice. 'Is there anything I can do?'

'No, thanks, I'll be okay. I'll have an early night, and if I feel the same tomorrow, I'll ring in sick.'

Holly threw her mascara wand at the opposite wall but kept her tone light. 'Okay, then. Listen, we can do it some other time — yeh? I hope you feel better soon.'

'Thanks, Holly. I'll probably see you in the morning. If not . . .'

'Okay. 'Bye.'

She replaced the receiver, a pensive look on her face. Could it be that his wife had come back and put her foot down? Or was she still away and Mark didn't want to miss her call? But, if so, why ask her out in the first place? Oh well, goodbye Indian cuisine and hello cheese on toast.

While she sliced the cheese Holly was reminded of her previous affair with a married man. All those promised meals and theatre trips, and the last-minute calls to say he couldn't make it. The mounting paranoia — was he telling the truth or simply using her? Was he *capable* of telling the truth when a lie could win him a night in her bed, no commitment necessary? She was still pondering over those things when the toast started to burn.

* * *

Cynthia Labrum left the Bridgetown Fish Bar with three portions of fish and chips burning her fingers through the white paper wrapping. She opened the door to her Ford Escort and put the package on the passenger seat. Traffic was light in the high street at 9.30 p.m. and she had no difficulty in pulling away from the kerb.

It was a ten-minute drive to the house she shared with her parents on the outskirts of the council estate, known to the tenants as the 'Posh End'. But the Bridgetown Fish Bar had the best fish and chips in town so Cynthia did not mind the journey.

Eventually the arc of her headlights lit up the row of rented garages situated in an alley behind her house. The road surface was far from even and the old car bumped along as Cynthia sped towards hers — the third on the right. She licked her lips; the hot vinegar smell was tempting her already sharpened appetite.

And then she saw a man at the end of the alley; he had stepped out of the shadows and raised his hand in acknowledgement. Cynthia's heart raced.

She pulled the car to a halt and climbed out, all the while searching the dark, her eyes narrowed. But she could detect no movement; the man must have gone. She relaxed, told herself she was over-reacting. That life was behind her now. He knew that. He wouldn't come looking for her.

Cynthia hurried to the garage, her footsteps echoing. Metal grated against metal, and the door squealed as she pulled it open. Then she turned back to the car and the man was there. He was so close, only inches separated their bodies.

'What do you want?' she demanded to know.

'Don't panic, Cyn, I only want to talk.'

'We've nothing to say to each other.' She tried to push past but he blocked her way. 'Leave me alone . . . please. All that's behind me now. Just leave me alone.'

'Not so loud.' His eyes raked the backs of the houses for signs of life.

And then he lunged. Cynthia let out a piercing scream. The sound swept along the alley, bounced off the garages and hurtled back.

'Shut up, you bitch.' With lightning speed, his hands went to her throat.

* * *

Almost twelve hours later Chief Inspector Ashworth was stopping off for his morning chat with Sergeant Martin Dutton who was manning the reception desk at Bridgetown police station. The sergeant looked thoughtful and more than a little worried.

'Good morning, Martin,' Ashworth said. 'You look like you've lost a pound and found a penny.'

Dutton gave a curt nod, his usual sparkle strangely absent. 'I've got a tricky one, here. A twenty-three-year-old girl's gone missing. She lives with her parents, went out for some fish and chips at about nine fifteen last night and didn't come back.'

'Anything suspicious about her disappearance?' Ashworth asked.

'Not really.' Dutton scratched his bald scalp. 'I don't think the girl's done a runner, though. For one thing, her garage door was open . . . Her parents think she must have come back from the chippy and was about to put the car away.'

'She could have left it open when she drove off for the chips,' Ashworth ventured.

'Would you leave your garage door open, nowadays, Jim? Especially if you lived on the council estate, as this girl does.'

'Point taken. Anything else?'

'That's about it, but it just doesn't gel with me. I suppose if she was doing a bunk she wouldn't have given the garage doors a thought, but . . .'

'But things like that become habit, don't they, Martin? What have you done about it?'

'What can I do? Officially it's a missing person case.' Dutton made a crude gesture towards the ceiling and Superintendent John Newton's first-floor office. Newton was a stickler for procedure and was not one to waste funds on flights of fancy.

'Martin, why don't you get a couple of your lads to make some house-to-house checks in the street where she lives? Should you get into trouble for it, you can tell the big chief I asked you to do it.'

Dutton grinned. 'That won't be necessary, Jim, I only wanted a second opinion.'

'You never know, Martin, you could end up with a medal for your swift action,' Ashworth said, making for the stairs.

'Never in a million years,' was the sergeant's sour reply. 'I doubt if Newton would put me forward for the cracked piss-pot award.'

* * *

Police Constables Gordon Bennett and John Masters had worked their way along Gypsy Lane, the address of Cynthia Labrum, with little success.

'Let's face it, Gord,' Masters remarked, 'most of 'em around here don't even want to see us, let alone talk to us.'

'I know, it's a waste of time,' Bennett said. 'We don't even know what we're looking for.'

They marched up yet another garden path and rang the bell. Two minutes later, they were about to give up when the door came open a few inches, a gold-coloured chain stretching across the gap, a grey-haired old lady peering out at them.

'Yes?' she said.

'Good morning, madam,' Bennett said.

'You'll have to speak up, young man, I'm hard of hearing.'

'Good morning, madam,' Bennett said again, louder this time. 'We're making enquiries to see if anyone heard anything suspicious between nine and nine thirty last night.'

'She's a fine one to ask,' Masters whispered.

The woman had a hand cupped to her ear, her face within the gap a mask of concentration. 'No, I didn't hear a thing,' she finally told them.

'Oh well,' Bennett said, 'thanks for your time, madam.' He touched his cap and turned to go.

'But my son did,' she called after them.

They hurried back to the door. 'What did your son actually hear?' Masters asked.

'That's right, my son heard something.'

'What did he actually hear?' Masters shouted.

'Oh, a lot of screaming in the alley round the back. And I think he said a car roared off just afterwards.'

'Where is your son, madam?'

'What?' the woman said, frowning. 'Speak up, why don't you? You young people all tend to mumble nowadays.'

Masters threw Bennett an exasperated look. 'I said, where is your son now, madam?'

'He's upstairs, in bed, drinking a cup of tea.'

'Listen, love,' Bennett yelled, 'can we have a quick word with him?'

They re-emerged ten minutes later with Bennett flicking the switch of the radio clipped to his tunic collar. 'Sarge, I think we've got a result. We've found a guy who heard some screaming and a car moving off at speed at about nine thirty last night. Perhaps CID would like to get here — if they're out of bed, that is.'

'I'll pass that on to them,' Dutton said with a chuckle. 'By the way, I hear Holly Bedford's on the look-out for a new boyfriend. Fancy your chances, Gordon?'

Bennett grimaced; as a man whose stormy marriage had put him on the wrong side of disillusioned, his hobbies did not include lusting after nubile female officers.

'Sarge, if I'm ever stupid enough to get hooked again, you've got my permission to castrate me — okay?'

CHAPTER 10

Ashworth surveyed the alley. On one side were the garages — seven, in all. On the other, high walls and gates leading to the back yards of the houses that made up Gypsy Lane. It was a blind alley, its only entrance approached via the main Bridgetown to Morton road which split the council estate into two halves. Ashworth saw that the garages would be visible from the upper floors of the houses; but at night, with its poor lighting, the alley would be a black spot.

'Well, Josh, we really don't have much. What do you think?'

'I'd say a big, fat zero.' They stopped by Cynthia's garage, its door now closed. 'Do we know who locked the garage up, guv?'

'The father, apparently. And who can blame him? They keep a lot of stuff in there — they didn't want it pinched on top of everything else.'

Josh cast his dubious gaze around the small area. 'I wouldn't imagine it's that unusual to hear screams around here, or cars moving off at speed.'

'You're probably right,' Ashworth said. 'Those noises might have nothing to do with the missing girl. In any case, we haven't got enough to start an investigation. All we can do is put out an all-cars alert for her Escort. Martin Dutton's got all the details on that.'

'Right, guv.'

Josh avoided the chief inspector's gaze. He knew only too well why Ashworth had chosen to attend this very routine enquiry, and why he had asked Josh to join him — he wanted to know something. There were times when discretion was not high on Ashworth's list of attributes.

Keeping in step on the way to Ashworth's car, Josh decided to pre-empt the question. 'I've got no idea, guv, and that's the truth.'

Ashworth shot him a startled look. 'You've no idea of what?'

'Whether Holly's having an affair with Mark Hartland.'

'I'm that transparent, am I?' Ashworth asked, smiling.

'At times, guv, yes. And I really don't see that it's any of our business.'

'When her love life starts to affect her concentration at work, then it becomes my business. She's a good copper, but when her mind's not on the job she'd test the patience of a saint.' He sighed. 'But it's not just that, Josh, I worry about the girl. I'd hate to see her get hurt again.'

'I know you mean well, guv, but Holly goes her own way and she's got enough pride for three. You know what she's like — if it all goes wrong she'll just shut us out for a while, say it doesn't matter, and then bounce back after a couple of days.'

But Ashworth disagreed. 'Josh, under that I-can-take-on-the-world front, Holly's a very vulnerable woman. Just one more serious emotional jolt could put her under for good. And her career along with her.'

They reached the car. 'Well, I've got no influence over her,' Josh said, waiting for Ashworth to unlock it. 'She's shut me out completely, and you've seen how she behaves around Mark.'

'I have.' Ashworth laughed. 'No doubt she thinks they're being very discreet and professional in the office, but we know her too well, don't we? I've also noticed her colourful language isn't on show when he's around — she becomes quite the little lady.' He shrugged. 'Anyway, we're hardly earning the Queen's shilling talking about Holly's love life. And, as you said, it's none of my business.'

'*Our* business, guv, that's what I said.'

* * *

Holly was at her desk, staring down at a report but taking in little of its content. Mere feet away was Mark's empty desk, and it troubled her. He had called in earlier to say that his cold had worsened and he would be staying at home. She was missing him already, and loud warning bells were going off inside her head.

In the years since her husband's death Holly had convinced herself that she would never fall in love again. Okay, her high sex drive was sometimes impossible to ignore. She had accepted that, had come to terms with it. But sex and love were entirely different animals — sometimes the twain did meet, and lucky was the woman when they did — and while a man might avail himself of the more basic parts of her anatomy, he would never find the path to Holly's heart. That had belonged to Jason; it was buried with him beneath six feet of earth.

Or so she had thought. Only now she realised it wasn't; it was still inside her, vulnerable, capable of being broken a second time. Holly felt that to give her all to another would be the final betrayal of her late husband. To do so would be an admission that her feelings for him had fallen short of love. And she wouldn't be able to live with that. But, what about Mark? She tossed the report to one side with an exasperated sigh.

'You all right, Holly?' Bobby asked from his desk.

'Why does everybody keep asking me if I'm all right?' she snapped. 'Yes, Bobby, I'm fine, I'm great, I couldn't be better.'

'Fair enough,' he said, holding up his hands. 'I couldn't really give a stuff how you are. I was only being polite.'

Holly found herself smiling. She had mothered Bobby through his raw recruit stage, then on to his confidence-building period when he had chased everything in a skirt. And finally she had watched him settle into the enquiring man he had become, always seeking knowledge and turning a deaf ear to any snide remarks from his fellow officers. He was tremendous fun to be with, but possessed an acid tongue when one was needed.

'Sorry, Bobby, I didn't mean it.' She reached for her shoulder bag. 'I'm trying to give up the ciggies and it's making me short-tempered.' She lit one and inhaled gratefully.

'Forget it.' Bobby grinned; he had suddenly remembered that Mark Hartland was a non-smoker.

Holly drew smoke into her lungs and welcomed its calming effect. 'So,' she said, 'where are we?'

'We've got an all-cars out on the missing girl's Escort . . .' He glanced at his watch. 'If it's going to turn up in today's taken-without-consents then it should be coming in any time now.'

'Do we know anything about the girl?'

'She's from a respectable family,' Bobby said. 'She works in insurance at the moment, but I put a few feelers out and it seems that up to three months ago she was unemployed and she may have been on the game, in a very small way. Still, not uncommon, is it?'

'When you're hard up, Bobby, you have to liquidate your assets. As you say, there's a lot of it going on.' The telephone on her desk buzzed and she reached for the receiver. 'DS Bedford.'

'Holly, it's Mark. I know you can't talk, but could I come and see you tonight? About eight?'

His voice sent a pleasant shiver coursing through her body. 'Yes, I can't see why not,' she said, with a smile.

* * *

62

The missing Escort turned up at 4 p.m. It was found along a dirt track leading to a local gravel pit. The chassis was completely burnt out but its metal number plates had survived, which was more than could be said for fingerprints, fibre samples or other clues, so it was of little use to CID.

Holly and Josh were despatched to the girl's home to interview her parents. It was a sombre journey, both of them aware that they could be returning in the not-too-distant future to break news of the girl's death.

Mr and Mrs Labrum were middle-aged and weary-looking, an ordinary couple who were clearly devoted to their only daughter. Holly counted no fewer than seven framed photographs of the girl when they were shown into the living room.

'I'm sorry to have to tell you this,' she said, lowering herself on to the beige and brown sofa, 'but we've located your daughter's car. It was found this afternoon, burnt out near the Billing-brook gravel pit.'

The couple exchanged a worried glance. 'What can that mean?' Mr Labrum said. His face was almost as grey as his thinning hair.

'I wouldn't worry unduly,' Josh jumped in. 'The car may have been stolen.'

'But where's Cynthia?' Mrs Labrum asked, a pleading tone in her voice.

'That's what we're trying to establish,' Holly said. 'Is there anybody she might be staying with?'

'What sort of question's that?' Mr Labrum spat. 'Listen, she went out last night to fetch us some fish and chips. She closed the garage door behind her — I know she did because I was in the kitchen and I heard it. When she wasn't back by quarter to ten I went out to wait for her and the garage door was open.' He looked from one to the other. 'Well, can't you see what that means? She came back and opened the garage.' He shook his head despairingly. 'But why would she drive off again?'

'She could have forgotten something,' Josh cut in. 'Any number of things could have happened; somebody she knew could have been coming along the alley . . . anything. Tell us about your daughter's friends — maybe they can throw some light on this.'

'Her friends have got nothing to do with it,' Mr Labrum said. 'You should be—'

'Don't lose your temper, Eric,' his wife chided. She turned to Josh. 'She didn't have . . . I mean, she doesn't have many friends, really. She's a very quiet girl, not one for gadding about.'

Holly took out her notebook. 'Where does Cynthia work, Mrs Labrum?'

'She's a receptionist at Allied Insurance in the high street. She's been there for about three months.'

'Right, we'll check there,' Holly said, jotting it down. 'Did she have any boyfriends?'

Mrs Labrum shook her head. 'I don't think so. She's had them in the past, of course, but nothing serious. Oh, there was someone a while back, when she was unemployed. We never met him, though; Cynthia never even told us about him, to be honest. But every Wednesday and Thursday night she'd get dolled up and go out—'

'I was worried, if you want the truth,' her husband interjected. 'I mean, just two nights a week . . . He could have been married for all we knew.'

'And when did that stop?' Holly quizzed.

'As soon as she started work — she stayed in every night after that.' He lifted his shoulders. 'We didn't say anything to Cynthia, we didn't want her to think we were prying.'

'And there was no one else that you know of?' Holly asked, writing it all down.

'No,' Mrs Labrum said, a little too quickly. Holly looked up in time to see the woman's imploring glance at her husband.

'Sorry, love, but I'm going to tell them,' he said, quietly. 'This is our girl we're talking about.' He turned to Holly. 'That Lee Swanson and his gang — they used to bother her a lot. They used to accost her every time she got out of her car. I used to see them from the back bedroom.'

64

'For what reason?' Holly asked.

'Cynthia just said he was always asking her for a date, wouldn't take no for an answer. Well, me and the wife didn't want to make too big a thing out of it, so we let it go. I mean, she's a grown woman — we can't mollycoddle her for ever, however much we'd like to.'

'So, Mr Labrum, you're saying that Lee Swanson was pestering your daughter,' Holly said.

'He was, yes, and I wish I'd done something about it at the time.' He clenched his fists, his anger almost palpable. 'It's about time somebody stood up to that scum. They've started to run this estate, and anybody who stands up to them gets a litre of petrol through their letter box.'

'When did he start pestering her?' Holly asked.

'As soon as she started work.' Mrs Labrum replied. 'Before that we had no idea Cynthia knew him. I remember saying to Eric, he only wants her now she's earning.'

'Right.' Holly closed her notebook. 'Could you let us have a recent picture of your daughter?'

Mrs Labrum crossed to the sideboard and selected one of the framed photographs. 'This is the best likeness of her.'

Outside, at the car. Josh said, 'What do you think?'

'Same as you,' was Holly's dejected reply. 'We'll be back here soon with the worst news those poor people are ever going to get.'

* * *

Holly only just made it for 8 p.m. Wearing fresh make-up and her new black dress, she'd hardly had time to sit down before the doorbell chimed. She sauntered into the hall and pulled open the front door.

'Oh, hi, Mark,' she said, smiling.

'Peace offering.' He held out a bottle of red wine. 'For last night.'

Holly took it with a grin. 'There was no need for this, Mark, honestly.' She smoothed down her dress. 'I don't know what you'll think of me — I've hardly had any time to get ready.'

'You look great,' he said, going through to the lounge. 'Shall I take the cork out?'

'It's okay, I'll do it in the kitchen. How's the cold?'

'A lot better. Must have been one of those twenty-four-hour things.'

The cork came out with a satisfying pop and Holly quickly filled two glasses, taking a long sip from her own in the hope that the alcohol would melt away her inhibitions. She found Mark making himself comfortable in an armchair. He looked so handsome in the soft lighting, and his sexy green eyes sparkled as they touched glasses.

'So, what's been happening at the station?'

Holly sat in the chair opposite and told him all about the missing girl.

'And nobody knows who she went off with?'

'No.' Holly sipped the wine. 'But the report we've had of her screaming suggests that she didn't go willingly.'

Mark mulled it over while Holly refilled the glasses. 'It's funny, you know, but working at the station has made me wish I'd gone into the police force.'

'It's okay,' was Holly's non-committal reply.

He took a long drink. 'I should have brought another bottle. This is really chasing my cold away.'

'Don't worry. I've got plenty more.' She laughed. 'Hey, you're not trying to get me drunk, are you?'

'Would I do that?' His eyes twinkled. 'You don't have any need to worry with me, you know.'

Holly smiled. 'I do know. It's just that I don't want you thinking I'm not tempted by your offer.' The wine was loosening her tongue. 'But, with you being married, well, it complicates things.'

'Unhappily married,' he reminded her.

'Yes, but still married,' Holly countered. 'And, in any case, I don't know anything about you. I don't even know if you've got any kids.'

66

He shook his head. 'Never tried for them. We didn't get on from the start, Holly, and I think we both realised that bringing kids into the world would have been a disaster for us.'

'Have there been any other women?' she asked, tentatively.

'Affairs, you mean?' He raised a forbidding eyebrow, but his eyes were laughing. 'Do we have to go into all that?'

'I'm not trying to pry,' Holly quickly assured him. 'I'm just trying to understand you, I suppose.' She gave him a warm smile. 'Mark Hartland, you are a very attractive guy, and if you've been unhappy for as long as you say there must have been other women.'

'Is this an official interview?' he complained with a grin. 'Aren't I entitled to have this recorded?'

Holly giggled. 'Sorry, my tape recorder's at the cleaners.'

'Okay, Detective Sergeant Bedford, there have been other women. I've been married for ten years — the first two were lousy, and from there it got worse.'

'But you never left her?'

He gave a shrug. 'Never saw the point. None of the others meant anything to me, and I suppose I always thought it could be a case of out of the frying pan and into the fire.' He drained his glass. 'Next question, please.'

'No more questions.'

'Your turn now, then.'

Holly sipped her wine and settled back in the chair. 'All right. I was married, but I don't want to go into that. Yes, I've had some affairs over the past few years, most of which I regret now.' She waved her glass. 'Even in this day and age, Mark, the attitude still prevails that if a man puts it about he's a jack-the-lad, but if a woman does the same she's a slag.' She finished her wine. 'Anyway, I'm going on too much. I'll fetch another bottle.'

They spent the rest of the evening talking, moving on to lighter subjects, enjoying themselves. Mark called for a taxi around midnight and offered her a chaste kiss before he left.

Holly was in love.

CHAPTER 11

Lee Swanson moved around the crowded pub as though he owned the place. This was his territory. No one would dare challenge him here. Cigarette smoke hung in a low haze, rap music thumped from the jukebox and people stood aside for him to pass while he scrutinised the drinkers. He finally found the person he was looking for in the lounge.

Helen Palmer was perched on a high stool by the bar. Four punters at fifty pounds a throw had left her flush and thirsty. She was already on her third double vodka and tonic and had planned on having a few more before she called it a day. Her face paled considerably as Swanson approached. She turned her back, hoping he wouldn't spot her, and her breath was held fast when he came to a stop by her side.

'Helen, my darlin',' he whispered, menacingly. 'You tryin' to hide from me?'

She swivelled around on the stool. 'Of course not, Lee. I'm just enjoying a drink.'

'Good girl.' He dug his hands deep into the pockets of his black bomber jacket. 'You've heard that Cyn's gone missing?'

'Yes.' Helen sipped her drink, her shaking hand causing the ice cubes to rattle against the glass.

'Tomorrow night the fuzz're gonna be all over this place, askin' questions.' He leant closer. 'I just wanted to make sure you remembered that I didn't know the bird.'

'If that's what you want me to tell them, Lee, then that's what I'll tell them.' She smiled brightly. 'Honest, Lee, I don't want any trouble with you . . . honest.'

'Good girl.' Swanson grabbed her delicate chin between thumb and forefinger, then squeezed hard. 'I like people I can rely on, Helen — know what I mean?'

She whimpered. 'You're hurting me. Please, let me go.'

He gave a coarse laugh. 'Don't know me own strength, see. But just as long as the other bastards do, eh?'

Swanson released her and took a small pill box from his pocket. He withdrew a yellow tablet and popped it into his mouth, washing it down with about a third of Helen's vodka.

'Cheers,' he said, handing back the glass. 'Now, you stay safe, you hear me?' The threat in his voice was all too clear.

While Helen watched him swagger off, an awful taste of loathing came into her mouth that no amount of vodka would be able to wash away.

* * *

Boris never minded the flat in the spring and summer months, when rising temperatures dried out the damp. A musty smell was left behind, a smell that was impossible to shift, but at least the rooms were warm.

Yet, a couple of hours spent in the comfort of Megan Rowntree's cosy little office, drinking tea from a bone china cup, was enough to make Boris realise that he and his father were living in a slum that was unfit for human habitation. According to Megan the terrace of houses was only standing because the council did not want the tenants on the streets, claiming for bed and breakfast accommodation.

With thoughts of Megan crowding his mind, Boris tip-toed into his father's room. The old man was lying on his back, fast asleep. Relieved, Boris quietly closed the door and stood for a while in the cramped passage.

He found Megan so easy to talk to. A smile of encouragement was forever on her lips, and his words flowed freely. He had told her of his early childhood in Russia, the hardships, the suffering, but also of the small joys that had sometimes brightened his youth. Not all was bad then. His father had been withdrawn, yes, disturbed, definitely, but not sick in the mind as he was now.

Boris had parried Megan's questions about his mother and brother, saying that to talk of such things brought too much pain. She had not pushed the subject, and he was grateful for that. Instead she had given him more tea and a huge wedge of cake. It was a delicious sponge with layers of jam and cream, topped with a fine dusting of icing sugar.

When he had needed the lavatory, voicing his request only when the discomfort became too great, Megan seemed not to notice his embarrassment. She led him gently into the corridor and pointed to a door on their right. Inside the lavatory Boris had gazed with an almost childlike wonder at the clean white tiles that covered the wall up to waist level, tiles that smelt faintly of fresh lemons.

He moved now along the dark passage, its brown wallpaper adding to the dismal aura, and felt for the light switch inside his own bathroom. The naked bulb flared into life, its harsh glare showing up every crack in the deep porcelain sink that served as a washbasin, picking out every bit of corrosion on the lavatory chain that hung from the old-fashioned water closet. There was no bath, no room for one; his father had to suffer the indignities of a bed bath while Boris managed with a stand-up wash.

Very quickly, he closed the door behind him, his nose wrinkling in distaste. The stink of the lake was still perceptible in that tiny enclosure; a dank, dirty water smell that would not go away. Dropping to his haunches, Boris tore open a small cupboard beneath the sink and pulled out a tightly rolled bundle. There on the floor he unwrapped the black suit, the black socks, the white shirt.

He fumbled for the hot and cold water taps. Water pressure was low and the sink took a while to fill, but when it had Boris plunged the clothing into it and took up a bar of green soap. Rubbing furiously, he watched a lather form as he worked on the coarse fabric.

'Come clean,' he sobbed, scrubbing until the skin on his fingers began to burn. 'Please . . . come clean.'

* * *

Ashworth had hardly settled at his desk next morning when Sergeant Dutton poked his head around the door of CID.

'She's turned up, Jim.' His gloomy expression told Ashworth that Cynthia Labrum had not been found alive.

'Where, Martin?'

'In the river, just outside town. Quite near to Beggar's Meadow. I've alerted the police surgeon, and Alex Ferguson and Forensic are on their way. The area's sealed, of course.'

'Good man,' Ashworth said with a brisk nod. 'Holly . . .'

She was already collecting her coat from the rack. 'With you, guv.'

They exchanged few words on the journey; Ashworth was in no mood for idle chit-chat. Could he be on the wrong track? If the body bore the same marks as that of the prostitute, Julie Stevens, then he would have to accept the possibility that they were hunting for a serial killer. They would be entering a race against time. The killer would have to be brought to justice pretty damn quick if a third or a fourth or a fifth death was to be prevented. And they could not afford to release details of the knife marks for fear of copy-cat killings; they could only state that the same man was being hunted for both murders.

Holly was mentally debating the best way to break the news to Cynthia's parents. It was the part of the job she hated most. No two persons reacted in quite the same way and therefore it was impossible for police officers to fully prepare themselves beforehand. Would they turn on her, unleash their frustrations for the fact that the killer remained free? Or would they crumple under the weight of her dreadful news? Well, she would soon know the answer.

Ashworth brought the Scorpio to a smooth halt a little way beyond the cordoned-off area of the riverbank. The police tent was in view as they clambered from the car. Ashworth cleared his throat and gave Holly a resigned look. They ducked beneath the yellow police tape and trudged across a meadow already alive with colourful spring flowers; their delicate perfumes, freed by a brisk breeze, wafted towards the picturesque waterway. Those splendid surroundings only enhanced the futility of another wasted life.

Alex Ferguson, waiting outside the tent, confirmed Ashworth's worst fears with his opening remark. 'Seems like your man's got a thing about water, Jim.'

'Who found the body?' Ashworth asked.

'A jogger.' Ferguson dug his hands into the pockets of his green body warmer. 'It was caught on some tree roots. Bit of luck, really — it wouldn't have come up for another couple of days, otherwise.'

'Luck doesn't seem like an appropriate word, Alex.' Ashworth nodded towards the tent. 'Same as before?'

'Exactly the same,' the pathologist confirmed. 'Take a look.'

The tent flap was pulled back and Ashworth got his first glimpse of Cynthia Labrum's death mask. Her eyes were closed now, but her mouth sagged open in a silent scream, her purple tongue distended. A thin red line ran down the centre of her face.

Ferguson said, 'She was strangled, then dumped in the water. Soon after she went missing — that's my guess. I'll be more precise when I've had a better look.'

'Are you sure the cut's the same as the one on the other girl?'

'Sorry, Jim, but it is. It starts at the scalp and goes straight down to the groin. It's strange, though . . .' Ferguson turned his gaze to the body.

'What is?' Ashworth asked.

The pathologist frowned. 'Well, you remember when the first body turned up, you made a remark about the killer undressing the girl, then cutting her and putting the clothes back on?'

'I remember.'

'Well, I'm almost certain that's what happened here. I've only done a quick examination, obviously, but there are no marks on the body that would suggest boisterous love-making, say, or a struggle.' He turned bewildered eyes back to the body. 'I'd say the girl was strangled, then the killer undressed her, used the knife, and put the clothes back on. Weird, isn't it?'

Ashworth had to swallow hard; the stench of death was already working its own special magic on his digestive system. He hurried out of the tent, ushering Holly before him.

'We've got a second body, now, guv,' she said. 'Still think it's Swanson?'

'Why not? Her parents told you that he was pestering her.'

'Oh, for God's sake . . .' Holly's ill-concealed impatience told Ashworth that she was in one of her no-nonsense moods. She said, 'Fine, let's bring him in, then. And if you're right we can put a stop to this, once and for all.'

Ashworth cast her a sharp look. 'We do have to find something to link Swanson with the girl's disappearance before we can question him, Holly — or had you forgotten that?'

'Okay, we pulled him once and the bastard got acquitted,' she said, tartly. 'What are you frightened of, guv — that if we do it again, or if we even dare to question him, his lawyer's going to make a complaint?'

'No,' Ashworth spat back. 'I'm guided by procedure, Holly. I'm not in the habit of dodging trouble with the lawyers of tuppenny villains.'

While the detectives locked eyes, Alex Ferguson thought it best to disappear. 'I'll be in touch, Jim,' he said, edging away. 'Post-mortem tomorrow. I'll call you.' Without shifting his gaze from Holly's face, Ashworth raised a hand in acknowledgement.

'We know Swanson was pestering the girl,' Ashworth said, sharply.

'We know he spoke to her on a number of occasions — that's not the same as pestering her, guv. And we've only got the parents' word for it, anyway.'

Ashworth pondered for a moment. 'Right, Holly, go and talk to some of the local prostitutes — see if you can establish a link between Cynthia and Swanson. Take Josh with you. Oh, and talking about the girl's parents, somebody's got to break the news to them.'

'Let me do it, guv. I'll take a WPC along with me.'

'All right. You might as well do it now. We're finished here.'

As Holly strode off towards the car, Ashworth lingered for a moment. Flashbulbs were popping with regularity inside the tent, the police photographer catching the body from every angle. Soon, the corpse would be bundled into a body bag and hauled to the mortuary vehicle — nicknamed the meat wagon, by some in the uniformed division — and then transported to the morgue.

How little people were affected by death nowadays, he reflected. In tonight's newspapers Cynthia Labrum would be front page news, but this time next week only those closest to her would remember.

CHAPTER 12

Holly went alone to the red-light district. She wanted to take her time, mingle with the prostitutes in a leisurely manner, all girls together — and she couldn't do that with Josh at her heel. Most of the girls knew Holly, felt easy with her; she was one detective who could look at them without contempt, could talk to them as if they were equals.

Holly was not expecting problems. However, most of the girls she tried to approach hurried away, glancing over their shoulders to make sure she wasn't following. This had never happened before, and Holly wondered what could have instigated such a change. This part of Bridgetown had never had a happy feel — too many of life's losers were eking out an existence on its streets — but there was now a sense of foreboding. Something was very wrong.

Holly decided to do another circuit of the area and then call it a day. Her footsteps, echoing dully on the empty pavements, matched the beating of her heavy heart. Breaking the news to Cynthia's parents had been a distressing experience. To start with they had been too shocked to speak, but then Mr Labrum had started to rant, spewing his anger into her face. Holly had tried her best to calm him, but grief and rage were not the easiest emotions to subdue. She couldn't even bring herself to ask which of them would identify the body; that would have to wait until tomorrow.

Despite it all, though, despite the dreariness of her task tonight, a small part of Holly's spirit was soaring. Mark had asked her out again. She'd had to refuse because of the job in hand, but she'd been overjoyed to see the disappointment on his face. Please God, could he be the one?

A hopeful smile was on her face when Holly glanced up and spied a girl at the entrance to the recreation ground. She was tall and slim, her long legs made shapely by high stiletto heels. Her outfit was scanty, her pose provocative. Holly hastened across the road, cursing her high heels and wishing she had worn her rubber-soled flats. But her luck held, and Holly was almost upon the girl before she turned.

'Oh, Jesus,' she exclaimed. 'Not you again.'

'Relax,' Holly said, holding up a hand. 'I only want to talk to you.'

'How nice,' the girl mocked.

'Drop the attitude, love, it doesn't suit you.' Holly took a pack of cigarettes from her pocket and offered one across. 'You know we never hassle you unless we get complaints from the public.'

'Oh yes, and how about when you book kerb crawlers?' the girl said, reaching for the cigarette.

'Same answer. If the good citizens complain, we have to respond.' She shrugged. 'Live and let live, that's my motto.'

The girl accepted that along with a light. 'Okay, what do you want?'

'Did you know Cynthia Labrum?'

'What do you mean, *did* I know her?'

'She's dead, I'm afraid.'

The girl's eyes widened. 'Shit . . . How? I mean, was it the same as the other girl?'

Holly nodded. 'Strangled, and then dumped in water.'

'But, why? She'd stopped doing the streets . . . she was out of it.'

'She had been on the game, then?'

The girl's cigarette glowed red as she drew on it. 'Oh, come on, leave her in peace. If her parents found out it'd probably kill them.'

'We have to get as much information as we can if we're going to catch her killer,' Holly persisted.

The girl was young, in her early twenties, but her eyes were old, their light extinguished long ago. She turned them towards Holly. 'Cyn was a nice kid. I tried to talk her out of it.' She gave a weary laugh. 'I'm a tart with a heart, see.'

'Yes?' Holly urged.

'She wouldn't have it. She was out of work and wanted to keep her car running.' Another drag of the cigarette, smoke mingling with the dark. 'She took a couple of regular punters, but that was all. And as soon as she found a job, she jacked it in.'

'Do you know who the two punters were?'

'No idea.'

'Think, love,' Holly urged. 'I know a lot of you girls run checks on your regulars just for safety's sake.'

'Well, if Cyn did, she never told me.'

'Okay.' Holly flicked away her cigarette; it landed in a cascade of sparks. 'Did Lee Swanson know Cynthia?'

The girl flinched. 'Leave it out, will you, I don't need my face marked. Look, this estate'd be better off without him, but until you put him away you won't find anybody round here willing to talk.'

'The bloody universe'd be better off without that scumbag,' Holly muttered. 'Okay, just a straight yes or no — did he know Cynthia Labrum?'

'Yes,' the girl whispered after some thought. 'He didn't want her to give it up. Work it out from there, why don't you?'

'Are you saying Swanson was Cynthia's pimp?' Holly quickly asked.

The girl peered at her watch and ground the half-smoked cigarette beneath her shoe. 'I'm saying nothing else, and much as I'm enjoying our little chat, I've got to go. Trade'll be on the main road, now.'

Holly watched the girl teeter away, her heels clickety-clicking. 'Watch your back, love,' she called. A hand was held high, a tiny wave, and then the girl was gone.

Holly leant against the tall black railings of the rec and sifted through the facts. At the very least they needed to find a reason to question Lee Swanson. At the very least, they needed that.

* * *

Helen Palmer had been seeing this particular client — the bondage freak — for three weeks now, and so far he had given her no trouble, no cause for concern. He was a pussy-cat, really, so she had decided to let him tie her to the bed. After all it was an extra fifteen quid and was, as she kept telling herself with a grin, money for old rope.

The guy was odd, in a nice sort of way. He never wanted her naked like the rest of them did. All she had to do was open her blouse, lift up her skirt and he was away. It was all over in a couple of minutes, and the money was handed across.

Helen took a minute to get herself ready. Then the bed dipped and his face was above her. There was something in his hand, but she couldn't see what it was because he was shielding it from her. Helen froze when he ran the object down her forehead and along her nose. It felt like a tiny point, but it didn't hurt because he was applying the lightest of pressure. It carried on under her chin, across her throat, then down towards her breasts.

When she saw what it was Helen wanted to laugh. It was a pencil. Why was the headcase drawing on her with a pencil? His features were rigid with determination, and his eyes were bright as he watched its progress. It neared her solar plexus, an area where she was particularly ticklish, and Helen had to bite hard on her lower lip to stifle a giggle.

* * *

Josh answered Holly's radio request for a lift back to the police station. He found her still outside the recreation ground, smoking a cigarette.

He leant out of the car window and waved. 'How much, love?'

'It's free for you, lover boy.' She climbed into the passenger side.

'Well?' he asked hopefully. She told him what she had gleaned. 'It's not enough to pull him in, Hol, much as we'd like to.'

'But, Josh, he could have been her pimp. If he was—'

'What proof have we got, though?'

'I think we've got enough to ask him to help with our enquiries. I bet the guv'nor will, too.'

'Oh yeh, and then we'll have to sit back and watch him walk. I'm beginning to wonder whether we'll ever get Swanson for anything.'

'We'll get him,' Holly said ruefully. 'We'll wipe that smug smile off his face.'

They fell silent, the engine still running. Holly finished her cigarette, flicking the end through the open side window while she glanced surreptitiously at Josh. He was staring at the speedometer as if its dial was suddenly an object of immense interest. She let out a loud sigh; they had been here before.

'I've been expecting this, Abraham. Honestly, sometimes you're more like a second mother than a best mate.'

'What?' he asked, defensively. 'I haven't said anything.'

'You don't have to. It's about Mark and me, isn't it? God . . .' She fell back in the seat. 'What with you and the guv'nor watching me all the time . . . I reckon you'd both like to see me fall arse over tit and land on my face.'

'Oh, come on, Bedford, that's not true,' Josh said, turning in his seat. 'You're not much but you're the closest thing I've got to a mate.'

Holly refused to smile. 'Look, I'm sure you mean well, but I don't need this.'

'I know you, Bedford, this isn't just a wham-bam-thank-you-mister — this one goes deeper.' He rested his hand on her shoulder. 'He's married, Hol, you could get badly hurt.'

'Josh . . .' She was just about hanging on to her temper. 'When I need your advice I'll ask for it — okay? Christ, I'm not even having an affair, yet.'

'Yet,' he echoed dully.

'That's right — yet.' She turned on him. 'If I do it'll be because I want to. And if I balls it up and get hurt, then that's something I'll have to deal with. Now just give me some space and let me get on with my life.'

'Fine,' he muttered. 'Sorry I spoke. From now on I'll keep my mouth shut.' Josh slipped the car into gear and pulled away from the kerb.

'Lighten up,' Holly coaxed, 'let me buy you some chips.' He said nothing. 'Oh, sod you, then.'

CHAPTER 13

Ashworth had arranged to meet Holly at the morgue at 9 a.m. sharp the next morning. Alex Ferguson had told him that Cynthia Labrum's post-mortem results would be ready by then and he wanted to be told the details face to face rather than on a disembodied telephone line.

By nine thirty the detectives had concluded their business with the pathologist and were positioned in a corridor, discussing the findings in whispered tones. Not that there was much to discuss. Ferguson claimed that the girl had met her death on the night she vanished and was dead before she went into the river. No extraneous marks had been found on the body — apart from the head-to-groin cut which was approximately four millimetres deep.

'Doesn't tell us much, does it?' Ashworth muttered.

'No, guv, but the cut is interesting. I could see what Alex was getting at. In both cases it was done with precision — a lot of care was taken to get it absolutely right.'

Ashworth nodded. 'Which is why I'm now wondering whether it *was* done by Lee Swanson — he hasn't got the attention span.'

'You don't want to pull him in, then,' Holly huffed.

'Not at the moment. We'd be better off seeing what door-to-door enquiries turn up.' Ashworth leant heavily against the wall. 'If only we could put him in the vicinity of Cynthia Labrum's abduction, it would be a start.'

'We still need her parents to formally identify the body, guv.'

'I know,' he said, sighing. 'You'd better get ready for another ear-bashing, Holly. It seems to me that blaming the police for everything is becoming a growing trend.'

'It's understandable, though — eh? I mean, their whole world's just been ripped apart. They're looking around for somebody to blame, and we're there.'

'Shoot the messenger.'

'Something like that.' She hitched her shoulder bag higher. 'Anyway, leave it with me, guv, I'll handle it.'

* * *

Boris was at the park again, and from the road beyond its perimeter he could clearly see the lake. Sunlight reflected off its surface, transforming the expanse into a blaze of dazzling orange. Even though the very sight of it made his stomach lurch, Boris found himself drawn to the water more and more. Every day he ventured closer, closer. Soon he would stand at the spot where . . .

He closed his eyes and strove to quell his rising nausea. Distant sounds came to him, a gang of boys playing football, their happy, enthusiastic yells soothing his troubled mind. He was moving towards them when an inner voice, a sixth sense, warned him that all was not well.

He swivelled on the spot and alarm welled in his chest. Lee Swanson and his gang of four were bearing down on him. Flight was uppermost in Boris's mind. He turned and ran, his heavy boots digging into the grass, sending clumps of fresh green shoots flying into the air.

The youths gave chase, whooping like a pack of wild Indians and shouting their customary abuse. Their lighter, younger frames gave them speed and soon they had Boris surrounded. He stood in the centre of the circle, his huge shoulders heaving, rivers of sweat streaming down his face.

'Why were you runnin' away from us, Boris? Don't you like us?' Swanson sneered. 'That ain't nice, mate. After all I've done for you, an' all.'

'Leave me alone.' The words were boldly said, but Boris had the air of a petrified animal as his fiery gaze darted left and right in search of an escape route.

Swanson merely grinned. 'You know somethin', Boris, I don't like people who don't like me.' He pushed his face close to the giant's chest. 'And people I don't like always get a kicking.'

'Leave me alone,' Boris said again.

'Now, the fuzz're gonna be askin' questions again — just like the last time. But if they ask you, you'll just say you don't know nothin'. That's right, ain't it, Boris?'

'I will say nothing . . . nothing.'

'Good.' Swanson grabbed him by the coat. 'Because if you do . . . Well, I know a lot of things about you, don't I? Like, what a naughty boy you are . . . I've said nothin' so far, but all that could change if you stopped behavin' yourself. Get my drift?'

Boris struggled to get free but he was grappled from behind and forced to his knees. Hard-toed shoes smashed into his sides, catching his ribs, forcing the breath from his lungs.

'Get off,' he screamed, rolling himself into a ball.

Swanson motioned for the kicking to stop. 'That's just a little warning, Boris. And, remember, I know a lot about you, so don't you start givin' me bother.'

* * *

The formal identification of Cynthia Labrum was a harrowing experience. Mr Labrum surrendered to his grief the moment the white sheet was pulled back and managed nothing more than a brief nod when asked if the body was that of his daughter. Refusing Holly's offers of help and comfort he dashed from the building, leaving her alone with the dead.

She searched around for the mortuary assistant, told him she was finished and then hurried along the corridor leading to the car park. Two mortuary visits in one day were two too many, and Holly hoped they would be her last for a very long time.

'Sorry, guv,' she murmured to herself, 'but you'll have to do without me for ten minutes. I need a coffee.'

Outside the hospital grounds she made for the high street and the appropriately named Coffee Shop. At fifty yards the rich aroma of roasting coffee beans reached her nostrils. Holly quickened her stride.

'Hey, what's the rush?'

The voice came from behind. Holly turned to see Donald Quinn hurrying towards her, a broad smile on his face. Her heart sank, while her mind raced to think up excuses.

'Can't stop, Donald, sorry, I'm on duty.'

His face fell. 'I was hoping to buy you a coffee. I have an apology to make.'

He seemed more casual, less intense and Holly found herself relenting. 'Okay, just a quick one.'

She sat in a corner, watching him pay for two coffees at the till while she delved into her shoulder bag. When her eyes settled on the 'Thank You For Not Smoking' sign Holly allowed the cigarette packet to slip from her fingers into the bag. The world was getting to be a smaller place for smokers, she reflected as Quinn placed the coffee cups on the table.

'How have you been?' he asked.

'Fine,' she said, rather awkwardly. 'And you?'

'Better than I was.' His smile was rueful. 'I really did behave like a first-class idiot, didn't I?'

'I wouldn't go that far.'

'You're too nice, Holly.' He shot her a cringing look. 'When I think about all those flowers and poems . . . I can tell you now, I even started following you about. I was outside your house on the night of your birthday, and I watched you kiss that guy as he dropped you off.' He exhaled sharply. 'I must say, I've never felt so jealous in my whole life.'

Holly dropped sugar into her coffee and stirred; she could think of nothing to say.

'I believe that's what brought me to my senses, actually,' Quinn went on. 'I realised I could be arrested for stalking you, so I decided there and then to pull myself together.'

'I'm sorry, Donald,' was her lame reply.

'It wasn't your fault. I didn't give myself enough time to get over the divorce.' He shrugged. 'I think I needed to feel wanted, and I longed for you to fall in love with me, I suppose.'

'I did tell you right from the start that I didn't want anything permanent.'

'I know you did, but I was in such a state, I wasn't listening.' He held up his coffee cup in a toast. 'But I feel much better now it's off my chest. I hope we can at least be friends, Holly.'

'Yes, of course we can.' She was smiling, but her tone was non-committal.

Quinn took a sip and lowered his cup, his eyes fixed on hers. 'When you saw me just now, your face said it all. Holly, I'd hate to have you dodging me all the time.'

'I wouldn't do that, Don,' she said, too quickly.

Quinn glanced at his Rolex watch and gulped down his coffee. 'Anyway, I must dash, I'm due in court in ten minutes.' He laughed. 'You keep arresting them and I'll keep trying to get them off when they come to court.' He winked as he stood up.

'Are you with anybody?' Holly asked, hesitantly.

'I'm seeing somebody, yes, but I'm taking my time. No more making a fool of myself.' He picked up his briefcase and backed away. 'See you around, then.'

Through the window Holly watched him weave between the slow-moving traffic, his calf-length mackintosh billowing behind him like a white cape. He was a really nice guy, no doubt about it, but he wasn't for her. Pity, really. The bleep of her radio cut through her thoughts.

'DS Bedford.'

'Holly, my lovely, it's your loyal admirer, Douglas, at Central Control. House-to-house have turned up a witness who saw Lee Swanson near Cynthia Labrum's house on the night she went missing. Jim Ashworth wants you and Josh to go to the young gentleman's home and ask if he'd be so good as to help us with our enquiries.'

Holly frowned at the radio. 'You been at the poetry again, Dougie?'

'The thought of you, DS Bedford, always makes me wax lyrical.' He chuckled. 'Where are you?'

'At the morgue,' Holly lied.

'Blimey, you must like bodies,' was his cheerful reply.

'Only male ones, Dougie . . . as I'm sure you've heard.'

He tut-tutted. 'Why do you have to be so base, Holly? It's most unbecoming.'

'Balls.' She grinned. 'Tell the guv'nor I'm on my way to get Josh.' She switched off the radio, stopping any further banter, and settled back to finish her coffee.

* * *

Forays into certain areas of the council estate were becoming increasingly difficult for the police, given the growing number of street gangs controlling their own small territories. Years ago those same gangs would have settled their disputes with fist fights or harmless raillery. But today they acted more like warring factions with their knives and petrol bombs — even guns were finding their way into the hands of these degenerates. And woe betide anyone who stepped in their way, be they police or members of the public.

By the time Holly swung her Micra into Kirkstone Crescent a group of youngsters was already on their tail. Their inane banter was innocent enough, but both detectives knew that careful handling would be needed if a nasty situation were to be avoided.

'Let's have a bit of fun, Josh,' she said, nodding towards them. 'Let's knock a few heads together.'

'If only we could,' Josh replied, struggling out of his seat belt.

They left the car and stood surveying the group. More than half were female, and all wore gold rings through their noses, ears, eyebrows — one girl even had them through her nipples. They knew that because the said body parts were poking through holes in the girl's black top.

'Christ,' Josh muttered, 'it makes your blood run cold, doesn't it?'

Holly grinned. 'It's all that female flesh, Abraham. It must be your worst nightmare.'

He managed a grin back. 'Come on, Hol, let's get this over and done with before the natives get hostile.'

It was Holly who banged on Lee Swanson's new white-glossed front door. 'Police,' she called through the letter box.

By this time the youngsters had grouped around the garden gate, their whistles and catcalls taking on a more sinister tone. A very tense moment passed before Swanson opened the door.

'You shouldn't mock the afflicted,' he called to his peers. Then, to Holly, 'Okay, what do you want?'

'We want you, down the nick.'

'You arrestin' me, then?'

'No, we just want you to answer a few questions.'

Swanson folded his arms and leant against the door jamb. 'Say I don't want to come? Say I've got other, more pressin', commitments?'

'Then we'll look again at what we've got, and if it's enough we'll nick you,' Holly said. 'Now, hurry up and shift your arse.'

'Not so fast, Sergeant, I think you're forgettin' something.'

She raised a quizzical eyebrow. 'Oh, really? And what's that?'

'You've already nicked me twice . . .' He grinned. 'And didn't you end up lookin' like a silly tart?'

Holly gave him her sweetest smile. 'So, you're refusing to come with us — is that what you're saying, *Mr* Swanson?'

'Now, would I say that?' he replied, a mocking light in his eyes. 'No, I'm always happy to help the police. And, let's face it, you lot need all the help you can get. Just give me a minute to ring my brief.' He straightened up and reached for the door. 'You can wait on my property, just so long as you behave yourselves. If you don't, then you'll have to wait in the gutter.' Swanson took a backward step and slammed the door.

'I will kill that prick,' Holly quietly fumed. 'I will tear him limb from limb. I'll—'

'Steady, Bedford,' Josh warned. 'Don't let him get to you — you'll only be falling into his trap.'

She threw him a accusing look. 'How the hell do you stay so calm?'

'Positive thinking, that's all. Positive thinking.'

'Oh, poofs are good at that, are they?'

'A damn sight better than nymphos, obviously.'

Holly laughed, and before she could think of a fitting riposte Swanson was opening the door.

'Right, you two, I'm ready for you, now.' He pushed past them and swaggered towards the gate.

'You drive, Josh. I'll sit in the back with Prince Charming.'

Holly handed him the keys, and while Josh quickly opened the driver's door and leant over to unlock the back the youths started to circle the car.

'Okay,' Holly said to Swanson, 'tell your friends to back off, and do it now. We don't want any trouble, do we?'

'If you say so, Sergeant.' He turned his sneering grin towards the group. 'Here, you lot, you're frightening the lady. Go on, piss off, and I'll see you later.' They dispersed immediately.

Josh was holding open the rear door. 'Mind your head, sir,' Holly said. As he ducked down to get in she placed a hand on the back of Swanson's neck, making sure that he collected a hefty bump as he was bundled inside.

'You bitch,' he spat, his forehead colliding with metal.

'Sorry, it was an accident,' she said, brightly, 'just an accident. But you can make a complaint at the station, if you so wish.'

CHAPTER 14

Ashworth paced reception while he waited for Swanson to be brought in. The youth's solicitor had already arrived; an oily little man by the name of Oliver Willis, from the same office as Donald Quinn. He was standing at the desk, trying to start a conversation with Sergeant Dutton.

There were times when Ashworth could actually feel his blood reach boiling point, and this was one of those times. Glaring at Willis, making no attempt to hide his dislike for the man, Ashworth wandered over to the desk, his scowl decidedly vicious.

'I hope you're going to let me question your client properly, Mr Willis.'

The small man, not in the least intimidated by the chief inspector's bulk, gazed up into Ashworth's face. 'I shall advise Mr Swanson of his rights, and that will include telling him which questions he need not answer.'

'I see.' Ashworth paused. 'How do you sleep at night, Mr Willis?'

'Very well, actually.' His thin bloodless lips pulled back into a smile. 'Chief Inspector, I'm sure I don't have to remind you of the fact that you accused my client of murder — a charge of which he was acquitted. You then accused him of burglary, but later had to drop the case and return his property — his *own* property together with an apology. When this latest flight of fancy of yours turns out to be groundless — as it surely will — I shall instruct my client to make an official complaint.' His cheery glance bounced from Ashworth to Dutton and back again. 'There, I think we both know where we stand now — don't you, Chief Inspector?'

The words stung Ashworth as surely as blows to the face. He turned abruptly and strode towards the double doors, his gaze frantically searching the car park. Within a minute Josh pulled in off the road and Ashworth watched while Holly manhandled their charge out of the rear seat.

Swanson was the first to enter reception. Ignoring the chief inspector he made straight for Willis and shook the man's hand warmly. Holly caught Ashworth's angry expression and gave a helpless shrug; Josh merely looked the other way.

'You should have heard the verbal he was giving us all the way here,' she said to Ashworth. 'And look at him, now — butter wouldn't melt in his mouth.'

'I could break his neck, Holly.' The words were squeezed out from between clenched teeth, but she got their meaning.

'I've just spent ten minutes in the back of a car with him, guv, and I could happily push his face through the back of his head.'

Ashworth gave a sudden laugh. 'It's just as well Willis is there to keep his client in one piece.'

'Actually, guv, I was thinking of Josh doing the questioning. He seems to be able to detach himself.'

'Why not? Holly, you stay in charge of the tape recorder, and I'll keep out of the way.'

'Chief Inspector,' Willis called. 'My client is waiting.'

* * *

Holly dealt with procedure at the tape recorder, and when all relevant information had been fed in, Josh began.

'Thank you for coming in, Mr Swanson,' he said, with an amiable smile.

'Listen, the first thing I want to do is make a complaint about her.' He flicked a morose glance towards Holly. 'She bashed my head against the car when I was gettin' in.' He turned to his solicitor and pointed to a tiny red mark on his forehead.

Josh leant across the table; his eyes screwed into narrow slits. 'I thought that was a spot,' he said, his expression deadpan. 'And I do have to say that things were a touch boisterous outside your house, what with your friends jostling us. Perhaps Detective Sergeant Bedford was a little heavy-handed in her haste to get you safely inside the car. Anyway, I'm sure Mr Willis will tell you how to make a complaint.' He settled back in his seat. 'Now, Mr Swanson, I believe you knew Cynthia Labrum?'

The youth stared into the middle distance, mouthing the name several times. Finally, he looked at Josh and shook his head. 'No, never heard of her.'

'We have a witness who says you used to pester her.'

'There's no need to say anything to that,' Willis jumped in.

Swanson glanced at his solicitor and then returned his smiling eyes to Josh. 'Then they're mistaken, ain't they?'

Josh made no response. He went on, 'You were seen in the vicinity of Gypsy Lane on the day and at the time when Miss Labrum was abducted.'

Swanson lit a cigarette and left the smoke to trickle from his nostrils. 'I live round there, don't I? Jesus, you're really scrapin' the bottom of the barrel this time.'

Josh waved away a cloud of smoke that was aimed deliberately at his face. 'So, Mr Swanson, you didn't know the girl and you didn't see her on the day she was abducted?'

He shrugged. 'How would I know if I seen her or not? I didn't know her, did I?'

'Steady,' Willis warned. 'Constable, my client is not aware that he knew the girl, and he most definitely did not see her on the day you mentioned. Now, if there're no more questions . . .' He made to leave.

Josh held up a hand. 'Please sit down, Mr Willis, I'm not finished yet. Now, Mr Swanson, we know that you own a Stanley knife—'

'So?' Swanson sneered. 'You've already checked it out once.'

'And it was given back to my client, together with an apology,' Willis said, brandishing a sheet of paper. 'Or so it says in this report.'

'Does your report also state that the knife was wiped clean of all incriminating evidence?'

Willis chuckled. 'Who's to say there was any evidence to wipe off in the first place?' He tut-tutted. 'There you go again, Constable, throwing doubt on my client's innocence without the slightest proof of guilt.'

'That Stanley knife,' Josh said. 'What do you use it for?'

'I've already told your guv'nor,' he said, sighing. 'I fit carpet, don't I?'

'Where do you fit carpet? Give me names and addresses.'

Swanson laughed. 'You what?'

'Do you get paid for these jobs?' Josh pressed. 'And if so, does the Social Security know about these payments?'

'Oh, come on, get real, mate. I do it for friends, family. I don't take no money for it. I ain't that mercenary.'

'What a first-class citizen, you are, Mr Swanson,' Holly said from her position at the tape recorder. Swanson answered with another of his grins.

The solicitor said, 'What's the purpose of this line of questioning, Constable?'

'I just want to give your client an opportunity to list all the ways he uses the Stanley knife, Mr Willis.'

'Well, he has, so now if you'll excuse us . . . I'm a very busy man.'

'I still have a few questions left, Mr Willis, so please bear with me.' Josh leafed through the papers he had brought with him and held two aloft. 'Witness statements, Mr Swanson, dictated and signed by Hilary Pierce and Gayle Briers. Remember them? Remember how they swore you slashed their faces with a Stanley knife? Miss Briers needed fifty-three stitches, if I remember rightly. Miss Pierce got off light — she only needed twenty.'

'You don't want to believe everything a pair of prozzies tell you,' Swanson said, breezily.

'And do you remember,' Willis said to Josh, 'that those two ladies withdrew their accusations before the case got to court?'

'Strange, wasn't it?' Josh said, looking pointedly at Swanson. 'As was the fact that they left Bridgetown shortly after the case was dropped.'

Swanson lifted his shoulders. 'Never can work some people out.'

Josh moved forward, his elbows resting on the table. 'You leant on them, and you were leaning on Cynthia Labrum. Tell me why, Mr Swanson. Wouldn't she do as she was told?'

'Constable,' Willis said, 'you will insist on going around in circles. I can only assume that you have nothing on my client and, therefore, I declare this interview is at an end.' He fixed Josh with a challenging look.

A grinning Swanson pushed back his chair and made for the door. Halfway there, he turned. 'Here,' he said to Josh, 'if that bird was strangled, how come you're lookin' for a knife?'

'Thank you, Mr Swanson, that'll be all,' Holly said. Then, for the benefit of the tape recorder, 'Interview terminated at five twenty-five. Mr Swanson and Mr Willis are leaving the room.'

Josh's shoulders slumped and he exhaled sharply. 'I ballsed that up, all right. We hadn't got enough to bring him in, Hol.'

'We had, but while that little creep, Willis, is around we don't get a chance to work on him.' She perched on the edge of the desk. 'You know, Josh, something tells me we're about to be warned off completely. And then what are we going to do?'

* * *

Ashworth often stayed in his office until quite late. He liked to sit in the dark and mull things over while he studied the lights of Bridgetown through the glass walls of CID. And this particular night there were many thoughts vying for his consideration.

Since the first murder, at his request, uniformed patrols had been keeping open their eyes and ears, especially around the area of the lake and, more recently, the banks of the River Thane. And two names in particular kept cropping up: John Allan and Boris Cywinski.

Mr Allan, father of the disabled murder victim, was, it seemed, forever around the lake; and since the discovery of Cynthia Labrum's body he had been spotted near the river on numerous occasions.

Boris Cywinski, or Bible Boris, as he was known, had been seen quite often in the park. Although uniformed had never actually found him by the lake, they had reported to Ashworth that the man was observed many times staring at the water from a distance with that odd, gentle gaze of his. There was no reason, of course, why either man should not be at those places. But . . . And it was a big 'but' as far as Ashworth was concerned.

Boris had never given the police any trouble; on the contrary he had always complied with their requests in a gracious and respectful manner. But the man, although capable of entering into intelligent conversation, was strange nevertheless.

A report had just filtered through that Boris had sustained a beating by Lee Swanson and his gang. On the pretext of asking him whether he wanted to press charges, Ashworth would at least have a chance to talk with the man.

His thoughts were rudely interrupted by the door to CID coming open with a flourish. Superintendent John Newton poked his head around it.

'You still here, Chief Inspector? And sitting in the dark?'

He flicked the light switch and Ashworth closed his eyes against the sudden burst of light. 'Just thinking a few things through, sir.'

Newton was a small man compared with most police officers, and he had a fussy way about him which rankled with Ashworth's more direct approach. Everything about him was precise, from the line of his carefully trimmed moustache to the sharp trouser creases in a uniform which always had that just-pressed look. The superintendent was probably held in high esteem by the county councillors for whom he religiously held back much-needed resources, but the officers within his command regarded him with contempt. Newton was a stickler for procedure and discipline, a totalitarian with little or no interest in the concerns of his staff.

'As you're here, I'd like a word,' he said to Ashworth.

The chief inspector visibly stiffened; they had crossed swords many times, but the last thing Ashworth needed now was a confrontation.

'Yes, sir,' he said.

'I've received a complaint from the solicitor of Lee Swanson. He's claiming his client is suffering from police harassment.'

'Sir—' Ashworth began.

'No, Chief Inspector, hear me out. And on the evidence of this morning's debacle, I'd be inclined to agree with him.'

'Sir, my officers were acting on information received.'

The superintendent, much to Ashworth's surprise, eased himself on to the edge of the desk, a warm expression replacing his usual bombastic look.

'As well I know,' he said. 'What we have here is a young man with cunning, animal cunning, and that's the most dangerous kind. He could have sued us, you know, after the murder trial — after the burglary charge, too, come to that.

But he didn't, he let it ride, and I can't help wondering why. Now he's claiming police harassment — and if you look at his file an independent review would find in his favour.'

'But surely we retain the right to question a person we suspect of involvement in a crime?'

'Chief Inspector, this is not a criticism of you, or your officers, I can assure you.' He caught Ashworth's astonished look, and went on quickly, 'I think I know what that man is after. He's trying to get himself into a position where we can't touch him, whatever he does, and that is not going to happen. So far we've given him exactly what he wants, so the next time he's brought in I want the evidence to be rock solid.'

Ashworth could only agree. He nodded briskly. 'But we may need money for witness protection, sir. Otherwise, we'll never get anybody to talk.'

'In that case I'll make sure it's available. Believe me, Chief Inspector, I want that thug behind bars just as much as you do.' He pushed himself off the desk and glanced at his watch. 'Shouldn't you be getting home to your good lady?'

Ashworth looked at the wall clock; it was 9 p.m. 'She's doing a stint at the Samaritans tonight, sir, so I'm at a loose end.'

'Oh well, goodnight, then, Chief Inspector.' He strode to the door and was gone.

'Goodnight, sir.'

Ashworth watched the door close with a broad smile on his face. If he could approach potential witnesses with something to offer in exchange for information, some guarantee of safety, then the ball might at last start to roll.

* * *

Holly had not the slightest wish to disentangle herself from Mark. She was comfortable, deeply content, and she loved to watch him sleeping. Occasionally he would murmur and cling to her like a frightened child. She wanted to touch him, to soothe him, but she lay still. Once awake he might decide to leave, to return to his own house, and Holly wanted him to stay.

What had passed between them had transcended mere sex. Together they had experienced a merging of the spiritual and the physical, a phenomenon that had driven all bitter memories from her mind. Never before had she known such fulfilment. Even now, an hour later, she chased it, clung to it, frightened that it might slip away, never to return again.

Mark stirred. He opened his eyes. 'Where am I?'

'You remember Holly Bedford?'

He gave a throaty chuckle 'Oh, yes, I remember her.'

'Well, you're in her bed.'

'That's right, you got me drunk and then took advantage of me.' He stretched lazily. 'What time is it?'

Holly's heart skipped a beat. Was this the end of it? She'd tell him the time, and he'd be off? Well, it had happened to her often enough — why should tonight be any different?

'It's eleven p.m.' In a move that spoke too much of panic, Holly wrapped her arms around his neck. 'Oh, Mark, do you have to go? Wouldn't you like to stay the night?' She held her breath and waited for his answer.

'You try moving me,' he grunted.

CHAPTER 15

Boris was being followed. For a while now he had been aware of a large man behind him as he skirted the rim of the park. The man always stayed at a distance and would avert his eyes whenever Boris turned to study him. With his heart beating loudly, his palms damp with sweat, Boris sat on a bench and waited to see what the man would do.

The spring air, drifting along on a warm breeze, held scents of the lake. It was refreshing, invigorating, but it made Boris shudder with loathing. Moments later that loathing was pushed aside by alarm for the man boldly approached and sat beside him.

'Boris Cywinski?' he asked, in a gentle tone.

The man's gaze was friendly and could not be avoided. Boris gave a guarded nod. 'I am he. Why do you want to know?'

The man offered his hand. 'My name is Ashworth. Chief Inspector Ashworth. We've met before — you may remember.'

'Ah, yes, the police.' Their handshake was brisk. 'I have done nothing wrong, I hope.'

'No, no, I just wanted to talk to you.' Ashworth hesitated, fearful of blowing this useful link by using the wrong words. 'It's just that, well, it's been brought to my attention that you were beaten up by Lee Swanson and his gang. I simply wondered whether you'd like to make a formal complaint.'

Boris turned from him, frightened that the chief inspector might see the horror in his eyes.

'Mr Cywinski?' Ashworth prompted.

'I am sorry, I have a lot on my mind.' He tried a smile. 'No, Mr Ashworth, I have no complaint to make. Really, it is of little consequence.'

'I heard this isn't the first time they've done it,' Ashworth persisted. 'You're a big man, Mr Cywinski — why do you let them get away with it?'

Boris gave a shrug. 'There are five of them.'

'Huh, if they'd tried it with me, four of them would be in hospital, and the fifth would still be running.' Ashworth took a moment to consider the man; he seemed very nervous, and a tiny muscle beneath his left eye twitched continually. 'Mr Cywinski, you must outweigh me by twenty-five pounds. Why do you let them do it? Have they some sort of hold over you? Is that it?'

'Do you have grandchildren?' Boris asked suddenly.

'I have four,' Ashworth said, with a puzzled frown. 'Two boys, and two girls.'

'And this is how I imagine you would talk to them.'

Ashworth shot him a penitent smile. 'You're telling me I'm treating you like a child — fair enough. But you must admit it looks odd. I think Lee Swanson does have a hold over you. I'm right, aren't I?'

Boris looked away. 'He has no hold over me . . . apart from his threats of violence. In that respect I am not alone — he threatens many people.'

Ashworth leant forward, rested his elbows on his knees, fingers linked, and said quietly, 'Mr Cywinski, I need somebody to testify that he uses those threats.'

'So that the courts can give him twenty-four hours of community service?' Boris scoffed. 'You do not offer a lot, Mr Ashworth.'

'I want Lee Swanson put behind bars for a very long time, but I need help to do that.' Boris remained tight-lipped, so Ashworth changed tack. 'You seem very drawn to the lake.'

Boris gave the water a glance, but quickly looked away. 'There are mothers walking their children around it, feeding the ducks . . . Are you going to say the same to them?'

'No,' Ashworth admitted. 'Look, Mr Cywinski, I confess to having an interest in you. So far, no one has come forward with information about the body found in the lake. I've been told you spend a lot of time here. If you could tell us anything, however insignificant, it would be of great help.'

Boris flinched. 'I would like you to leave me alone. Please stop treating me like a mental patient and afford me the same rights you would any other citizen.'

'Certainly.' Ashworth got to his feet. 'I'm sorry I had to bother you. If you do need to speak to me about anything, you know where I am.'

As Ashworth walked away, Boris brought a hand up to his burning forehead and shuddered. The police suspected him. It was only a matter of time before they banged on his door, searched through his belongings. And, what then?

* * *

Flood water from its upper reaches had swollen the River Thane, turning it into a swirling mass of bubbling black. The water eddied and boiled, smashing its way along the deep channel. John Allan stood watching it from the bank, a desolate figure staring into the murky depths. He was motionless but his mind was racing, dwelling on the one person who was always there — his son, Clive.

Time heals, they say. But they were wrong. Almost eighteen months ago, his son was killed. And in those months not a night went by when he didn't lie there in his bed, staring into the darkness, imagining the brutal attack. Night after night the scene was played out in his mind, reel by reel, each one freeze-framed. And not even the whisky could stop it.

Oh no, time heals nothing. John Allan's pain was still strong and getting stronger.

It was different for Mildred, though. Clive's body was hardly cold in its grave and she was getting over it. Shopping, and cooking, and eating. And bloody knitting! Her only son dead, and she could still take pleasure from seeing the sleeve of a cardigan grow, or the front of a jumper.

People cope in their own ways, she said, we're all different. Just because I'm getting on with life, she said, doesn't mean I'm not breaking up inside. Two-faced, that's Mildred. That's all women. Two-faced, and shallow.

* * *

Ashworth stomped up the station steps, his mood turning blacker than the river with each stride. That was a wasted opportunity, if ever there was one. But he couldn't force Boris to press charges. And he couldn't demand information unless in an interview situation. He was getting nowhere fast. And wasn't Swanson loving it?

Boris was not wholly responsible for Ashworth's bad temper; lack of momentum on the cases in hand played a part, too. The chief inspector had two unsolved murder files on his desk and as far as he was concerned those in CID were showing precious little interest. A part of Ashworth realised he was being unfair to his team. After all, with nothing to go on, all they could hope for was a helping of inspired guess-work — a large helping, at that.

The moment Ashworth set foot in reception, Martin Dutton signalled him across to the desk. The chief inspector took in a deep breath and prepared for another of the sergeant's revelations.

'What's happened to Holly?' Dutton asked. 'The lads are a bit put out. She's not much sport in the canteen, now-adays, gone all prim and proper. Rumour has it she's in love with somebody in CID.' He gave Ashworth a pointed wink.

'I don't delve into the private lives of my detectives,' Ashworth huffed. He did, of course, but he would never admit such a thing to the sergeant. 'As long as they're performing their duties, Martin, that's all that should concern me.'

'Steady on, Jim, I'm only passing the time of day. Is something bothering you?'

'Nothing, apart from global warming, the third world . . .' He gave the sergeant a contrite look. 'Sorry, Martin, I shouldn't take my moods out on you. I've got two unsolved murders, a tearaway who's all but running an estate, and a team that doesn't seem too worried about it.'

'Calm down, Jim. Your team are working their socks off to clear your increased workload. Their clear-up rates are the highest in the county.'

Ashworth smiled. 'All right, Martin, I admit I'm out of order, but I can always rely on you to put me in my place. The thing is, I like a clean sheet—'

'Those days are gone. Most forces nowadays are over the moon with a forty per cent clear-up rate.' He paused, his mouth get in a serious line. 'I do share your concern about the council estate, though. Patrol cars, ambulances, fire engines — they're all getting stoned there. It won't be long before we have a full-scale riot — you mark my words.'

Ashworth nodded. 'It only takes one to get away with murder, and they'll all think they can. That's how it always starts, and there's somebody out there who's doing just that.'

'Nothing turned up on the two murders, then?'

'Nothing. We're missing an obvious motive in all this, Martin. And yet I can't help feeling that Swanson's tied up in it, somehow.'

'I shouldn't be saying this, Jim, but a lot of my lads are putting their money on Bible Boris. Funny, really — when somebody's a bit weird, a bit different from the norm, we always suspect them of something, don't we? Even if they've got a squeaky-clean record. Mind you, he has got a social worker taking a lot of interest in him, and they don't waste their time on fine, upstanding members of the public.' He tapped his nose 'Get what I mean?'

Ashworth's eyebrows arched. 'How did you come by that information?'

'My daughter works at Social Services. She told me.'

'And do you happen to know the name of the social worker?'

'No, but I could easily find out.'

'I'd be grateful if you would, Martin. As you say, we do take extra interest in weird people . . . because they're more likely to do weird things.'

* * *

Boris was sitting in Megan's cramped office. And while she made fresh tea, he thought again of the talk he had had with the chief inspector. He longed to discuss it with Megan, to tell her he was afraid. But he dared not; to make much of it would imply guilt. Only those with terrible secrets needed to be fearful of the police. She would ask questions. Too many questions.

He would have to cope alone, bear his worries in silence. But it was so hard; and on top of that his father's health was deteriorating to such an extent that he would soon need constant care. Boris had guessed days ago that the old man's sight was failing, for not once had he mentioned the neatness of his clipped beard.

Earlier on, before he left for Megan's office, Boris had broached yet again the subject of medical help, and yet again his father had refused. He would suffer to the end, and he would make sure that Boris suffered along with him.

'Hey, cheer up,' Megan chided, as she carried in two cups of tea.

'Sorry.' He took one of the cups which clattered against its saucer until it was balanced on his knee.

'Your beard's shorter,' Megan said.

Boris shyly ran thick fingers around his chin. 'I was thinking of shaving it off. And having my hair cut, too.'

'That's a great idea.' She placed her cup on the desk and stared at him intently. 'Listen, I could get you in with my hairdresser, if you like.'

A grin crept slowly across his face. 'All right, I would like that very much. Megan, I would so like to stop being Bible Boris. I want to become a normal person who does not get stared at by everyone he passes.'

'Let's make a start, then. Tell me again about your childhood in Russia. And, remember, Boris, you must tell me everything.'

Megan sensed a breakthrough was imminent. Prising information from Boris was proving to be difficult; in fact, she sometimes thought it would be easier to get blood out of a stone. Perhaps today would prove her wrong.

After a moment, Boris began to relate in his quiet, hesitant voice the story of his childhood. Megan noticed that he began the story, as he always did, after his fifth birthday, and she wondered what had happened during those missing years, before his schooling started in the remote rural area of the Soviet Union.

'The soldiers always arrived in the dead of night to search for signs of religious worship,' he said. 'So Bibles were hidden under stone floors, and all of our neighbours would hold their breath until the soldiers marched away.'

'Poor Boris. It must have been awful for you.'

'Sometimes they stayed for hours searching the hovels. And sometimes they beat up the men and . . . and . . . raped the women.' He faltered, his head falling forward.

'Please go on,' Megan encouraged. 'Get rid of your ghosts, let them go, and I promise they'll never bother you again.'

He nodded. 'One day my father said, we must go far away, to a country that will recognise our faith. I was a young man then, strong, already towering over my father. Oh, but, Megan, that trek across Russia, without compass or maps, almost killed us. We had no food, no water — to be all the time hungry is such a terrible thing. And the cold . . . The Russian winter is cruel, so cruel, especially in the barren wastes where there is no shelter. We had only the clothes we were wearing when we left — no thick winter coats, no boots . . .'

'Go on,' Megan prompted, when he stopped.

'With God's help we somehow made our way across Europe to England. And . . . well, you know the rest.' He looked at her, his eyes pleading. 'Do you think I could become normal, Megan? Do you really think so?'

She moved from the desk and took his hand. 'Boris, for years now you've been repressed, never allowed to be your true self. It'll take time — I can't pretend it won't — but one day your true character will emerge.' She paused. 'You'll have to let everything out, though. I still sense there's a lot you're not telling me.'

Boris avoided her eyes. 'There are certain things I have banished from my mind. I do not want to remember them.'

She stooped down by his side. 'Boris, your life didn't start when you were five years old. What happened to your mother and brother?'

'Oh, please, please do not press on those things.'

'But I must press you, Boris. Those things, however terrible, have got to be faced if you're to go on.'

'No, no . . . *no*.' The words came from deep within his throat. And then Boris was on his feet, large hands clamped over his ears. So sudden and so violent was the movement that Megan recoiled, sprawling backwards as he stumbled across the small space.

'I cannot stay here,' he yelled from the doorway.

Megan heard him thudding along the corridor, the floorboards beneath her vibrating with his heavy steps. And then the outer door slammed so loudly that she yelped with fear, her whole body a-tremble.

Outside, Boris took in a number of deep breaths to compose himself. His head hurt; a blinding pain was behind his eyes and it shot darts of torment into his brain.

He needed a woman. He needed to sin.

CHAPTER 16

'Okay, I admit it — I'm going home because I'm expecting a call from my wife.'

Mark was pulling on his trousers with angry tugs. The intimacy they had so recently shared was gone, pushed aside in a second by Holly's reproachful glare. She was wrapping her bathrobe around herself, suddenly wanting to deprive him of her body. The deeper the love, the deeper the hurt. And Holly was hurting, now.

'Oh, well, that's just great, isn't it?' She threw his sweatshirt at him, and then his socks. 'You'd better hurry up and get dressed. You wouldn't want to miss her call.'

Mark ducked swiftly to miss a shoe. 'For, God's sake, Holly . . . She phones once a week. It doesn't mean anything.'

'If it doesn't mean anything, why do you have to be there?'

'Because I don't want her to suspect anything — why do you think?'

'Mark, you told me there was nothing left between you and your wife. So, why should she care what you're doing?'

'It's more complicated than that—'

'You still love her,' Holly flared. 'You love her and you don't want her to find out you're having a bit on the side. Wouldn't want to upset poor Mrs Hartland, would we?'

'I can't understand your attitude, Holly, this is only our second date.'

She stood before him, her face pink with rage. 'What are you doing here, then — trying me out? And if I don't come up to scratch, you'll carry on living with somebody you can't stand the sight of?'

'You're not being fair,' he said, shrugging on his jacket. 'I just meant I've hardly had time to get used to us.'

'You've had all the time you're getting, Mark.' She sagged on to the edge of the bed. 'I'm sorry, it's my fault, I promised myself I wouldn't do the married man bit again.' Her composure had returned, but the gaze that settled on his face was still stony. 'Get rid of her, Mark, and then come and see me.'

'This is an over-reaction,' he said, his tone pleading. 'I'll tell her when she comes home, I promise.'

Holly save a slow shake of the head. 'Tell her tonight. Save her the trouble of coming home.'

'But there's the house to consider. It'll have to be sold, and the money divided up.'

'What the hell are you waiting for? A rising property market?'

It was then that Mark made the fatal mistake of looking at his watch.

'Oh, just piss off,' she screamed, hurling a pillow at him. 'Go on, get out, you might miss her call.'

He backed out of the room, and the next thing Holly heard was his car engine revving outside. She threw herself across a bed that was still warm from their lovemaking. Urgent tears threatened but she fought to keep them at bay. She must pull herself together, that's all. Better to know the truth now than in the weeks and months ahead. She would survive — she always had. And then the tears rolled down her cheeks, unhindered. All he had to do was say he'd stay. Was that too much to ask?

* * *

108

Helen Palmer washed the aspirins down with neat vodka while she paced around her tiny flat. She had been pacing for most of the evening, down side streets, along main roads, and seemed now to be incapable of stopping.

One lousy punter in four hours' traipsing the streets. Fifty lousy quid. Gratefully kicking off her four-inch stilettos, Helen finished the vodka and poured herself another large measure. If things didn't improve soon she'd have to cut down on the drink. But, could she? Most days it was all that kept her going. The worse her plight became, the more she relied on it. Still, the bottle was almost full so tonight was taken care of — another couple of large ones and then bed. Who knows — the lunchtime trade might be frantic tomorrow.

Helen was about to refill her glass when the front door-bell sounded. Very carefully, she parted the curtains and peered into the street. It was one of her regulars — the bondage freak. He'd pay through the nose to have her tied up, so maybe the day wouldn't be a complete waste of time, after all. Easing her aching feet into the tight shoes, Helen rushed to let him in.

* * *

Mildred Allan cast another worried glance at the clock. It was 10.30 p.m. and her husband was still not home. She sipped her hot milky drink and contemplated the disaster that was now her life. Even the horror of her son's death had faded. In the months since his murder her world had fallen apart and nothing seemed to matter anymore. She lived in a void without meaning or direction.

Never had she needed her husband more than in the months immediately following Clive's death. But John had pulled away from her, had become more and more distant until it seemed that he almost blamed her for what had happened. Since then the gulf had widened, and she no longer had the will to attempt to bridge it.

With the mug grasped tight Mildred padded towards the door, eager to get to bed before his key turned in the lock. John's late-night walkabouts were always followed by whisky, glass after glass drawing him steadily into a maudlin stupor. And she didn't want to witness that. Not again. To have those eyes that had once shone with love turn on her with drunken fury was too much to bear. Let him have his whisky and his hatred, and good luck to him.

* * *

Helen lay still on the bed, smiling broadly despite her discomfort. She was spread-eagled, the rope around her wrists attached to the headboard, the man squatting heavily across her thighs. It was exactly like the last time, only now the rope was pulled tight — too tight. Already her hampered circulation was bringing pins and needles to her fingers. Never mind, though, it was worth putting up with a little discomfort for eighty-five pounds.

His face above hers caused Helen to stiffen. Gone was his customary flush of embarrassment, the unsure glint in his eyes. In their place was a steely determination that drew back his lips in a silent snarl.

He reached across to the bedside table, and Helen fought back a laugh. Here we go — he's gonna cover me with pencil marks again, stupid bastard. Think of the eighty-five quid, girl. Money for old rope . . .

That fixed smile was still in place as she closed her eyes. But before darkness descended she was aware of something catching the light. A metallic flash? It certainly wasn't a pencil.

* * *

Boris ran down the steps to his flat, almost tripping in his rush to get inside. With the key poised before the lock he stopped to get his breath. The air was heavy with exhaust fumes that made his eyes water and his nostrils quiver. And the night was alive with sounds: a distant hum of traffic, the repetitive drumbeat of a rap record drifting from an open window in the flats; and somewhere nearby drunken laughter quickly turned into angry yells.

With a huge effort Boris kept his nerves steady and inserted his key in the lock. Once inside he threw the bolt then leant against the door, his heavy frame a quivering mass.

Tonight would be the last time. Never again would he give in to his immoral cravings, to the weakness of his flesh. Never again. His duty now was to look after his father, to ease his passage into the next world.

With leaden steps Boris trudged along that stark passage. Already he could detect the sour scent of death. It was lurking somewhere in the shadows. And death always got its way.

* * *

Holly was ready to put the telephone down when the receiver was snatched up at the other end and Mark's voice was in her ear.

'It's me,' she said, hesitantly. 'I didn't think you were there. The phone must have rung a dozen times.'

'I was in the shower.' He, too, was hesitant, as if trying to gauge her mood. 'Have you rung to confirm it's all over?'

Holly twirled the telephone flex around her fingers, the words not coming easily. 'No. Actually, Mark, I wanted to say sorry. I realise now I was being a little unfair.'

He exhaled sharply. 'Thank God for that.'

'Listen, I . . . Well, I think it's time for us to be upfront about this. I'm . . .' She took in a long breath. 'I'm getting pretty heavy feelings that I'm not used to.'

There was a long pause. 'I'm getting them, too. Is it still called falling in love?'

Holly lay back against the pillows, a teasing smile on her lips. 'Are you telling me you're in love, Mark?'

'I think so. You know the cleaner at the station, the one with the crêpe bandage round her knee . . . ?'

She laughed. 'You sod, Hartland.'

'Sorry, but I'm finding this embarrassing. Oh what the hell . . . Holly Bedford, I've got feelings for you — exciting feelings — and I don't know what to do about them.'

'Mark, I think we need to get some things straight here — if you're really serious about me.'

'I am, Holly. Oh, God, I am.'

'Then this has to progress. I mean, it can't just stay as sex — enjoyable as that may be.'

'I hear what you're saying, but you must give me time. A couple of months — yes? — that's all I need. I've got myself into a real rut, I know. She's at her mother's most of the time so it's not like we're really married, but now I've got to make the break—'

'I know it's difficult,' Holly cut in, 'but just think how it could be afterwards. We could live here, and—'

'Just give me a couple of months. Okay?'

'Yes, okay.'

'Holly . . . I love you.'

Tears fell for the second time that night, but these were definitely preferable to the last. 'Love you, too,' she whispered back.

CHAPTER 17

Helen Palmer was first missed at lunchtime, fifteen hours after she had opened the door to her client. She rarely failed to show on a Thursday in the saloon bar of the Mitre. Thursday was pay day for the local construction workers, and the weekend usually started there.

The girls were always nervous when one of their numbers dropped out of sight, but especially now that a murdering pervert was on the loose. Even so, while they sipped their drinks and waited for punters, most of the girls had already found reasons for Helen's absence. She could be ill, or entertaining one of her regulars; she could have simply moved on to richer pickings. Two of the girls remained unconvinced, however, and decided to check out her flat at the end of the lunchtime session.

But first things first. The grapevine was buzzing with news that an increased police presence would be on the streets over the next few weeks. And the girls wanted to bolster their earnings in case an enforced holiday was on the cards.

* * *

Boris was up early that morning. All night he had tossed and turned, his body hyperactive with nervous energy, his thoughts centred on his main concern — the bundle of clothing. He must get rid of it today.

Even before first light had broken his father had started his fevered ranting. Delirium was setting in, and for that Boris was thankful. The old man would soon be oblivious to his own pain — and more importantly — unaware of his son's furtive movements.

Hurrying past his father's bedroom like a guilty child Boris collected the clothing from its hiding place beneath the bathroom sink. With it concealed inside his coat he went out into the yard beyond the kitchen, his frightened gaze flitting all ways. The small space was made more cramped by dense brambles that had taken over long ago, leaving any plant that might once have grown there little chance of survival.

Boris pushed past the prickly stems until he came to an old metal dustbin that stood rusted and abandoned beside a disused lean-to shed. The shirt was thrown into the dustbin first, the socks next, and finally the black suit. A lighted match soon followed, but the clothes were too damp to burn. Boris tried stuffing layers of dry newspapers between them, but still they would not ignite.

He felt blind panic constrict his chest, felt his breathing deteriorate to a series of laboured gasps. And the twitching curtains in neighbouring windows did little to deaden his fears. Were they watching? Had they seen?

He darted into the lean-to shed and threw aside long-forgotten items — half-filled rubbish sacks, empty paint pots, corroded garden tools — until he came upon a paraffin can. He shook it fiercely and almost cried with relief when its contents spattered against its sides.

With little concern now for watchful neighbours Boris soaked the clothes with the paraffin, then stood back and tossed a flaring match into the bin. A sheet of flame shot heavenwards, causing him to stagger back, a hand shielding his eyes. He stood and watched as orange sparks crackled and died, crackled and died. Presently the fire lost its vigour and Boris was able to move closer. The clothes were little more than dying embers, a pile of red-hot soot that could have been anything. Satisfied that the bundle was completely destroyed, he went back inside the flat.

Boris washed the black grime from his hands in the kitchen sink and prepared his father's breakfast porridge. In the bedroom the old man's rheumy eyes followed his son's shadowy figure until the tray was placed on his lap.

'I have talked with God,' he said, his voice cracking. 'He is not yet ready to forgive you, Boris. Hell and brimstone will be yours if you do not repent.'

Boris spooned the porridge into his father's mouth, resisting a strong urge to ram the spoon down the skinny throat and at the same time muttering prayers for forgiveness for having such thoughts.

The old man sipped his black coffee. 'I am not long for this world. Soon you will be rid of me.'

'I will stay with you, father. I shall shop for food, but apart from that I will stay with you.' He picked up the tray and headed for the door, his father's voice following him.

'You have no feelings, Boris. You murdered your mother and your brother, and now you are going to watch me die but your voice is so matter-of-fact.'

Oh, for an end to this torture, an end to his father's cruel words. At that moment Boris could quite happily have wrapped his strong fingers around that scrawny neck. And, why not? Why not silence the old man, once and for all? Boris knew he had sinned enough already: he would never be welcome in God's land. Would one more dark deed make any difference?

The breakfast things rattled violently on the tray as Boris scurried out and shut the door on temptation.

* * *

Holly had taken a telephone call that had brought her to the bar of the Mitre. The sleazy feel to the place made her uncomfortable, and she determined to keep her visit short. The public house had changed little in the past twenty years. Hope and optimism had stopped drinking there long ago. Only despair and failure rubbed shoulders with the miserable few now settled at the rickety tables, their pint glasses sipped at infrequently so that one round might last for an hour or more.

Holly glanced about until her gaze settled upon the prostitute she had met at the gates to the rec.

'Hi,' she said, her smile easy. 'So, what's all this about?'

'This is Joyce,' the girl said, pointing to her companion, 'and I'm Mandy. We only use first names — all right?'

Holly sat down and shrugged. 'Doesn't give me a problem. Okay, what can I do for you?'

'Listen, at the rec, you looked half-decent — all right? — which is why we decided to call you . . .'

'Yes? What do you want to tell me?'

'One of our girls has gone missing.'

'Missing as in vanished?' Holly asked with mounting interest. 'How long's it been since she was last seen?'

'It was only the day before yesterday,' Joyce piped up.

'A bit early to start worrying, don't you think?'

Mandy gave her a scathing glance. 'Slags move about — is that what you mean?'

'Not quite how I would've put it, but you must admit—'

'Yeh, I know, but Helen wasn't like that — was she, Joyce? If she was going off somewhere, she'd have told us.'

The barman had been keeping a watchful eye on Holly from the moment she sat down. He lifted the counter flap and picked a path to their table.

'Here, love, this ain't a bleedin' charity,' he said to her. 'What you having to drink?'

She looked him up and down; he was sixteen stone of flab covered by a T-shirt and jeans. 'I'm all right, thank you,' was her cool reply.

'No, you ain't. If you just want somewhere to sit, go to the library. If you're in my pub, you buy a bleedin' drink.'

She fished her warrant card from her bag and shoved it in front of his nose. 'Just lose yourself — all right?'

116

The barman glowered at her. 'Yeh, well, it won't be long before you can't come on to this estate anymore, and good riddance.'

'Don't hold your breath,' Holly replied, with a smile. 'No, on second thoughts, please do. Now, go on, bugger off.'

The barman's flab rippled with indignation as Holly turned back to the girls. Swearing to himself, he shuffled back to the bar.

'Sorry, girls, but there's not a lot I can do about this.'

'But we went to her flat, yesterday, and couldn't get a reply,' Joyce said, earnestly. 'Honest, we're really worried something might have happened to her.'

Holly had a moment's thought. 'Okay, give me her name and address. I'll ask around, but there's not a lot more I can do.'

'Her name's Helen Palmer, and she lives at Flat 3 Vale View.' Mandy let out an impatient breath. 'I bet you'd be able to do something if she was a copper's daughter, or if she lived in one of the posh houses.'

'Mandy, it's got nothing to do with Helen being a pro. And we don't even know if she is missing, do we? I can't waste police man-hours unless I'm certain something's wrong.'

'But she never misses the Thursday lunchtime trade. Say that bastard pervert's got her, eh?'

'Is there anything you can give me that might suggest she's in some sort of danger? Has she been threatened recently? Has she had any weirdo clients?'

The two girls exchanged a look. 'Well, she was seeing this bloke who's into bondage. He sounded weird, and no mistake. Helen said he liked to draw on her with a pencil.'

Holly chuckled. 'That's novel — I wonder what he got out of that.' She dropped her notepad into her bag and made to go. 'Leave it with me, girls. If she doesn't turn up in the next few days, I'll do my best to get a look inside her flat. Is there a number where I can get hold of you?'

'Not bloody likely,' Mandy said. 'We'll make contact with you. I'm not inviting a visit from your lads in blue.'

'Fair enough.' Holly got to her feet. 'Contact me in a few days.'

She was making her way to the door when she saw a familiar face in the growing crowd of drinkers. Unable to believe her eyes, she shouldered her way to the bar.

'Don?'

His back was towards her, and his shoulders were hunched as if he were trying to disappear within himself. A sheepish look was on his face when he turned, but within a second that smooth, professional smile was in place.

'Holly, what are you doing here?'

'I might ask you the same thing? I'm working, actually.'

'Same here,' he said, his tone hushed. 'A lot of my clients come from this estate.'

She gave him a puzzled look. 'But surely they go to your practice to see you?'

He shook his head. 'Not always. I'm a bit embarrassed about seeing you, to tell the truth.'

'So I'd noticed,' she muttered to herself.

'But the world's changing,' he went on. 'Some of my clients insist on meeting me here. If I don't comply they take their legal aid elsewhere.'

'I see.' She glanced at her watch. 'I'd better be off, Don, nice to see you.'

'You, too. See you around.'

As Holly manoeuvred her way towards the door, Quinn's haunted gaze never left her back. And pinpricks of perspiration were showing on his upper lip as he knocked back the remains of his scotch.

* * *

Josh and Bobby were hovering over computer printouts when Holly burst into the CID office.

'Where's the guv'nor and Mark?' she asked, dropping her shoulder bag beside her chair.

118

'I'll answer that in order of importance,' Josh said, with a grin. 'Mark's gone to the canteen, so if you want a ciggie, now's the time. And the guv'nor's in a meeting.'

Holly stuck out her tongue and made a grab for her cigarette packet as she settled at her desk. 'Right, boys,' she said, exhaling smoke. 'I've just come from the Mitre. Two of the local pros are worried about their friend, one Helen Palmer. They haven't seen her for a while and they're worried that the big, bad serial killer's got her. I said I'd look into it if she hasn't surfaced in the next few days.'

Josh snorted. 'Holly, a pro's gone walkabout. It's hardly grounds for starting a nationwide hunt.'

'Maybe not, but she had a client who was fond of tying her up and drawing on her with a pencil—'

'Well, what do you know?' Josh said, slapping his thigh. 'This guy is dangerous. You can do a lot of damage with a pencil.'

'Especially if it's just been sharpened,' Bobby chipped in.

'Watch it, you two,' she said, with a good-natured grin. 'You've got to admit, though, it's pretty weird behaviour.'

Josh let out a caustic laugh. 'I never thought I'd have to explain perverse sexual practices to you, Hol, but there are guys out there who pay to have their balls nailed to the floor. Now, that's not my idea of a night out — I'd rather have a lager and watch *News at Ten* — but it doesn't make them murderers.'

'Okay, Abraham, thanks for enlightening me.' She sat back, her brow furrowed. 'Do you think a solicitor would meet his clients in the bar at the Mitre?'

Josh shot a confused glance at Bobby. 'Are you on something, Hol?'

'No, I'm being serious. Do you think a solicitor would?'

'I suppose he would, if his client wanted him to. I haven't given it a lot of thought.'

Holly stubbed out her cigarette and reached inside her shoulder bag for a mint. When Josh tittered she threw the wrapper at him and was on the verge of making an obscene remark when Ashworth strode in.

The chief inspector was not a difficult man to read. When his face looked like thunder, when a pulse raced in his forehead and he slammed the door behind him, they knew it was time to keep their heads down. He was standing by his desk, inhaling deeply and studying the map on the wall.

'Right, you lot,' he said, at last, 'Superintendent Newton has called a meeting in the newly formed incident room for all divisional sergeants and CID.' He scowled. 'Now, the superintendent will explain what it's all about, but I just want to say this — if any of you feel like voicing objections, I'll back you to the hilt.' He ignored their startled expressions and marched towards the door. 'Come on, His Lordship's waiting.'

The incident room was housed in a large office at the rear of the building. A number of desks equipped with telephones and fax machines, computers and modems, were positioned near the back wall; and five wooden benches stood in rows before a large blackboard. The superintendent, looking rather like a peacock, was strutting to and fro in front of the blackboard; and half a dozen uniformed sergeants were sitting on the benches when Ashworth and his team bustled in.

'Ah, Chief Inspector, now you and your crew are here, we can make a start,' Newton said, pointedly.

They sat down and Newton gazed into the sea of faces. 'You'll no doubt be wondering what this is all about. Well, I shall tell you . . . It has been brought to my attention that we're experiencing considerable difficulties on what we all know as the council estate.' There were several nods of agreement. 'We also know that this estate is the main source of drugs in the town.'

Ashworth raised a hand. 'I'd have to disagree with that, sir. There are drugs on that estate, certainly, but no more than on any other.'

'But they are more openly on sale,' Newton countered. 'And therein lies the problem. We're losing control. These

121

youngsters are laughing at us. They think they're above the law.'

'The majority of people on that estate are law-abiding,' Ashworth said. 'It's just a small minority who cause the trouble, and I don't believe that drugs are the problem.'

'Drugs aren't the problem?' Newton scoffed. 'Of course they're the problem.'

'Sir, I can see what the chief inspector's getting at,' Holly broke in. 'If we take a dealer off the streets we're removing, say, five hundred pounds' worth of smack, and there's a dozen more waiting to take his place. It's the real suppliers we need to get.'

Newton glared at her. 'That is not something I agree with,' he said, stiffly. 'If we keep hitting the street dealers, they're going to realise it's not worth the effort and sooner or later they'll stop trading.'

'Sir, that estate is a tinderbox at the moment,' Ashworth argued. 'One spark and it could go up. If we go in there, heavy-handed, then we'll be providing that spark.'

'He's right, sir,' Sergeant Dutton called out. 'My lads are only getting stones thrown at the patrol cars at the moment, but they could just as easily be petrol bombs.'

'And why do your . . . *lads* . . . allow these youngsters to throw stones at the cars?' Newton demanded to know.

'Sir, the yobs run off and lose themselves in a maze of alleys. What can our lads do — leave the cars and give chase? The cars would be stripped by the time they got back.'

'Thank you, Sergeant, you've just reinforced my opinion that the whole area is getting out of control. Now, what I want is a fairly low-key operation. Surveillance first — which is CID territory — and when that is complete, one swift raid and we take in as many dealers as possible.'

Ashworth had closed his eyes with the intention of counting to ten; but such was his anger, he had now reached thirty-three and still Newton's voice continued to drone.

'In the meantime,' he was saying, 'I want a much-reduced presence on the streets. Let's lull these people into a false sense of security.' He clapped his hands briskly. 'Has anyone any questions or comments?'

'Yes, sir.' Ashworth spoke with great restraint. 'I would like to register my doubts about this operation. I think it's ill-timed, carries too great a risk, and will not solve the problem.'

'Thank you, Chief Inspector, but I have already taken the decision,' Newton replied, icily. 'So, if no one else has anything to say, I will bring this meeting to an end.'

'Get the riot gear ready,' Ashworth murmured to those in front.

* * *

'Guv . . .' Holly called to Ashworth, her high heels clattering loudly in the stone-floored corridor.

His hostile expression softened slightly when she told him about Helen Palmer. She had expected the same half-hearted response she had received from Josh and Bobby, so was surprised when Ashworth showed genuine concern.

'Do we know anything about this girl, Holly?'

'Only that she was on the game, guv, and she appears to have vanished.'

'Do you know her address?'

'Yes, it's a flat in Vale View.'

'In that case it's probably rented privately. Find out who the landlord is. If the woman doesn't turn up in a couple of days he could get worried about his rent and let us take a look inside. You know you're on duty tonight?' She nodded. 'We'll work in pairs. You come with me, and Josh can go with Bobby.'

* * *

Later that afternoon, Ashworth was shown into an office by a casually dressed young secretary and was greeted with a warm smile by an equally casual Megan Rowntree.

'Please, do take a seat, Chief Inspector.' She cleared files from a chair and, finding little space on her cluttered desk, she abandoned the pile on the floor. 'Oh dear, I'm not the tidiest person in the world, am I?'

Ashworth waited for Megan to take her seat before he sat down. Making himself comfortable, he said, 'You may be wondering why I'm here.'

'I may, indeed,' she said, eyeing him coolly.

'I've come about Boris Cywinski.'

Megan's face darkened with dread. 'Boris? Why, what's he done?'

Ashworth, surprised by her reaction, said, 'He hasn't done anything . . . as far as I know, anyway. I followed him in the park. I needed to have a chat with him.'

'Do you make a habit of accosting people, Chief Inspector?'

'I hardly accosted him,' Ashworth retorted.

'My choice of word,' she said, smiling. 'Look, shall we make it easy for ourselves and admit that you haven't a lot of time for social workers, and I haven't a lot of time for the police?'

'That's blunt, which I like.' Ashworth tried to relax. 'Miss Rowntree, Boris has taken a severe beating at the hands of some local hooligans — no doubt you would regard those youths as merely misguided — and I was simply inviting him to press charges.'

'And then proceeded to question him about everything under the sun, I suppose. You haven't the right, you know.'

He gave a rueful grin. 'Miss Rowntree, as a social worker, you spend a considerable amount of your time delving into the pasts of your clients in order to explain their current behaviour. Whereas I, as a police officer, have to spend all of my time dealing with the consequences of that behaviour.'

'Point taken,' she said.

'So, would you mind telling me why you're spending so much time with Mr Cywinski?'

'None of your business, really,' she said, shrugging. 'But, if you must know, the plight of Boris and his father came to our attention some time back. Even then his father was in need of medical and psychiatric treatment, but he would accept neither. They live in substandard housing—'

'Then close it down,' Ashworth interjected.

'It's all so easy to you people,' was her terse reply. 'The truth is, most of the council accommodation isn't much better than what they've got now. In any case, if we close these places down, we're only putting the tenants on the streets.'

'And from there your interest in Boris grew?'

She nodded, her smile self-mocking. 'You see, Chief Inspector, I'm a real do-gooder, a real woolly-hat merchant.'

'And what have you discovered, Miss Rowntree?'

'Very little, up till now.'

'In that case, you're in grave danger of having your woolly hat confiscated,' Ashworth said, drily.

Megan let out a hearty laugh. 'I like you, Chief Inspector, I've tried not to, but . . .' She was suddenly serious. 'I do know that Boris is trying to blot out the first few years of his life. And they're very important years. Negative influences in those early years can manifest themselves in a number of ways in later life — social awkwardness, anti-social behaviour—'

'Maybe even murder?' Ashworth cut in.'

'In extreme cases, yes.' She met his eyes, her expression forthright. 'Is that what you suspect Boris of? Murder?'

'I have no evidence pointing in that direction.'

'But you have suspicions?'

'Let me put that question back to you,' Ashworth said, shifting uncomfortably in his seat. 'Do you have any suspicions?'

'Of course not,' she said, quickly.

'Are you sure, Miss Rowntree? When I first said I was here about Boris, you appeared fearful. Why was that?'

She became edgy, took to fiddling with her pen. 'I admit that just for a moment . . .'

'Yes?'

'My last session with Boris ended badly, Chief Inspector. I went too far with my questioning, and Boris rushed out of here. He was in a very bad state.'

'Between ourselves, Miss Rowntree — and, believe me, this will go no further . . . Do you think that Boris Cywinski is capable of violence?'

She considered the question. 'Between ourselves?' Ashworth nodded. 'I really don't know, Chief Inspector. Until that last session I believed that Boris would be incapable of a bad thought, let alone a violent act. But, now . . . I'm not so sure. Perhaps future sessions with him will reveal the truth.'

'You'll be seeing him again?'

'Of course. I can't let him down, now.'

Ashworth got to his feet. 'Which brings me to the real purpose of my visit. That is, to warn you to be careful.' He smiled down at her. 'There, you're not the only one with good intentions.'

* * *

Ashworth's Scorpio was parked a little way down from the Mitre Pub and away from any street lighting, which meant that they had a good view of the building's frontage while enjoying a fair degree of anonymity. He watched with Holly while money changed hands in exchange for small brown envelopes, their contents promising the desperate purchasers a short escape from the real world.

'I think we can safely say that man's selling drugs,' Ashworth grunted, irritably.

'Yes, guv, as they were at the half a dozen other sites we've been to tonight.' She let out a loud sigh. 'How long have we got to do this before Newton orders the raid?'

'Your guess is as good as mine.' He glanced out of the side window. 'They know who we are, you know. They just couldn't care less.'

'Huh, that just strengthens Newton's hand to order a crackdown.'

'I suppose so,' he grudgingly agreed. 'You know, Holly, I often wonder whether I oppose Newton's plans because I don't agree with them, or simply because I can't stand the man.' He took in a sharp breath. 'Here comes trouble.'

Holly glanced up and saw Lee Swanson and his four friends swaggering along the street. Swanson spotted their car straight away and lost no time in pointing it out to his gang. They passed slowly — some waving two fingers, others shouting abuse and banging on the car's roof — and went on towards the pub, yelling, 'Let's have a revolution.'

Ashworth exhaled noisily. 'I think we'd better call it a day.'

Holly was reaching for the ignition key when she spotted Mandy emerging from the pub. 'Hang on a minute, guv, there's somebody I want a quick word with.' She jumped out of the car and ran across the street, calling the girl's name.

Mandy fidgeted on the spot, her face a mask of worry. 'I don't need this, you know. You'll get me marked.'

'All I need is a phone number where I can get in touch with you.' The girl hesitated. 'Oh, come on, Mandy, we're not going to hassle you, and it might help us find Helen.'

'Okay, give us a pen.' She found an envelope in her handbag, ripped off a corner, and scribbled down the number.

'And write down the address of Helen's landlord, if you know it.'

'Bleedin' hell,' Mandy exclaimed. 'I've got a punter in tow — you'll scare him off.'

'Just one more thing and you can go,' Holly said. 'That guy who used to draw on her with a pencil. What did he do, exactly?'

Ashworth watched Holly sprint back to the oar, felt the cool night air rush in when she opened the door.

'We're in business, guv. That guy who used a pencil on Helen Palmer — he drew a line starting at her forehead and going straight down the centre of her body.'

'That sounds like our man,' Ashworth said, his mind racing. 'Do we know who her landlord is?'

'Yes, a Mr Philip Holland, and this is his address.' She handed him the scrap of paper and pulled out into the traffic. 'I'll phone him as soon as we get back to the station — yes?'

'No,' he said, glancing at his watch. 'Mr Holland may not be too happy if we disturb him at this time of night. To get in there, Holly, we'll need his cooperation, so we'd better leave it till the morning.'

CHAPTER 19

Holly knew that things were not quite right the second she opened her front door; some sixth sense warned her that another person was in the house. She turned on the light, bathing the tiny hall in a soft glow, and hurried to the lounge. The room was exactly as she had left it. Next she tip-toed towards the kitchen, her breathing shallow, and slowly pushed open the door. It banged against the wall while she searched for the light switch. The fluorescent strip flickered twice and then jumped into life.

Her jaw sagged with surprise. The table was set for two, and a small vase at its centre held a single red rose. Mark pulled the cork from the wine bottle, a grin spreading across his face.

'Thought I'd surprise you.'

'You nearly gave me a heart attack.' Her gaze went again to the table.

'You were the one who wanted me to have a key,' he said, smiling. 'Come and go as you please, you said.' He put the bottle on the table and crossed to the oven. 'Now, there's chow mein and prawn crackers—'

'Oh, Mark, this is great, but you shouldn't . . .'

He pulled her close. 'What I'm trying to say is, there's more to us than just bed.'

'Thanks,' she said, happily. 'I really appreciate it.' She tore the tops off the foil containers and drooled. Only now did she realise how hungry she was. Eagerly, she scooped the food on to plates.

'She's coming home in a couple of weeks,' Mark said, lightly.

Holly flinched at the words, and some of the food missed the plate. Her heart felt heavy but she was loath to let it show. With her back towards him, she continued to dish out the meal.

'And that's when I'm going to tell her, Holly. I promise.'

She turned to him. 'I hope you mean that, Mark.'

He poured the wine and handed her a glass. 'I've made up my mind. I'm determined to do it. I want to spend the rest of my life with you, Holly Bedford.' He raised his glass in a toast. 'You make every day seem special.'

'You're a true romantic,' Holly said, laughing. 'It won't be easy though, will it, Mark? Telling her, I mean?'

He sipped his wine, his gaze fixed on her face. 'I've been over and over it in my mind, and I know what I'm going to do. I'll come straight out with it and then leave the house.'

* * *

Boris sat in his bedroom, head in hands, a thousand worries deepening his despair. He knew he should get medical help for his father. A good son would at least try to ease the pain, however much venomous abuse was spat in his face. So, why was he dragging his heels? Did a small part of him enjoy witnessing his father suffering? Was he so evil that he could delight in an old man's pain?

His father was dying. It would not be long, now. Over the past twenty-four hours his symptoms had worsened. He did nothing but writhe about in the sweat-sodden sheets, calling to his wife and conducting one-sided conversations with others long gone. Was he hallucinating, or were those dead souls actually there, preparing the old man for his final journey?

Boris stared out of the window — a grimy square at pavement level — and focused on the disused factory and warehouse that stood opposite. They seemed to be mocking him, their smashed windows like smiling eyes, their splintered double gates like a broad grin that was aimed at him, at his dismal existence.

He shook his head to dispel the folly and turned his thoughts to Megan. She made him feel sane, normal. But she was always probing into his past. Was she trying to trap him? That policeman was — he was certain of it. Boris wanted Megan to be a true friend, for friendship was a blessing he had never known. She would come here looking for him, he knew she would — and, what then? He could not let her into this hovel; he could not let her see how he lived. And she must never set eyes on his father, for if she did the old man would be taken straight away to hospital and Boris would for evermore hear his curses echoing from beyond the grave.

Just then a rowdy disturbance made him swivel his eyes to the right, made his heavy heart beat rapidly. Lee Swanson and his gang were coming along the street, throwing stones and empty beer cans at the few panes of glass still left in the derelict factory. They were noisily chanting racist slogans, and at the same time giving Nazi salutes. A deep loathing suddenly engulfed Boris and made him catch his breath; a loathing so intense that it hurt his chest.

* * *

It took Holly and Josh less than an hour to track down Helen Palmer's landlord, next morning. They found Philip Holland to be an uncooperative man with a shifty gaze. Heavy gold jewellery decorated his neck and wrists; and on almost all of his fingers he sported a chunky gold ring. He owned thirty properties in all and had recently returned from a six-week holiday in America. He was unwilling to let them into his luxury apartment, let alone surrender the duplicate key to Helen's flat.

'Sorry, but I don't think this is a police matter,' he said, the rings glistening as he waved them away from his door. 'And you've no right to expect entry, either.'

'No, we haven't,' Holly said. 'But we do have reason to believe that a crime may have been committed, Mr Holland, and your help would be much appreciated.'

'Then apply for a search warrant.' His fleshy face broke into an oily smile. 'Sorry, but I do have my other tenants to think about, and it wouldn't do my reputation any good if it got around that I let the police into their flats on the flimsiest of excuses.'

'Okay, we'll get a warrant,' Holly snapped. 'And then we'll really turn the place over.'

Holland let rip a raucous laugh, his mouth wide open, and they saw then that his love of gold had spilled into his mouth; gold fillings abounded, and even two of his upper incisors had been crafted from the precious metal.

'You haven't enough to get a warrant, and you know it,' he said.

Josh caught Holly's sharp intake of breath and jumped in quickly to avoid a scene. 'Listen, sir, we're trying to be nice about this. As you say, at the moment we can't demand entry, but if we wait until the girl's officially recognised as missing then we'd have every right to look at her flat.'

'Okay, then, you do that,' the man blustered.

'There is another way of looking at this,' Josh continued in the same persuasive tone. 'If this girl's just decided to up and leave, you'll have lost a lot of rent by then.'

Holland frowned. 'Do you think that's likely, Constable?'

'That's the way I read it, sir.'

'Well, I could go and have a look . . .'

'You could, sir, and you'd be perfectly within your rights. But, say Helen Palmer's in there and doesn't feel like opening the door to your knock — how's it going to look to your other tenants, you letting yourself in and out of their homes whenever you feel like it? If we go in, low key, looking for a missing person . . . Well, if Helen's there, no harm's been done.'

The man thought it over. 'It will be low key?'

'You have my word, sir.'

'All right, I'll meet you there in an hour.' He closed the door in their faces.

Holly grinned. 'You're a manipulative bastard, Abraham.'

'Personally, I'd have said charming, but you always did have a foul mouth.'

* * *

An hour later, to the minute, Ashworth ushered Holly into Helen Palmer's flat. Philip Holland waited outside, peering nervously through the open door. Not knowing what they would find made them both uneasy.

'If she just decided to do a moonlight flit, guv, she left without doing the washing up,' Holly called from the tiny but immaculate kitchen.

Ashworth's gaze took in the pile of dishes in the sink, and he stooped to sniff two spirit glasses on the draining board. Taking great care not to touch them, he delivered his verdict.

'Vodka in one, and scotch in the other.' He studied the glasses closely. 'If she has been murdered, would it be too much to hope that our man might have left us a set of his prints?'

'It'd be handy, guv.'

They searched the lounge next and found that nothing had been disturbed. The compact space was neat and tidy. Helen Palmer was clearly house-proud, which made the layer of dust covering every surface all the more puzzling.

The small bathroom yielded no clues, either. And Ashworth was staring in astonishment at the shocking-pink suite when Holly gave an urgent call from the bedroom. Three strides took him across the hall.

'Look at the bed, guv.'

His gaze fell immediately on the double mattress. Its quilt had slipped on to the floor at its base, and the bottom sheet was stained with blood.

'Not a large amount,' he commented.

'But I bet there's enough for a shallow cut from the head to the abdomen.'

'Hmm.' He straightened up. 'Holly, I reckon this is number three.'

Without waiting to be told Holly activated her radio. 'Holly Bedford,' she said, urgently. 'We're at Vale View, flat number three. We need Forensic — it's a real tooth-comb job — and send uniformed for the door and the street.' She released the switch and glanced around the room, her gaze settling on the wardrobe. 'Do you think she could still be here, guv?'

'I'd say it was unlikely, but we'll have to check.' He pulled a handkerchief from his pocket and made for the wardrobe. 'No, Holly, our man has a thing about water,' he said, peering inside. 'One body turned up in a lake, another in a river . . . I've no doubt the third will be found in similar surroundings.'

'I'll go and tell the landlord,' Holly said. 'I bet he'll be chuffed.'

'He'll get over it,' Ashworth grunted.

* * *

Megan parked her car and walked the last two hundred yards to Boris's flat, considering as she went the dingy facades of the houses. It was not difficult to imagine the splendour that had long since gone from the Victorian terrace. The buildings were all five-storeyed, with balconies around each of the uppermost windows. Below ground, where Boris lived with his father, would have been the servants' quarters.

Where once grandeur had thrived, only decay prospered. Most of the window sills were crumbling — the paint that remained, peeling from the woodwork — and the glass panes were heavily grimed by traffic fumes. The tree-lined avenue, which had once carried sedate carriages pulled by well-groomed horses, now vibrated with the flow of heavy goods vehicles. Megan heaved a sigh; it was such a shame when areas like this were left to rot.

Boris was at his window. Having to spend most of the time entombed in the flat was eroding his sanity; and whenever his father slipped into a fitful sleep he hastened to that small pane, that threshold to the outside world, and drank in the passing images as eagerly as a thirsty man consumed water.

But even that small pleasure could throw up its share of terror. For was that not Megan swiftly approaching? Boris rested his cheek against the cold glass, straining to watch her every step along the weed-strewn pavement. For a brief moment he almost believed that she was there for some reason that had nothing to do with him. Perhaps one of her cases lived nearby, or his street was merely a short-cut to her next destination. But Megan stopped directly outside his flat, her eyes flitting from the number on his door to a page in her notebook.

Highly alarmed, Boris raced into the dark passage to check that the bolts were in place. They were, but he still leant against the door, using his bulk as a barrier against the outside world. He heard and felt her knock; it sent tiny tremors through his body.

'Boris,' she called. 'Please open the door. I need to speak to you.'

Fearful that her voice would wake his father, Boris strained his ears for the slightest sound. All he could hear was the dry, rasping cough that now afflicted the old man, racking his pathetic body, bending it double.

'Oh, go away,' he mouthed, his features contorted with fear. 'In the name of God, go away.'

Megan knocked again. 'I'll come back, Boris. I'll keep coming back until you open the door.'

Three more knocks followed, each one louder than the last. Surely his father could hear them? Sweat broke out on his forehead, and he was about to relent when a slip of paper fluttered from the letter box and landed softly on the stone floor. Then, thankfully, Boris was listening to her retreating footsteps. He picked up the paper and scanned the scrawled note.

'Boris,' it read, 'I urgently need to talk to you. I still want to be your friend, and I'm sorry if I've done anything to offend you. My telephone number is on the reverse of this paper. Please ring me.'

Boris screwed up the note and was hurling it along the passage when a loud thud came from his father's room. He ran, his eyes wide with horror, and threw open the door. The old man was crawling across the floor, babbling incoherent words, a stream of saliva issuing from his lips.

Boris gasped, and rushed to his side. 'Father, you must get back into bed.'

The old man clung to him; Boris could feel those long bony fingers digging into his arm.

'Do not let them in,' he rasped. 'They say they are from the hospital, but they are the police. They will torture me, try to make me admit my faith. And they will take my son . . .' His grip tightened. His whispered words became frantic. 'My son has blood on his hands, so much blood. But he is all I have . . . all I have.'

CHAPTER 20

Ashworth feared he had another full-scale murder enquiry on his hands. And this time the odds against him were stacked a mile high, for this time there was not even a body to give him a helping start. It was tempting to simply file the murders away. No one would make much of a fuss. It was a sad fact that the death of a prostitute did not seem to attract the same public outcry as the murder of a model citizen.

He wandered down to the incident room where photographs of the first two murder victims were pinned to the blackboard, their meagre details written beneath. Soon Helen Palmer's picture would be there, too. Ashworth frowned. There had to be a connection between the three girls. But, what could it be?

The fact that they had all worked as prostitutes was a smokescreen — he was sure of it. They were focusing too heavily on that detail and failing to see some other, more important, factor that could lead them in an altogether different direction. After all, if the killer simply harboured a deep hatred for women who sold their bodies, why did he murder Cynthia Labrum? She had given up that life, had taken a job. No, it didn't fit, as far as Ashworth was concerned. There was something else linking the girls. There had to be.

'Guv, we've got the details you wanted on Helen Palmer,' Holly said, as she bustled in with Josh.

Ashworth settled on the nearest bench and waited while she flicked through her notepad.

'She was born in Bridlington-on-Sea on twentieth June 1962, which makes her . . . thirty-five. She left Bridlington about five years ago, when her marriage broke down. She had no job training, no qualifications, so she started selling the only thing she did have — herself. Things were quiet up north, so she moved to London but the going was too tough and she drifted into the Midlands. She'd been in Bridgetown for about two years. She'd got a couple of convictions for soliciting, but otherwise she was clean.' Holly closed the notepad abruptly and pinned a small photograph to the blackboard. 'We found this snapshot of her in the flat.' She scribbled brief details beneath it, then added the word 'Missing'.

'Anything from Forensic?' Josh asked.

'No,' Ashworth said, with an absent shake of the head. 'I'm not holding out too many hopes there, anyway. All they're likely to tell us is whether the blood on the bed's the same group as Helen's, and if any of the fingerprints found in the flat are known to us. There's been too much people traffic through the place for anything else to turn up.'

'But we don't know her blood group,' Josh said.

'We will, if her body turns up. Otherwise, we trawl round the local surgeries until we find her GP.'

'And are we looking for Helen?' Holly asked.

'Not in any organised way.' Ashworth aimed a scowl at the ceiling. 'The powers that be say she's missing, no more than that.'

Holly knew better than to pursue the point; clearly the chief inspector's application for manpower to search for the girl had been overruled by Superintendent Newton.

'One thing's for certain, though,' Ashworth said. 'We've got to step up this investigation, get some results. It could mean a lot of extra hours — unpaid, of course.'

'Tell us when, guv, and we'll be ready,' Holly said. 'We'll leave you to it, then.'

He gave a nod, not really listening. 'She'll turn up in water — that much I do know,' he muttered quietly, staring at the blackboard. 'And the answer's on there, but I'm damned if I can see it.'

* * *

Only a fraction of Holly's attention was on the missing girl. Mark was avoiding her, and all of her powers of deduction were working on the reason for it. Throughout the day there had been none of the usual secret glances between them, glances that made her tingle with anticipation.

She searched her mind. Had she done something that might have put him off? Had he thought over his promise of the night before and decided against leaving his wife? Those worries and others went round and round inside her brain until a dull ache stretched across her forehead. Holly deliberately left any confrontation until late in the day. She told herself that work must come first, but the truth was she dreaded hearing his excuses.

It was 5 p.m. and she was heading back from the canteen. Turning into the corridor outside CID she found Mark leaving at the end of his shift. Was it her imagination, or did he almost do a half-turn at the sight of her, as if to head off in the opposite direction?

'Hi, Mark. Listen, is anything wrong? You've been avoiding me all day.'

His eyes seemed fixed on a square of wall above her head. 'She came home this morning,' was his quiet reply. 'No doubt hoping to surprise me with someone.'

Holly's smile slipped; she felt as if a cold lump of lead had suddenly lodged itself in her middle. 'But you left my place to come to work.'

'I know, but I called in at the house . . . to make sure things were all right. And thank God I did,' he added, with an awkward laugh. 'I hadn't been there five minutes when she turned up.'

'What the f . . .' Holly bit back the retort and peered down at her shoes as a group of uniformed officers passed them in the narrow corridor. As soon as they disappeared through swing doors at the end she rounded on him. 'What do you mean, Mark? You sound pleased that she didn't catch you out. You're going to leave her — remember?'

'Keep your voice down,' he muttered, glancing left and right. 'We don't want this all over the nick.'

'But I've got to know where I stand.'

He was edging away. 'You'll just have to give me time. I promise I'm going to tell her. Look, if I can't get to you tonight, I'll give you a ring.'

'Don't bother, I'm working,' she said, moodily. 'So, there's no way she'll catch you out tonight, is there?'

'Please don't be like that, Holly. I love you. What time will you finish?'

'I've no idea.' She shot him a terse look. 'This isn't a nine to five job, you know.'

'I'll be in touch,' he said, backing away. 'It'll just be for a few more days.'

'I said, don't bother.' She rushed into the office without another word.

* * *

The murder investigations might be slow in bearing fruit, but the drugs raid went better than anyone at Bridgetown police station had dared to hope. Owing to the stack of information gathered during the surveillance work each unit had a specific target. They were to move in on the pushers and get them off the streets and into waiting police vehicles before anyone had time to react. That was the plan, and it worked perfectly.

Only Holly and Josh experienced difficulties. Their brief was to take out a dealer named Wee Joey Spencer, an acne-covered delinquent who worked the slot machine arcades. Joey was known to be violent, a characteristic fuelled by his need for the substances he sold, and Holly guessed that her martial arts expertise might be tested to the full.

They sat in Josh's car, waiting for Joey to put one foot on the pavement. For the past hour and a half he had been much in evidence inside the arcade; and it would appear that trade was brisk for he was continually approached, his dealings conducted in full view of all. Much money was taken and many small packages changed hands.

Josh had been worried about Holly's mental state all evening. She had hardly said a word in the car, and every time he tried to start a conversation she merely answered in monosyllables. This type of work carried a certain degree of danger — yes, when the time came it would be two against one, but there was always the unexpected to contend with . . . a swiftly pulled knife aimed at the stomach, or a well-concealed gun suddenly nudging the chest — and he could only hope her mind was sufficiently on the job to cope with it. When Joey finally left the arcade and stood for a moment to light a cigarette it was obvious by the way he swayed that he had sampled quite a lot of his own merchandise throughout the evening — a state of affairs that could only hamper the operation.

'Let's go and get him,' Josh said. 'If we handle it right, he shouldn't play up.' He reached for the door handle. 'Just remember, he stays placid as long as you don't lean on him.'

'Piss off, Abraham, I don't need you to brief me.'

They left the car and managed to approach Joey without being seen. Soon they were positioned at either side of him, and Josh grabbed an arm and propelled him across the pavement.

'Nice and easy, Joey,' he said. 'Let's just walk to the car and get in.'

'I don't want to get into no car, man.' His accent was faintly Scottish, his tone completely amiable.

'Don't mess us about,' Josh said, opening the rear door. 'Just get in, Joey, we don't want any trouble.'

'Hey, leave me, will you? I want to stop here.'

Joey made a half-hearted attempt to break free, but Holly pushed him from behind. 'Just get in the car and shut it.'

He rounded on her. 'Do that again, you cow, and I'll do ya.'

'Yes, and I'll break both your fucking legs unless you get into the car.'

She grabbed him by the collar and manhandled him on to the back seat. They were causing quite a commotion, what with Joey's loud protests and Holly's even louder retorts. Soon, a crowd of youngsters had drifted out of the arcade to see what was going on.

'You're over the top, Bedford,' Josh warned. He skirted round to the driver's side, a careful eye on the crowd.

'I don't need your opinion, thanks very much. I'm the detective sergeant, don't forget, and you're the detective constable.'

Josh glanced at the crowd: it was getting restless. 'Well, okay, Detective Sergeant, just get your mind off your personal life and on to the job, because it's my life you're risking as well as your own.' They jumped into the car and sped off just as the first bottle was thrown.

* * *

The reception area at Bridgetown police station was buzzing with activity. While a smug Superintendent Newton paraded about, looking very pleased with himself, Ashworth stood with Sergeant Dutton and watched the never-ending procession of drug dealers being led by uniformed officers to the downstairs office of the custody sergeant.

'That's twenty-nine,' Dutton said. 'We haven't got enough cell space — we're having to use the cells under the magistrates' court.'

Ashworth gave a humourless laugh. 'Never mind, Martin, they'll all be out on bail in the morning, and dealing again by lunchtime.'

'Here's number thirty,' Dutton said, when Holly and Josh led Joey through the doors. 'Well, well, Wee Joey Spencer . . . pathetic little bugger.'

Joey's face was ashen, his eyes were downcast, and he made little protest as Josh ushered him down the stairs to the cells.

'Well, that's it,' Newton said, clapping his hands, excitedly. 'The end of an extremely successful operation. I think we'll see a marked improvement on that estate from this moment forward.' He advanced to the reception desk. 'Sergeant Dutton, perhaps you could pass on my congratulations to your troops — they've done a fine job.'

'I certainly will, sir. I'm sure it'll mean a lot to them.'

Newton searched the sergeant's face for a hint of sarcasm but was met with a deadpan expression.

* * *

'Josh, thanks for not saying anything in there.'

He was hurrying down the steps to the car park when Holly called to him. He stopped and waited for her to catch up.

'Come on, what do you think I am?' He cast her a warning glance. 'But don't ever put me in a situation like that again, Holly. You know as well as I do, in this job you have to have complete confidence in your partner.'

She lit a cigarette and turned away to exhale smoke. Her expression was penitent when she turned back. 'Okay. It won't happen again, I promise. I've got a lot of things on my mind, that's all, but I'm sorting them out.'

'Glad to hear it.' He started down the steps again.

'Josh. I hope this isn't going to come between us.'

He sighed heavily and turned to face her. 'Put yourself in my place for a minute. You're having an affair with Mark and it's going wrong, by the looks of it.' Holly opened her mouth to protest but Josh shouted her down. 'No, listen, Holly, you're not being fair. You bottle everything up inside yourself and you shut me out. If I try to get past the barriers you put up, you tell me to mind my own business . . .' His tone softened. 'Look, Holly, all I'm trying to say is, I'll stay out of your private life — it's nothing to do with me — but if you need a mate, I'm here.'

'Thanks, Abraham.'

'But no more stunts like that one — okay? — or you're on your own.'

CHAPTER 21

The first signs of unrest surfaced on the council estate at
10.30 p.m. Police Constables John Meadows and Gordon
Bennett, patrolling the streets in their police vehicle, noted
with alarm the large numbers of youngsters gathered outside fish and chip shops and takeaway restaurants. They were
not particularly hostile, and the officers had only the usual
shouted abuse to contend with, but the numbers involved
were worrying. Small groups were pretty easy to disperse,
even when drugs had been taken; the youths saw baiting the
police as a form of light entertainment, something to enjoy
when nothing better was on offer. But get a crowd over a
certain number and control was less tenable, difficulties more
likely.

'Do you think we got away with the drugs raid?' a nervous Bennett asked.

'No, they're just biding their time, getting a good stack
of petrol bombs in,' Meadows quipped.

He took a sharp left and steered the car into a side street.
The light was bad there, the buildings on either side cloaked
in shadows.

Bennett peered out of the side window. 'Something's
wrong here, John.'

'Yeh, I know, half the bloody street lights don't work.' He flicked the car's headlights on to full beam and inhaled sharply. 'Jesus Christ, there's a bloody great mob coming towards us.'

Bennett glanced urgently through the windscreen. Youngsters, some as young as eight, were bearing down on them. They seemed to be coming from everywhere, dashing out of the gloom like rats scrambling from danger.

'Back up, John,' Bennett shouted. He reached for his radio. 'Central Control, it's Gordon Bennett. Come in . . . quick.'

Meadows braked and slammed the car into reverse at the very moment that the missiles began to fly; bricks and bottles showered on to the vehicle's roof as it shot backwards.

The radio crackled. 'What's up, Gordon?'

'We're in Gladebury Avenue, sarge. We're under attack from a crowd of youths — could be as many as a hundred.'

The tyres burned on the road, and Meadows was about to turn into the main street when a brick hit the windscreen, turning it white while a thousand pieces of broken glass stayed in place. The mob was running now, advancing on the reversing car.

'Can you get out of it?'

'I think so, sarge.'

Meadows reversed into the main street and punched out the windscreen while he swung the wheel. Bricks were smashing into the bodywork even as the car sped away.

'We're clear, sarge,' Bennett said into the radio, 'but the motor's badly damaged.'

'Get back to the nick.'

* * *

Holly was rummaging in her shoulder bag for her front door key when the telephone started ringing in the hall. The key was within her grip, but her fingers seemed to increase in number as she fumbled to insert it in the lock. Swearing loudly she got the door open and kicked it shut while she grabbed the receiver.

'Hello?'

'Hi, Holly, it's Mark.'

'Oh, hello.' She kept all emotion from her voice, but tears were stinging her eyes. 'Where are you?'

'In a phone box. I've been to the pub. I had to find some way to talk to you. I've been phoning on and off for the last couple of hours.'

'I've just this minute got in.' She took in a deep breath. 'Your wife's at home, I take it?'

'Yes, she . . . Listen, Holly, I want to go on seeing you.'

Holly bit on her lower lip, bit it hard so the sob that threatened to escape might wither away. 'Mark, I've felt so lousy since that row. I nearly fouled up tonight. I just can't carry on like this.'

'It's the same for me, but . . . well, there's something I haven't told you. Her mother's in the latter stages of cancer. I can't spring this on her, not out of the blue, I can't be that insensitive . . .' His voice cracked, and Holly guessed he was crying.

'I don't suppose I'd love you if you were. Mark, we will be together, won't we?'

'Of course we will,' he was quick to say. 'It'll only be for a few months . . . weeks, even. Oh, God, that sounds awful — I'm waiting for somebody to die so I can start my life again.'

'It's okay, I know what you mean, but we've got our own happiness to think about.' She paused. 'Mark, what's she like?'

'I don't want to talk about her, Holly, I want to talk about us.'

'I only want to know what she looks like. Christ, you don't know how awful it is, thinking of you with her.'

He gave a bitter laugh. 'You've got no worries on that score. She has her hair cut really short, and she hangs around in jeans and jumpers all the time. She really turns me off.'

147

'Yes, well, just make sure it stays that way.'

'It will, I promise. Look, I've got to go, there's a queue of people waiting to use the phone.'

'Okay, I'll see you in the morning. Love you, Mark.'

'Love you,' he said, and then the line went dead.

Holly dropped the receiver and immediately picked it up again. She punched out 1471 and listened to the mechanical voice telling her that she was last called at 10.31 p.m. on 1 July, but the caller did not leave their number.

'At least he was telling the truth about phoning from a call box,' she muttered, replacing the receiver.

This whole affair was pulling Holly in two different directions. One half of her wanted to believe him, was desperate to believe him, but a tiny, rational part of her mind was screaming out: 'Pull the other one, it's got bells on it.' She had told Mark that she couldn't go on like this for much longer, and she had meant it. Trouble was, she had fallen so deeply that the thought of losing him was too much to bear. And now it could be months before they were together.

Holly shrugged off her coat and made for the kitchen, her thoughts tumbling over themselves. Was the story about his mother-in-law true, or was it simply a delaying tactic? Did she want it to be true? It would be better, for the woman's sake, if it *were* a lie. Oh, this way of thinking was doing no good at all; she was just tying herself in knots. All it did was highlight the one worry that was ever-present at the borders of her mind — she knew hardly anything about Mark, so how could she trust him so completely? Short of spying on him, there was no way of finding out the truth. She would simply have to go with her feelings and hope that, just this once, she wouldn't fall flat on her face.

* * *

When John Meadows's patrol car limped into the station car park, nearly every available uniformed officer was boarding two black riot vehicles. There were forty officers, and all were armed with protective visors, riot shields, and CS2 gas canisters.

Although no one would have admitted it publicly, most of the officers were welcoming a confrontation that night. There were scores to be settled after months of being spat at, verbally abused, stoned and — worst of all, perhaps — made to feel totally impotent.

There was a real buzz in the back of the vans where taut nerves and adrenalin rushes were tightening resolve. Three patrol cars led the procession along a route that covered most of the council estate. But the unruly element had already weighed the odds and decided against a continued disturbance. So the streets were quiet and brooding.

CHAPTER 22

The forensic report on Helen Palmer's flat was waiting on Ashworth's desk when he got to the office the following day. He found, as he scanned the pages with Bobby, that his earlier assumptions of its details had not been far wrong. The blood found on the sheet was indeed of the same group as Helen's — Dr Patel, at Bridgetown's main medical centre, had grudgingly confirmed as much, while muttering on about patient confidentiality.

Traces of blood had also been found on the carpet by the side of the bed, but nowhere else in the flat. No fingerprints already on police records had been found. And every one of Helen's clients would have to be located — an impossible task — if all fibres and hairs were to be identified and eliminated.

'Our man's too clever to leave clues all over the place.' Ashworth concluded.

Bobby frowned and leant his elbows on the desk. 'This is a long shot, guv, but he may give us something just as important.'

'I'm not following.'

Bobby turned back to the first page of the report. 'There's blood on the bed, which we assume came from the cut the killer made — his trademark, as Holly calls it — and there's blood on the carpet beside the bed, but no traces anywhere else in the flat. That could mean that when the killer removed the body from the bed he wrapped it in something.'

'Yes, but how does that help us? Her coat could have been lying nearby, or her dressing gown. What are you getting at, Bobby?'

'I did say it was a long shot, guv — but, say the killer used something of his own.'

'Why?'

'Helen was only five foot two, wasn't she? Well, the killer would obviously have wanted her completely covered so he wouldn't leave a trail of blood all the way to his car. So, he'd be more likely to use a larger garment—'

'He could have used a sheet out of the airing cupboard,' Ashworth said, shortly. 'He could have used a spare curtain. I'm more interested in how he got the body out of the flat and into a parked car without anybody seeing him do it.'

'Ah,' said Bobby, 'there was a famous case in New York in 1938—'

'Bobby, stick to the here and now. I'm not—'

There was a loud knock, and Sergeant Dutton entered the office. 'Your body's turned up, Jim. Acton gravel pit. Alex Ferguson's already there, waiting for the police surgeon.'

'Thanks, Martin.' Ashworth scooped up his car keys. 'Right, Bobby, let's go and meet Helen Palmer.'

* * *

Acton gravel pit was reached by a heavily rutted bridle path about two miles in length. Recent heavy rain had made it nothing more than deep mud in places, and Ashworth muttered hotly as dirty brown spray covered the bodywork of his Ford Scorpio. The vehicle took the path at a ponderous fifteen miles an hour, pitching and rattling over the uneven ground until its way was blocked by a five-bar gate. They left the car in a clearing that anglers used as a car park and climbed the gate, and a uniformed constable quickly pointed out where the body had been discovered.

The pit was some forty acres of water, and today its still, slightly oily surface was dimpled by the light drizzle that had been falling relentlessly since dawn. They walked about a mile before the temporary white tent could be made out in the distance. Ashworth strode along while Bobby struggled to keep abreast, and at the scene they ducked into the roped-off enclosure. Alex Ferguson had watched their progress, and a grim look was on his face when he crossed to greet them.

'Well, it's turned up,' he said, in his usual detached manner. 'And a little the worse for wear, I'm afraid.'

'It's our man again, I presume?' Ashworth said, stopping just short of the tent.

'I think so, Jim, but there's a slight variation, this time. Like the first two, she was strangled. And, like the first two, she was cut from the back of the scalp to the thighs. But this time — and I can't be a hundred per cent sure until I've done the post-mortem — this time it looks like the cut was made while she was still alive. And there are marks on the wrists that suggest she was tied to something. It would seem your man is getting into his stride and finding out what turns him on the most.'

'It also seems he's getting over-confident,' Ashworth mused.

'There's no need to look at the body, unless you want to,' Ferguson said, catching the chief inspector's reluctant glance towards the tent. 'The photographers are about to move in.'

'I'd like to take a look,' Bobby said.

'Help yourself.' Ferguson opened the flap and stood aside for him to enter.

'Who found the body?' Ashworth asked.

'An angler hooked into it. It was a good way out, but apparently some of these specialist chaps are casting well over a hundred yards these days. He had to be taken to hospital, suffering from shock, but he'll have a good tale to tell about the one that didn't get away.' He was about to chuckle, but Ashworth's icy glare stopped it dead.

Bobby came out of the tent and wandered a few yards along the bank. He stood staring out across the vast stretch of water, his face a ghostly white. The chief inspector excused himself and moved across to join him.

'You all right, son?'

Bobby turned quickly, as if only now aware of another presence. 'I will be in a minute.' He made a face. 'It's the first time I've seen a dead body.'

Ashworth laid a sympathetic hand on the constable's shoulder. 'Books don't always prepare us for the reality, Bobby.'

'I did have an idea, while I was in there, though. I think he's pretending to cut the bodies in half. Two halves of the same. Twins — don't you see? I reckon we're looking for somebody who has a twin, or has a thing about twins. It's something to do with twins, anyway.'

'It's a plausible theory, Bobby — but where does it get us?'

He shrugged. 'I don't know, guv. Nowhere, I suppose.'

On the way back to the car they passed the two undertakers heading for the crime scene. And as the Scorpio bumped and skidded its way back along the bridle path they passed a third man, a very familiar man, negotiating the route on foot. It was John Allan.

* * *

Wee Joey Spencer had spent the night in the cells, a particularly noisy night for the effects of the drugs had worn off well before 2 a.m. By morning he was sweating profusely and shaking so badly that he was unable to hold the cup of tea that had grudgingly been offered. The duty sergeant had deliberately turned a deaf ear to Joey's repeated requests to see a doctor, and during his court appearance the cramps in his stomach had almost bent him double.

He was bailed, and the minute he was free Joey went back to the estate and tried to call in some favours in return for a fresh supply of heroin. But his luck had run out. It seemed that no one thought they owed Wee Joey anything at all. So, by evening his need for a fix had become desperate. He sat in the bar of the Queen's Head, the sickly-sweet smell of his sweat permeating the air, the crippling nausea holding on tight to his empty stomach.

He'd have to do a job, a break-in, to get some money. But how could he, in this state? He couldn't stop shaking long enough to pick his nose, let alone a fuckin' lock.

'Joey . . . good to see you.'

Joey glanced up to see Lee Swanson and his friend, Carl Dunkley, slide into chairs on the opposite side of the table.

'You look bad, Joey, you should see a doctor.' Swanson slid his hand into the pocket of his leather jacket and pulled out a small white package. 'But a doctor couldn't give you this, could he?'

So fierce was his need that Joey made a grab for the packet. But Dunkley caught his wrist in a vice-like grip. Joey winced.

'Don't be so eager,' Swanson said, with a disapproving shake of the head. 'I'm lookin' for a favour.'

Dunkley released his wrist and Joey slumped back in the chair, never once taking his eyes off the package in Swanson's hand.

'I'll do anything, Lee. Just give me the smack, man.'

'I'll give you this, and more, Joey, if you say you heard things in the nick . . .'

'What things, Lee?' His voice cracked. 'Oh, shit, man, I need it bad. I'll say anything.'

'Tell everybody the fuzz're gonna come down heavy on the pushers. Tell them there's gonna be a nine p.m. curfew on the estate. Tell them we're all gonna have electronic tags . . .' Swanson grabbed the front of Joey's T-shirt and yanked him close, their noses almost touching. 'I don't give a fuck what you tell them, Joey, but get them mad. Get them *mad*.'

'Yeh, yeh, I'll do it,' Joey said, grinning wildly. 'I'll do anything, man, you know me.'

Swanson reached into his pocket, and this time he produced three more packets. 'Right, Joey, we've got a deal. The fuzz mean business this time — got it?'

Joey reached for the drugs, nodding eagerly, and disappeared in the direction of the lavatory.

'That should get everybody fired up and ready to go,' Swanson said.

'What you after, Lee?'

His eyes narrowed. 'I want a riot, and I want to waste one of the pigs, then watch them go ape shit when they can't prove it was me.'

CHAPTER 23

The light rain persisted throughout the night and well into the next day. It was running in rivulets down Ashworth's waxed cotton jacket and dripping on to the knees of his trousers by the time he reached the spot on the River Thane where Cynthia Labrum's body had been found. John Allan was crouched on the bank, staring dully into the now slow-moving water. He glanced up when the chief inspector approached, then looked away quickly.

'I saw you at Acton pit yesterday,' Ashworth said.

'So?'

'Why were you there, Mr Allan?'

'I wanted to see what was going on.'

'How did you know anything was going on?'

Allan huffed. 'What is this — twenty questions? I was out walking and I saw all the police cars heading for the pit. I wanted to know what was happening, that's all.'

'Is it your hobby, Mr Allan, visiting crime scenes?'

'Murder interests me,' Allan spat. 'Or had you forgotten?'

'Is that why you spend so much time here?'

The man's gaze returned to the water. 'I'm trying to find the guts to throw myself in, if you must know.'

'I hate water, it frightens me,' Ashworth said, grimacing. 'Funny, that.'

Allan gave a bitter laugh. 'Shouldn't you be arresting me, now? Saving me from myself?'

Ashworth squatted on his haunches and gazed out to the opposite bank. 'Not much point in that. In my experience, if somebody's determined to throw themselves in a river or under a train, they do it.'

'Thanks for the sympathy,' Allan huffed.

Ashworth turned away and pretended to study the water. His heart was bleeding for the man, but he knew that sympathy would only fuel his self-pity.

'You don't understand what it's like,' Allan was saying. 'Having to face every day . . .'

'I know that what happened to you . . . *and* to your wife . . . would threaten anybody's sanity,' Ashworth said, gently. 'If you both live to be a hundred, I doubt if the pain will ever go away. So, maybe you should be trying to find the guts *not* to throw yourself in the river.'

Allan turned on him, his tone angry. 'But what have I got that's worth going on for, Mr Ashworth? What?'

'Try facing it square on and you might find out. I imagine that, like the rest of us, you promised to look after your wife, for as long as you both shall live?'

'My wife?' Allan covered his eyes and shook his head. 'God, Ashworth, only you could come up with a twee answer like that.'

'Maybe. But have you ever thought, for one minute, that while you've been wallowing about in your self-pity, like some gutless . . .' He stopped; he was going too far. 'Mr Allan, that woman needs you desperately, needs something to cling to, and if you can't see that . . . If you can't see that and face up to the responsibility, then there's the river — do everybody a favour and jump in.' He straightened up and walked away smartly.

* * *

Megan had been back to Boris's flat half a dozen times but had still not gained entry. Each time he had hidden at the window, watching her pace up and down on the pavement, praying for her to go away.

This time, as she walked off, his heart felt heavy for she had looked back and he had seen her worried expression, her frantic eyes. He was the cause of her distress, but what could he do? It would be better to break their friendship, now; better for him, and certainly better for Megan.

Even in the sanctuary of his bedroom Boris could hear his father's laboured breathing. It was so loud, it seemed to fill the flat. He cradled his head in his hands, his despair sinking to new depths. He must get the old man to a hospital where they would at least take away his pain. Whatever grudges he held against his father, he must do that small thing. Everyone had the right to a peaceful death. Didn't they?

* * *

John Allan got home at 4 p.m. At the sound of his key in the lock Mildred abandoned her knitting and stood with nervous hand to her throat while he took off his coat and outdoor shoes. Recent times had taught her not to be a nuisance, to stay out of his way; and she was clearing her things from the settee, ready to leave him in peace, when he came into the lounge. But instead of sinking into his armchair as he normally did, his blank expression fixed on the fireplace, he carried on to the conservatory and settled in one of the loungers. Puzzled, she edged towards him and asked in a hesitant voice, 'Would you like a cup of tea, John?'

'Yes . . . please.'

Mildred almost tripped in her hurry to get to the kitchen. He had said, please; not his usual, if I want one I'll get it myself. He had actually said, please. Willing the kettle to boil quickly, she took out a plate and searched the larder unit for biscuits. Oh, why hadn't she got dark chocolate digestives? John loved those. Never mind, bourbons had always been his

158

second favourites. She arranged them carefully on the plate, made the tea, and took it through on a tray.

'Now I know you think I fuss,' she said, placing the tray on the table, 'but I've put some biscuits out. There's no need—'

'Haven't we got any chocolate ones?'

Mildred hid a smile; that's what he always used to say, before . . . 'I'll get some tomorrow, if you like.'

He dunked a biscuit and took a bite. 'I was by the river today, and I bumped into Jim Ashworth. He gave me a right rollicking.'

Afraid that his hatred for the chief inspector might surface and spoil their feeble truce, Mildred jumped in quickly. 'He's a good man. John. We've both been so rude to him, so bitter, yet he still keeps coming to see us.' She feared she had said too much, but the words would not be denied. 'I . . . I realised a long time ago that he's not making excuses or trying to come to terms with his own conscience, he really cares.'

'I know.'

Mildred shot her husband a startled look while his own gaze swept over the unkempt garden whose path had all but surrendered to the weeds.

'I was thinking,' he said. 'Tomorrow, if it's not too wet, we could get out there and re-establish the borders, maybe cut the grass. If it's not too wet, that is.'

'It won't be,' she said, her eyes bright with tears. 'I can get the wellingtons out.'

'And something else — I thought we could get some hanging baskets from the garden centre. You know, the ones that are already planted. It's not the same as growing your own . . .' He stopped and turned to look at her. 'Let's try and come through this, eh? Let's try and have some sort of life.'

'Oh, John.' She grasped his hand and gave it a squeeze.

'It won't be easy, Mildred, some days I feel there's nothing left inside me.'

'We'll make it,' she said, softly. 'If we try hard enough.'

* * *

Sergeant Dutton was preparing to go off duty, but he did so with none of the usual feelings of satisfaction for a job well done. He drained the last of his tea, his jovial expression replaced by a concerned frown, and reflected on his lot. Superintendent Newton was like a cat with two tails. It was even rumoured that he had smiled once or twice.

Newton's good humour was due to the fact that the council estate had been quiet since the drugs raid, and he put it down to the action he had taken. But officers like Dutton, with thirty years' service behind them, knew differently. This was merely the calm before the storm. It wouldn't be long before all hell broke loose on the streets. He just thanked God that the force had been issued with its own riot gear.

He cast an impatient look at his watch and let out a heavy breath. Where was his replacement? Why on earth couldn't these youngsters watch their timekeeping?

* * *

Gordon Bennett and John Meadows were the closest when the call came in. Bennett grabbed the radio.

'We're in Berkshire Crescent, sarge.'

'Get yourselves to Barrack Avenue. There's a break-in in progress at the post office. Believed to be four men inside the premises. I'll get back-up there as quick as I can.'

Wanting surprise on their side they left the siren switched off and parked some distance away from the post office, covering the last fifty yards on foot.

'You take the back, Gord, and I'll do the front,' Meadows whispered.

Bennett sprinted along an alley running parallel with the premises and found that the piece of garden at the back was surrounded by high wooden fencing. He used that cover to get as near as possible to the rear exit.

'In place, John,' he said into the radio.

Meadows saw that the main door to the post office was ajar. It had been forced open, the wood surrounding the lock hacked and splintered. He gave the door a gentle push and grimaced when the twisted hinges creaked. He listened intently, but only silence bounced back at him.

Switching on his torch he shone the thin beam around the interior. The shop appeared to be empty, its stock undisturbed. He tiptoed to a rear door that led to . . . what? Living premises? A storeroom? With his ear against the wood he listened for the slightest sound, but could hear nothing.

Becoming bold now he tried the handle and the door swung inwards. The room beyond was empty apart from stacks of files and papers lining the walls in an orderly fashion. Everything looked fine to Meadows.

'I think somebody's pulling our plonkers, Gord,' he said into the radio attached to his lapel. 'The front door's been forced, but there's nobody on the bottom deck.' He glanced towards the stairs. 'Any sign of life on the first floor, from where you are?' The radio gave off a burst of crackled interference, but there was no answering call from Bennett. 'Talk to me. Gord. This is no time to be throwing a moody.'

'Jesus Christ!' Bennett's voice had risen above the static. 'We've got trouble, John. There's a mob coming along the alley. Get back to the car.'

Meadows wasted no time in racing through the premises, and he just about made it to the street when a petrol bomb arched through the air towards him. As a sheet of fire spread across the road, he could only watch with mounting fear.

CHAPTER 24

Megan had decided to try one more time to get in touch with Boris. If that attempt failed, she intended to give it up as a bad job. After all, if he was determined not to see her there was little she could do to change his mind. And her workload was large enough as it was, without adding to the burden with visits to a lost cause.

Out of habit she parked the car a hundred yards away from the flat, making sure that it was properly locked. And as she walked Megan became aware of belching black smoke casting dark shadows on the horizon. Something was wrong. No ordinary fire would rise so high, and garden refuse or attic rubbish would not produce such thick, acrid smog. She was trying to decide what lay in that direction when a sudden commotion caused her to reel round on the spot. A group of youths — perhaps ten of them — were following the path she had taken. They wore balaclavas and gripped makeshift weapons that appeared to be bricks in knee-length socks.

They stopped by her car, rocked it from side to side, its small chassis a mere toy in their destructive hands. Megan's first reaction was to run back, to chase them off, but even as she dithered the car turned on its side in a loud crash of shattered glass and crumpled bodywork. Petrol poured from its ruptured tank and Megan watched in horror as some of the boys threw lighted matches at the puddle that was forming fast. Eager flames shot several feet into the air, engulfing the car in a matter of seconds, turning it into a giant ball of fire.

The youths scattered seconds before the petrol tank exploded. Black smoke spewed from the inferno and weaved an almost elegant path towards the sky. All of a sudden Megan knew what had caused the smoke on the horizon. Terror gripped her throat, sucked the strength from her legs. She was alone on the street; she had passed no one, had seen no one. She was alone with that group of vandals.

Megan tried to run, tried to sprint that last short distance to Boris's flat, but her slow stilted strides were the stuff of nightmares. She had travelled but a few feet when the boys spotted her and charged as one along the road like a pack of hunting hounds ready for the kill. But Boris's flat was within reach and she fled towards the steps, hurling herself down them without thought of injury. But she landed badly, hands outstretched to break her fall. She toppled, her shoulder jarring severely against the front door, a searing pain taking away her breath.

But rest was a luxury she could ill afford, the chanting mob was almost upon her, the edges of their words blurred by drink and drugs. Megan jumped to her feet and pounded on the door, pleading as she had never pleaded before.

'Let me in, Boris,' she yelled. 'Oh, please, let me in. Boris . . . please.'

They were so close now, almost behind her. Not daring to look back Megan fell against the door, so terrified that her body would no longer move by command. Her head was spinning, the noises fading, slipping away into the distance.

And then the door came open. Boris put out a huge hand and grasped her wrist, then pulled her inside and along the passage. Megan landed in a heap, aware of the door slamming shut, of bolts being drawn. Aware too of the sounds of tortured breath being pulled into dying lungs. Pitiful sounds that were so loud, so dominant, it seemed to Megan in her confused state that the whole building was breathing.

* * *

A knot of panic gripped Sergeant Doug Bentley in the pit of his stomach as he sat in Central Control, speaking urgently into the microphone.

'All units in the area of the council estate — come in. Come in.'

'Jim Ashworth, here.' The strong, firm response made Bentley jump.

'Jim, the estate's gone up. Gordon Bennett's got cut off from John Meadows. He's on foot and about twenty-five of the bastards are after him.'

'He's in radio contact?'

'Heard from him five minutes ago — nothing since. He was heading towards the disused industrial site.'

'Right, Doug, I'll go in from Fullmount Road and try to get him out. What's happening on the estate?'

'Our worst nightmare, that's what. Petrol bombs, torched cars being used as barricades. All available officers are on it, or on their way. Reinforcements are coming in from all over the county. The fire brigade's getting through, but they're drawing a lot of flak.'

'All right, Doug, I'm on my way. If you make contact with Gordon, tell him to stay on the industrial site.'

* * *

'I thought I was going to die out there,' Megan cried. 'Those kids are like wild animals.' She was still shaking violently, her stark gaze fixed on Boris across the narrow passage.

'They have always been wild animals,' he replied, almost savagely. 'You are simply seeing them as they really are for the first time. Years ago, in my country, they would have been executed, or made into generals.'

'You have a twisted view of the world, Boris.'

He jerked his thumb towards the door. 'That is the world. It is not all sweetness and light, where everything can be put right by treating people nicely.'

She listened to the breathing. 'Your father?'

He nodded, pushing past her. 'Come with me.'

She followed him to a door at the end of the passage and shivered when Boris pushed it open for the awful gasps became louder. He invited her to look inside.

With hesitant steps Megan entered the room and found the old man lying in bed. The face on the pillow was a death mask; its skin was without colour, almost transparent, and no flesh cushioned it from the skeleton bones. The sheets covering his sunken chest rose and fell in convulsive jerks and told of the effort with which he dragged in his life-force.

'He's dying,' Megan whispered.

'I do know that,' Boris replied, flatly.

'You should get him to hospital. They could at least make him comfortable there.'

Boris moved to the edge of the bed and patted smooth the sheets. 'I was about to, but it will not be possible tonight, not with the trouble on the streets.'

'You shouldn't have left him so long. He might have got better if—'

'This was what he wanted. It was his last wish before he faces God.' He ran a hand across his forehead and turned dull eyes towards her. 'And in spite of all he has done to me, all he has said, he is still my father and I must obey his wishes.'

* * *

'Central Control, it's Bennett, here. Come in, please.'

Sergeant Bentley pounced on the microphone. 'Gordon, where are you?'

'In Somerset Close. The kids are still following me. I'm knackered, sarge, I don't think I can go much further. But every time I slow down they come charging after me, throwing stones and bottles and Christ knows what else. I can't get away from them.'

'Hang on, Gordon, Jim Ashworth's coming in after you. He's heading for the old industrial site. Now, the reports we're getting say it's still fairly quiet there. Are you anywhere near it, yet?'

'About five minutes away, sarge.'

'Get there as fast as you can.'

'I'll try. Oh, shit, I've got to go.'

Radio contact came to an abrupt end, but not before Bentley caught the words, 'Death to the pigs,' coming from somewhere near Bennett. Unable to stay still, the sergeant moved across to the wall map and located Bennett's position. Until reinforcements turned up, the officer was on his own.

'It's down to you, Jim,' Bentley murmured, worriedly.

* * *

Gordon Bennett paused just long enough to glance back. Yet again the youths were stampeding towards him, their war-cries becoming more charged, more deranged by the minute. Spread across the road and pavement in one continuous line, they raced towards him, stopping now and then to pick up any missiles that came to hand then tossing them at his retreating back.

He had been running for what seemed like hours with little respite, unwilling as he was to take refuge where others might be. The last thing he wanted was to involve innocent members of the public in this game of hate. All he could do was keep on running and hope that their collective attention span was nearing its end.

His rubber-soled shoes pounded noiselessly on the tarmac surface as he headed towards the derelict factory. Whether he could make it that far was a worry he was reluctant to face. His legs ached badly, their muscles knotted with cramp, and his lungs felt as if they might burst, but still he ran on.

The noises behind him seemed to be fading slightly, but when he looked back they were still there, still intent on pursuit; only the sounds of their voices were waning, snatched away by a sudden stiff wind. Bennett pushed himself harder, for he realised now what would happen if he was actually caught. They were after blood.

A painful cramp tugged at his right side, just below the ribs, and Bennett was forced to slow to a trot. But he had made it to the old industrial estate and, please God, help would be waiting. An old, abandoned leather factory stood to his left and Bennett waded through waist-high grasses to reach it.

The area was dark, pitch black; every one of the street lamps had been broken. Over to the east, however, the night sky was alive with orange flames. Bennett staggered into the building where the smell of leather was still strong, even after fifteen years of disuse. The place was empty of equipment, but old wooden benches and packing cases littered the floor. Bennett darted behind the largest of the cases and collapsed on to all fours, dragging dusty air into his lungs. The chanting mob soon brought him to his feet, though. They couldn't have seen him enter the factory, but he was unwilling to take risks. His best chance, he reasoned, was to choose a good hiding place and hope that they wouldn't find him in the derelict maze. But before he had time to move loud yells could be heard directly outside the broken windows.

Bennett cowered in a corner, pushed back against the wall, and tried to lose himself in the darkness while the mob skirted round to the main entrance, their raucous din unabating. They approached swiftly, kicking at the doors, smashing the few remaining windowpanes, wreaking havoc with every step.

Over in the corner Bennett held his breath and waited for them to burst in. He could just make out the tops of their balaclavas bobbing past the windows, heading for the doors, heading for him. But the doors remained closed; the pack was moving on to the adjacent building. And then all sound stopped abruptly, as if someone had thrown a switch to turn it off.

Bennett rested his head against the wall and took in a grateful breath. He was so happy to be alive that he failed to question their movements, never for a moment wondered why they had suddenly gone quiet. All he had to do now was wait for Jim Ashworth. He would give it five minutes to make doubly sure he was clear and then get across to the main road.

CHAPTER 25

At the very centre of the estate the police presence was having a hard time. They numbered around seventy, and although they were decked out in riot gear, they were no match for the three-hundred-strong crowd before them. From behind a barricade of burning cars the youngsters lobbed petrol bombs that exploded around the feet of the officers, making them jump back. Even broken paving stones flew through the air to be caught against riot shields.

Superintendent Newton was pacing to and fro, well behind the battered thin blue line. Anxiety flushed his features; that priggish expression of his had departed hours ago. A screech of brakes sounded behind him and he turned quickly to see a river of officers pouring from the back doors of two police vans. More reinforcements from surrounding towns. The bill for this little lot would be horrendous.

'Right, get down to the action,' he ordered, briskly. 'And spread out. I want the rioters driven back, I want those barricades removed, and I want a baton charge to break up the mob.'

One officer at least was little impressed by the superintendent's authoritative demands.

'Who's that then?' he asked his neighbour. 'Fucking Errol Flynn?'

Newton shot a glare in the direction of the van. He could not for the life of him see how their dire situation should warrant such uproarious laughter.

* * *

Ashworth noted Megan's burnt-out car, the embers still smouldering, and he felt his own tyres crunch on a carpet of broken glass. Apart from the car and the vandalised street lights, everything on the avenue was as it should be. Not a soul was in sight, and the only movements to catch his eye were the pulling aside of curtains as anxious residents peered out into the night. He parked halfway along the road and stared at the disused factory and warehouse.

'Hurry up, Gordon,' he muttered. 'I don't fancy having to go in there after you — not tonight.'

Nothing in the avenue moved.

* * *

Gordon Bennett was still crouched in the darkness, immobilised by fear. The events of that last hour had been worse than anything he had experienced during his ten years with the force. A knot of tension was still tied tightly in his middle, its tentacles spreading up to his shoulders and neck where they retained a vice-like grip.

He tried to relax, tried to think clearly. One thing was certain he couldn't stay where he was. Ashworth would never find him there. He would have to get to the main road, and pretty quick. As soon as he was certain the mob had gone, he could use his police radio — he had switched it off for fear of advertising his whereabouts — and report in to the sergeant.

Bennett pushed himself from the wall, and loose stones and rubble scrunched beneath his shoes, the sound amplified in the hostile silence. With tentative steps he headed for the doors, and he was almost there when he stopped dead. He could hear the scraping of a shoe on tarmac, and then running feet coming closer, beating a tattoo on the ground. Whispered instructions followed, the words incomprehensible.

So, they hadn't gone. They were still out there, waiting to ambush their prey the minute he stepped outside. At that moment a gritty resolve began to blossom in Bennett's chest. Further flight was now impossible, so he would have to fight. Ducking down behind a bench he drew out his truncheon and waited. Seconds became minutes, and the only sound to break the insufferable silence was his racing heartbeat.

Why didn't they make their move? What were they waiting for? They were at the windows, looking in — he could see their dark shapes. Exactly what were they contemplating?

And then he knew. It was all around him, a gushing, gurgling noise that started at the doors. Bennett shot a fevered glance in that direction and could just make out a widening pool of black that spread lazily. It advanced towards the middle of the floor, moving stealthily around packing cases, under benches, building up behind rubble and then spilling over and coursing its way in channels between stones and other debris.

The strong smell stung his nostrils and nudged his memory. His mind played a game of association and threw up images of garages and articulated lorries. Bennett swallowed loudly. That dark lake, moving ever closer to his huddled form, was diesel fuel.

* * *

The bleep of Ashworth's radio cut through the quiet like a knife. He snatched up the handset.

'Jim, Gordon's in the old Curtis shoe factory. They've poured diesel fuel in and torched it.'

At the very moment those words were uttered Ashworth found himself staring at a sudden explosion of flames perhaps sixty yards in front of him.

'I can see it,' he said, hurriedly. 'Is he still in radio contact?'

'No, he told us what was happening, then shouted Jesus Christ and went off the air. There's a fire unit on its way, but I don't think it's going to be in time, Jim.'

Ashworth was already starting the car's engine. 'Just get it here, Doug, on the double.'

Without checking his rear-view mirror Ashworth pulled out into the road and pushed down hard on the accelerator. By the time he reached the slip road leading to the industrial estate his speedometer was touching sixty. Refusing to waste one precious second he maintained his speed and took the bend on two wheels, jarring his body badly when the vehicle righted itself with a thump on the straight stretch. Up ahead a small white van was pulling away, and Ashworth's racing mind was quick to register the number.

He got as close to the factory as he dared and gazed for a moment in disbelief at the grisly scene before him. The whole of the ground floor was ablaze, the heat from the fire immense; flames were making their way rapidly to the first floor. Even from the car Ashworth could detect the scent of melting metal as fierce heat licked at the iron window frames.

He scrambled out of the car and forced himself not to panic but to think clearly, to act swiftly. He knew that the building was five storeys high with a central staircase. Bennett, if he had escaped from the ground floor in time, would be on one of the top floors. The windows would do little to aid them; each was made up of forty small panes — too small for a man to squeeze though — criss-crossed by thick iron supports.

He raced around to the other side of the building, the searing heat burning the left side of his face, making his clothes hot to the touch. Part of him wanted to wait for the fire engines, but he knew that if Bennett was still alive each second could be vital to getting him out of that inferno.

Luckily, Ashworth knew the factory lay-out well; he knew too that there was just one small chance of reaching Bennett and he had to take it. The right-hand wing had been the office block, separated from the factory by a thick wall.

That part, as far as he could see, had not yet succumbed to the blaze so maybe he could get to the fifth floor that way.

A relatively cool breeze soothed his skin as Ashworth approached the door. Taking in a deep breath to bolster himself, he eased it open and went inside. To his left was a long passageway that led to the factory proper, and Ashworth could see that swathes of grey smoke were already escaping from beneath the thick teak door that separated the two areas.

The staircase loomed before him, and he took the stone steps three at a time. The pungent stink of burning timber grew stronger by the second, and Ashworth brought a hand-kerchief to his mouth while his lungs heaved. He had reached the first floor when an horrific crash came from the factory, and he guessed that the ceiling had finally surrendered to the flames, leaving them free access to the floors above.

Ashworth pushed himself harder. By the time he reached the fifth floor he was fighting for breath as the all-consuming heat snatched oxygen from the air. His head felt light, his senses were spinning. Afraid that he might pass out Ashworth rested for a moment, his back against the wall, waiting for his eyes to focus clearly again.

With faltering steps he negotiated a long passage that was identical to the one on the ground floor. Its door opened grudgingly before his hesitant push and for a second or two he surveyed the scene. Smoke was seeping up through the bare floorboards, weaving itself into columns that drifted around the vast empty room like ghastly spectres. Already he could feel a powerful heat beneath his feet.

'Gordon.'

Ashworth had bellowed the name, but his voice was weakened by the smoke and he doubted whether it would be heard over much of a distance.

'Gordon,' he called again, bringing on a fit of hacking coughs.

He fell to his knees, spitting out sour-tasting saliva, the air almost too hot to inhale. Smoke was rising fast now with visibility down to a few yards, and outside eager flames lapped at the window sills. Ashworth's hope was fading fast. Bennett must have perished on the ground floor. But then a slight movement caught his attention, a meagre scuffling music to his ears.

'Gordon, is that you?'

'Over here,' a pathetic voice called through the twisting, swirling fog.

CHAPTER 26

Holly and Josh were behind the police line, keenly following the officers battle to establish some sort of control. There were now one hundred and fifty of them coming at the rioters from all four sides, hoping to drive them into a manageable square. Experience had taught the police that when cornered the mob would start to break up, start to think as individuals again instead of a mindless pack. Only then would their instincts send them scurrying away in search of escape routes. And only then would the police be able to move in and make arrests.

Those arrested, of course, would plead that they were merely innocent bystanders, caught up in the orgy of violence and destruction. And in most cases the police would be unable to prove otherwise, ending up with perhaps a handful of convictions from a night that had filled the hospitals and caused damage that would run into hundreds of thousands of pounds.

One of the officers who had only seconds ago diverted a large piece of paving slab with his riot shield was now stooping to pick up the offending item with the intention of throwing it back into the crowd. And Holly was loudly voicing her approval when Bobby, his face drained of colour, came running towards them.

'Gordon Bennett's trapped in a factory on the old industrial site,' he told them, breathlessly. 'They've soaked it in petrol and set fire to it. They reckon the guv'nor's going in to try and get him out.'

'Jesus Christ,' Holly exclaimed. 'Can we get through to it?'

'Just about, with a bit of luck.'

'Right, come on, we'll take my car.'

* * *

Ashworth found Bennett curled up in a corner, his face blackened by the smoke, his eyes glazed with shock.

'On your feet, son, we've got to get out of here.'

Bennett turned a blank stare towards him and shook his head. 'No, leave me, I don't want to move.'

'You've got to,' Ashworth yelled. 'On your feet — now.'

'No,' Bennett screamed back. 'I'm so bloody shit scared, I *can't* move.'

A snarl crossed Ashworth's face as he hauled the sobbing Bennett to his feet. 'I haven't got time for this, son. We're both going to die in here if we don't get moving.' He dragged the protesting officer towards the door, then pushed and shoved him into the passage. Slamming the door shut behind them, Ashworth grabbed Bennett by the front of his tunic.

'Listen, Gordon, we've got one chance and it's a slim one.'

But Bennett wasn't listening. He was heaving silent sobs, his tears leaving clear vertical tracks along his blackened cheeks. Ashworth shook him roughly.

'Gordon, listen to me. We need to get down to the ground floor. If the fire still hasn't spread to this part of the building, then we can get out. Do you understand?'

Bennett nodded, sending more tears tumbling from his brimming eyes. Ashworth took his arm and guided him along as quickly as the dazed officer would allow. The smoke was worse than ever; it was thick and black, curling in front of them so that the steps were hard to find. If the windows had not been shattered by vandals then they would have easily been overcome, and Ashworth found himself thanking God for those wrongdoers.

Pushing Bennett ahead, Ashworth stumbled down the steps. The lower they went, the hotter the atmosphere became. His eyes watered relentlessly, making it almost impossible for him to negotiate the steep flights. Bennett was a dead weight, hardly lifting his feet as Ashworth propelled him along.

He lost count of the number of floors they had descended, but he knew they must be somewhere near the bottom. As they rounded the final corner tiny flames were snaking along the floorboards, their presence telling Ashworth that the fire had indeed spread to the office block.

He had never known fear like this, had never felt so weary. Every inward breath was a torment, every forward step an insurmountable test of strength. He stumbled on to the bottom of the stairs. He had no need to glance along the corridor to know that the fire had taken a hold here, for as Bennett's inert form literally dragged him over the last step, heat from their right almost knocked him off his feet.

He took a moment to get his balance and then, keeping himself between Bennett and the fire, Ashworth paused to assess the damage. He found that the teak door was no more and the fire, now unhindered, was working swiftly towards them.

Propping Bennett against the wall, Ashworth struggled out of his jacket and beat at the nearest flames that blocked their escape route, subduing them momentarily. Then he grabbed the officer's arm and thrust him towards the outer door. The handle was red hot but he paid it no heed, his thoughts now centred on getting far away from that furnace which could so easily have become their grave.

And then the door was open and glorious cool air was quick to greet them, quick to fuel the fire, too. Behind them, while they wove an erratic path across the grass, the inferno let out a mighty roar, its flames hungrily consuming the fresh supply of oxygen. Darkness was no match for the burning building which lit up the area with a dazzling brilliance. And within that false daylight Ashworth lowered Bennett to the ground and then sank to his knees, coughing and retching, bringing up black phlegm until his middle hurt.

A pounding of feet nudged its way into his consciousness, made him glance round. And then confident hands were lifting him and carrying him a safe distance from the fire. Ashworth liked the feel of those hands, for they meant that others were in control now, others could take charge of the decision-making. With those thoughts in mind, he let his eyelids fall shut and sank into a deep oblivion.

* * *

From the balcony of his penthouse apartment, twenty-two storeys above ground level, Donald Quinn had a perfect view of Bridgetown and its surrounding countryside. That evening, with drink in hand, he gazed down at a town under siege, its many fires no more than flickering candle flames in the distance.

Safe as he was in that lofty haven, Quinn found himself almost enjoying the impromptu entertainment, but frowning tetchily whenever the tiny particles of black carbon that filled the atmosphere drifted up to settle on his white bathrobe. He brushed off the specks and sipped his whisky and soda. If the police had made plenty of arrests that could only be good for business. The legal aid side of his practice was booming in these unlawful times, and who was he to worry?

Turning his back on the outside world, Quinn went inside. And while he placed his empty glass on the coffee table he wondered why he always got the lowlife cases, the prostitutes, the pimps, the minor villains and yobs who couldn't commit a crime without leaving a hundred and one pieces of personal evidence at the scene. Losers, the lot of them.

Defending Lee Swanson and his bunch for the murder of a disabled man hadn't really done him any favours. He was now known as the villains' lawyer — not a good tag to collect. But he had met Holly during that case. As her image flashed into his mind Quinn's mouth became a morose line and he quickly poured himself another large scotch, topping it up with the tiniest dash of soda.

Holly had come too quickly after his divorce. He should have known that, should have made allowances for it. Not that he had loved his wife; she had simply been an ornamental acquisition, a beautiful accessory to have on his arm at all of the various functions that came with his profession. He doubted whether he loved Holly either, but he needed to possess, needed to know that a woman was his and his alone. But now they had both run out on him; his wife taking half of everything he owned in the divorce settlement, and Holly robbing him of what little self-confidence he had left.

Quinn shrugged and drained his glass. After locking the balcony doors he collected the bottle and his glass and took them into the bedroom. He shrugged off his bathrobe, slid between the cool silk sheets, and was reaching to turn off the bedside lamp when his gaze fell on a photograph of Holly that was propped up against its base. It was Holly at her most provocative: chin resting on clenched fist, the corners of her full mouth flicked up in a half-smile, and those eyes, those gorgeous green eyes staring straight into his soul.

That pose, which he had once found go alluring, now seemed to mock, to jeer at his inadequacies. And that teasing smile, which angered and aroused Quinn in equal measures, only intensified his insecurities. She thought it was over, but he hadn't finished with Holly yet . . . nowhere near finished.

* * *

Ashworth was prostrate on the grass, awake once more but dreadfully tired. His face and hands were still a harsh red from the heat of the fire and his clothes were crumpled and grimy, the jacket lying by his side peppered with small burn holes.

179

'So, we've got a hero for a guv'nor, then,' Holly said to Josh, as they stood over him.

Ashworth looked away, embarrassed. 'I wouldn't say that. Where's Bobby?'

'Parking the car.' Her mischievous smile slipped. 'You all right, guv?'

'Of course I am.'

He started to get to his feet, the effort bringing on that hacking cough. Behind him three fire crews were tackling the blaze, at last bringing it under some sort of control, but not before the third floor collapsed in a spectacular display of crimson and orange.

'The ambulance should be here at any minute,' Josh ventured. 'You will be going to hospital, guv?'

'No, of course I won't.' He straightened up, but was none too steady. 'There's no need for me to take up a bed, I'm fine. It's Gordon I'm worried about. That lad's been through hell, tonight. Where is he?'

'Over there.' Holly pointed to where Bennett was sitting on the ground, a thick blanket donated from a nearby house wrapped around his shoulders. 'I think he's in shock.'

'So would I be,' Ashworth said, gruffly, 'if I'd been in there with them pouring petrol all around me and then setting it alight. I'd better have a word with him.'

They watched him limp away. 'He's in shock as well,' she said to Josh. 'Only he's too bloody proud to admit it.'

Bennett's face was still black with dirt and smoke, the path of tears he had shed still visible. His expression was one of startled disbelief, caused in part by the night's events and by the fact that his eyebrows and thin moustache had been singed out of existence. He glanced away sharply when Ashworth appeared before him.

'I'm sorry, sir, I lost my bottle in there. I was just so bloody scared.'

Ashworth crouched beside him. 'And you think I wasn't? You did all right, son, you've got nothing to be sorry about.'

Bennett managed a smile. 'Thanks for coming in to get me.'

'Just forget it,' Ashworth said, waving a dismissive hand.

The wail of an ambulance siren grew steadily louder as the vehicle sped onto the estate. Moments later it was screeching to a halt, the paramedics leaping from its cab. 'Where's the casualty?' one of them shouted.

'Over here,' Ashworth responded.

Behind him, more of the factory collapsed. He turned to look at it. The flames, violent twisting forces of danger, were quickly quelled by the water only to leap back as soon as the flow moved or slowed. It was then that the self-control Ashworth used to keep himself in check began to evaporate. Suddenly his legs began to shake, the severity of the trembling taking him by surprise.

There were people milling around him: paramedics helping Bennett onto a stretcher, uniformed officers, the fire crew. He felt terribly claustrophobic. He had to get away; a couple of stiff malts would soon have him right.

Ashworth began to walk, but could manage only a few steps. His chest felt tight — the smoke coming from the fire was irritating it again. The cough started up, pulling at his sides, aggravating his aching diaphragm. He pitched forward, landing on all fours, still coughing and hacking. Looking up he saw that Holly's concerned face was staring down at him.

'Hospital, guv?'

He gave a resigned nod. 'Hospital.'

CHAPTER 27

Events like a riot and a near-death situation in a blazing building were hardly conducive to a good night's sleep, and so it was a bleary-eyed Holly who walked into the police station at 8 a.m. next morning. Mark Hartland was waiting just inside the swing doors and the moment she entered, he pounced.

'I've been so worried about you,' he said in a terse whisper. 'I couldn't get to a phone last night.'

Holly shot a brief glance towards the reception desk and found Dutton watching them with a quizzical frown.

'I'm okay,' she said, calmly. 'Just tired.'

He studied her face. 'You seem distant.'

'I am, I suppose.' She took in a long breath. 'Look, Mark, last night was pretty rough. A lot of things go through your mind at times like that.'

'Yes? What are you trying to say?'

'I don't like what I'm becoming, that's all.'

'But, Holly—'

'No, listen.' She glanced again at Dutton and lowered her voice. 'Your mother-in-law's ill, Mark — for God's sake, her death's one of the conditions for us being together. I can't take that . . . I can't. If you ever find yourself free of commitments then, great, come and see me. But I don't want

182

any part of this — too many people stand to get hurt and I don't want it on my conscience.' She started to back away. 'So let's just leave it where it is — okay?'

'Fine,' he said, clearly shocked. 'You've made it very plain.'

Holly hurried to the reception desk, aware that Mark's eyes were still on her. 'Morning, Martin,' she said, cheerily.

'Morning, Holly.' He nodded to a pile of custody forms in front of him. 'Ten arrests last night, all waiting to be interviewed.'

'Okay. Has the estate settled down?'

He huffed. 'Last night most of the residents greeted us like conquering heroes, but this morning it's suddenly all our fault. The community leaders are already mouthing out the usual things — the kids need facilities, something constructive to do to turn them away from crime. Sometimes I wonder why I carry on.'

'They do have a point, Martin. A lot of it was our fault.'

'His Lordship's, you mean?' He rolled his eyes towards Newton's office. 'I suppose you're right. But our good superintendent will be telling the media, later today, how it was his swift action that contained the trouble.'

Holly gave a bitter laugh. 'I can hear him saying it, as well, the smug bastard. Any of your officers down?'

'Only Gordon's in hospital — he's in for shock, slight burns and smoke inhalation. Some of the others have got cuts and bruises, but I think they'll work through them. What about Jim?'

'Same as Gordon — shock and smoke inhalation. That's all I know, so far. We're visiting this afternoon. I'll let you know more, then. See you later.'

She was halfway to the stairs when Dutton had a sudden thought. 'Oh, Holly, I nearly forgot,' he said, hitting his forehead with the palm of his hand. 'Somebody phoned for Jim this morning. Megan Rowntree — she's a social worker with the council. The message was a bit garbled but she said she'd got something to report, only she couldn't come in because she was at the hospital.'

'Megan Rowntree?' Holly shook her head. 'The name doesn't mean anything to me. Oh, well, if it's important I'm sure she'll call back.' She hitched up her shoulder bag and carried on to the stairs.

* * *

Early afternoon found her scurrying along a corridor with Josh and Bobby *en route* to Ashworth's sick bed. They rounded the last corner to find Sarah leaving his room, a relieved smile on her face.

'Hello, Mrs Ashworth,' Holly said, rushing to her side. 'How is he?'

She smiled. 'Complaining about everything, dear, so he must be on the mend.'

'We're not chasing you away, are we?' Josh said.

'Of course you're not — don't be silly. I've had half an hour with him, and I can come back tonight.' She patted his arm. 'Anyway, I know he wants to see you lot, so I'll leave you in peace.'

'How are you getting home, Mrs Ashworth?' Bobby asked.

'I'll phone for a taxi in reception, dear. Oh, I'd better warn you that Jim and the sister have apparently crossed swords a couple of times.' She dropped her voice to a conspiratorial whisper. 'She can be a bit sharp.'

Leaving them with a sunny smile Sarah marched off down the corridor. And they were about to enter Ashworth's room when a loud voice hailed them from behind.

'Excuse me . . .' Holly turned back with a questioning look. 'Yes . . . you.'

It was the sister, approaching at a gallop. She was large-framed woman of fifty, and her flesh wobbled eagerly as she bounced towards them on her thick rubber-soled shoes.

'Only two visitors at a time. See? It states it very plainly there.' She pointed to a notice on the wall. 'Please abide by the rules. It makes life go much easier for the nursing staff.' Holly pulled a face at her retreating back.

184

'I'll give Mrs Ashworth a lift home while you two go in,' Bobby said. 'Give me the car keys, Holly, and I'll catch her up.'

Ashworth's face broke into a smile the moment they entered the room. 'Ah, there you are. Sarah saw you pulling into the car park.'

'Bobby's giving her a lift home,' Holly said. She started to pile fruit into a bowl. 'There you go, guv — apples, oranges, and grapes.'

Ashworth viewed the bowl with little enthusiasm. 'Thank you,' he said, weakly.

'Get a few of those down you, guv, they'll soon clear out your system.'

'A clear system's always been one of my ambitions, Holly. Anyway, how's Gordon?'

'Not too good,' Josh told him. 'We've just been along to see him. The doctors say he should soon get over the physical injuries, but most of his problem's up here.' He tapped his forehead. 'It's early days yet, of course, but it could be he'll never work in the force again.'

'Damn,' Ashworth exclaimed. 'He's a good copper, too. I was trying to tell him last night that that sort of thing probably only happens once in a career, that he's got to put it behind him.' With much reluctance he picked off a grape and tossed it into his mouth. 'So, what was the outcome of last night's riot, in terms of arrests?'

'Ten.' Holly pulled up a chair and sat down. 'And it's a wonder any of them got nicked — to hear them talk they weren't even there. Anyway, they've all been interviewed and charged, but it's only minor stuff, guv.'

'Who's representing them?'

She lowered her eyes. 'Donald Quinn. He wasn't there in person, but his people were.'

Ashworth scowled. 'That man's getting to be as bad as the criminals he represents. And that reminds me . . .' He leant across and took a tissue and a pen from the bedside locker. 'This is the registration number of a white van,' he said, scribbling on the tissue. 'I want to know who owns it. Check it out with Swansea.'

'Will do, guv. Oh, and here's Alex Ferguson's report on Helen Palmer. It arrived just as we were leaving.' Holly fished it from her bag and handed it across.

Ashworth brightened considerably as he read the report. 'So, Alex was right. The cut *was* made while she was still alive. And she *was* tied by the wrists — very tightly, too, it would seem. Minute traces of white and grey fibres were found embedded in the contusions. They came from whatever was used to secure the girl.' He glanced at them. 'At last we've got something to work on.'

'What do you want us to do, guv?' Holly asked.

'Make a list of all firms manufacturing materials such as twine, rope, string . . . Stick to a twenty-mile radius, to start with. If we can find out who supplied the rope, and to where, we might get closer to our killer.'

* * *

Back at the station Holly sat at her desk wishing, not for the first time, that she had kept her romantic life completely separate from work. She had already sent Bobby off to start work on the list of rope manufacturers and was trying to concentrate on the interview statements, but Mark's gaze was upon her, making her feel very uncomfortable. Several times she looked up, and each time he turned away. It made for a very frosty atmosphere which no amount of fooling from Josh could hope to thaw.

Going back to the statements Holly hoped that she would get over Mark. For the first time in God knows how many years she had done the sensible thing, and she had no intention of going back on her decision.

'Holly,' Josh called suddenly from his desk. 'I've got a result on that registration number. It's a Ford van, and guess what? It's registered to our old friend, Lee Swanson.' Holly pondered for a moment, chewing distractedly on the end of her biro. 'Well, do we do anything?'

'No idea, Josh. The guv'nor didn't say why he wanted to know, did he? I'd better get in touch and ask him.' She was reaching for the telephone, when it buzzed. 'DS Bedford.'

'Holly, it's Martin, I've just had an interesting phone call on reception.'

She grinned. 'If it was a heavy breather, and he phones again, Martin, give him my number.'

A chuckle travelled down the line 'It was a prostitute called Mandy — sorry to disappoint. She said to tell you that the three murdered girls had all been working for Lee Swanson at one time or another. She said she trusted you to keep your mouth shut about where the information came from, but if you mentioned her name she'd deny it, even under oath; and the next time you wanted to know anything you could go and fuck yourself.'

'When did you get the call, Martin?'

'A couple of minutes ago. I'll let you have a copy of the transcript as soon as I've written it out.'

* * *

Late in the afternoon Megan had gone in search of a call box to telephone for an ambulance for Boris's father. She had scuttled nervously along the road, her gaze never leaving the scorched shell of the leather factory, and was thankful that the public telephone, at least, had escaped the vandals' hands. To start with the ambulance service was reluctant to send out a vehicle.

'Love, the hospital's jam-packed with casualties from last night,' the man had said. 'If he's in the shape you say he is then you'd be better off calling for his GP.'

Although he stopped short of saying the actual words, Megan had heard in his voice the message that hospital was not the place for no-hope cases.

'But he should be admitted to hospital,' she had insisted. 'He's in a great deal of pain and he needs constant attention which is just not possible where he is now.'

'All right.' A loud sigh on the line. 'I'll get an ambulance there as soon as I can.'

On her way to the call box Megan had deliberately avoided the scene of her burnt-out car, but walking back she forced herself to view the remains. Goodness knows how she was going to replace it but she would have to find the money from somewhere. Her job was impossible without transport.

A mixture of anger and sadness had filled her as she took in the full extent of the damage done to the area. She had always been of the view that violent and criminal youngsters in our society were simply in need of a little tender loving care and she had never been ashamed to say so. But now, perhaps for the first time, she had an insight into the victims' lot, could see their side of the argument. And what she had learnt now made Megan question her convictions.

With a heavy heart she had trudged back down the steps to Boris's flat and her melancholy only deepened when his father's audible distress met her at the door.

* * *

Over at the hospital the querulous chief inspector was fast making himself unpopular. Ashworth was a man not used to inactivity. Bed was for sleep; once awake, he got up. He grunted and growled through the routine visit of the doctor on his rounds, during which he was told that smoke inhalation could have serious side effects but, luckily, all signs indicated that he should come to no real harm.

'So, when can I go home?' he asked, hopefully.

The doctor's face brightened. Having a patient eager to vacate his bed was always a bonus. 'Well, Chief Inspector, physically you're quite sound. When I do my rounds tomorrow, if all is still as it should be, there's no reason why you can't be discharged.' The corners of Ashworth's mouth flicked up into a smile. 'But, of course, you've been through a very traumatic experience, so I do feel that counselling will be necessary.'

'No counselling,' he said, the smile becoming a scowl.

'I would advise—'

'Doctor, if and when I feel the need to talk over what happened last night, I shall do so with my wife rather than with some perfect stranger who'll probably diagnose me as suffering from heaven knows what post-syndrome something-or-other just because I encountered a traumatic experience in the natural course of my duty.'

The doctor exhaled sharply. 'Have it your way, Chief Inspector, I was only trying to help. I'll see you in the morning, then.'

As soon as the door closed on the white-coated figure Ashworth climbed out of bed and reached for his dressing gown. He viewed the garment with disdain. Why did Sarah have to buy him a new one to bring in? He liked his old one; it was comfortable, worn in. Whereas this . . . this . . . *thing* — with its blue and black stripes, its awful grey collar, and the tassels on the end of its tie cord — was a monstrosity. He stomped out of the room like a giant sulking schoolboy and set off to the payphones to ring Holly.

'Guv, thank God you've phoned. I've been trying to get in touch with you.'

'Any luck with that registration number?'

'Yes. Would you believe that the van belongs to our old friend, Lee Swanson?'

'I thought it might. I saw it pulling away from the old shoe factory just after it went up in flames.'

'And that's not all, guv.' She told him about Mandy's call.

'Well, well, that is interesting.'

'Do you want us to pull him in?'

'Not yet. Give me a while to think about it. Next time we have him in that station, Holly, we've got to make damned sure he can't wriggle out of anything.'

* * *

On the ground floor of the hospital, almost directly below the payphones, Boris's father was in the process of being admitted. The registrar, a young man who looked dead on his feet, was conducting an earnest discussion with Megan.

'We're doing what we can to ease his breathing and make him as comfortable as possible, but it's only a matter of time.'

'How long?' Megan asked.

'Hours, I'd say. Twenty-four at the most. He really shouldn't be in here; we haven't got the beds. His own doctor could have done everything we can.'

'But the hovel he lives in isn't fit for human habitation,' she snapped. 'What's happening to the health service when it can't provide much-needed help for a dying man?'

'I've been on duty for thirty-six hours,' he hissed. 'The phone keeps ringing with people asking, can I have a bed for this or that?' He gave her a stern look. 'Don't ask me what's happening, I just have to cope with it.'

Megan's hostile expression softened immediately. 'I'm sorry, doctor, I didn't mean to get at you personally, it's just that . . . oh, it doesn't matter. Will it be all right if we wait?'

'Of course.'

She left the registrar in the middle of a fractious telephone conversation and wandered back to Boris to tell him what had been said. He seemed to accept the news calmly enough, slowly crushing the plastic cup he was holding but showing no outward emotion.

'So, I have to wait here for death to arrive,' was all he said.

'Boris, we should report what we saw last night to the chief inspector,' she said, changing the subject gently.

'No.' He was resolute. 'I will not leave this hospital while my father is still alive.'

'Okay. Listen, I'll ring the station and get them to come here.'

'No . . . *no.*'

His voice had risen sharply, and other relatives of the sick turned in their seats to stare at him. Megan gazed with alarm at the plastic cup that was almost torn to shreds within his huge fists. Why had the mention of the police affected him so strongly?

She decided to leave it there and crossed instead to the drinks machine along the corridor. Glancing back she saw Boris rocking in his seat, looking for all the world like a lost child. He was a mountain of a man, it was true, but a mere innocent, nonetheless.

And of course he was frightened of the police. How could he not be after the life he had led? Locked in that narrow existence with his father; spending his days reading from the Bible while all around him mocked; forever being told to move on by suspicious uniformed officers. Those very facts alone were probably responsible for the healthy distrust he now held for the forces of law and order.

CHAPTER 28

To be officer in charge of CID was rather exhilarating, and the challenge at least took Holly's mind off her love life. There were lines of enquiry to follow up that might possibly lead to the apprehension of the perpetrators of the riot. Holly doubted it, though; hours of video footage would have to be studied if any of the culprits were to be identified. And then there was the footwork — getting out among the people, interviewing petty criminals, junkies, and the like. Although very little worthwhile information was gathered during the course of their investigation, a large quantity of looted property had been unearthed and several arrests made. All of which would look good on the CID's clear-up rate.

But alone at home, Holly found thoughts of Mark crowding her mind, and deep depression only a whisker away. She would have to get busy — that was the only way to keep her thoughts at arm's length. After picking at fish and chips, she washed up, vacuumed the house from top to bottom, then loaded the washing machine and sat down for a cigarette.

One of the pluses about not being with Mark was the fact that she could smoke as many as she wanted. Perhaps she should be concentrating on the positive, looking on the bright side, instead of acting as though her life was finished. She stubbed out the cigarette and lit another.

It was later, in the bath, when depression finally overwhelmed her. While soapy water lapped around her chin she began to dwell on her love for Mark. There was guilt mixed in with it, too, for she realised now that she loved him far more than she had ever loved her late husband. Those times with Mark had been so wonderful, unreal, like a lovely dream. But now it was over, all gone.

Maybe love was something she would touch fleetingly but never own. Maybe those girls, tramping the streets, had the right idea. They never gave freely, they always got something back.

And some got more than they bargained for.

The thought jolted Holly back to the present. She must stop feeling sorry for herself and start getting her head round the murders. And she must start right now. Ashworth always gave her a lot of rope, but on this case she was in danger of hanging herself with it.

With the bath finished and her hair dried, Holly poured herself a large gin and tonic. And while she sipped it, her thoughts turned, of their own accord, to the following day. 9 July. Mark's birthday. She had day-dreamed for hours about the present she would buy, the restaurant at which they could celebrate.

Realising that the gin was responsible for her dismal thoughts Holly decided to go to bed. But would she sleep? Probably not. One more drink might help. After a moment of indecision she chose the easy option and refilled her glass. Drifting off to sleep a while later Holly imagined an expensive restaurant, Mark toasting his wife across a tiny candle-lit table while she whispered adoringly, 'Happy birthday, my darling.'

* * *

Holly's head was pounding next morning, her mouth still dry after five cups of coffee. She kicked shut the door of

193

CID with her heel and threw her shoulder bag on the desk. Josh and Bobby, all too familiar with the signs, kept their heads down and tried to look busy. Only Mark stared at her, hoping to catch her gaze. But she ignored him and glanced instead at the birthday card standing on his desk. It did nothing to improve her mood.

'Right, what have we got this morning?' she demanded to know.

'There's a Megan Rowntree and a Boris Cywinski waiting to see you,' Josh said.

'And what do they want?'

'No idea, sarge,' he said in that mocking tone which infuriated her. 'They wanted to see the guv'nor, but were told they'd have to make do with you.'

Holly glared at him. 'Where are they?'

'Martin Dutton put them in interview room one.' He turned back to the computer keyboard, but not before she had caught his sarcastic grin.

Holly stormed along the corridor. God, there were times when she hated Josh. He always waited until she was in a bad mood, and then he made all sorts of little digs. She was desperate for a cigarette, too, but with Mark in the office she would have to wait until later. Suddenly her step faltered. Hold on a minute — what was she doing? She had finished with the man. He was out of her life. And yet he still dictated whether she smoked or not. For one fleeting moment Holly felt like burying her face against the wall and weeping like a baby, but by the time she entered the interview room she had on her public face.

'Good morning.' She gave them an encouraging smile. 'I'm DS Bedford.'

They were sitting in silence at the table. Megan glanced up when Holly came in, but Boris carried on staring at the tabletop.

'I see they've looked after you.' Holly nodded towards the cups of tea. 'Now, what can I do for you?'

'We want to report something,' Megan began, hesitantly. 'Something we saw on the night of the riot.' Holly pulled up a chair and motioned for her to go on. 'I was at Boris's flat in Gladebury Avenue when it happened — we needed to get his father to hospital, that's why . . .' She stopped and shot a worried glance at Boris.

'Go on, Miss Rowntree.'

'I'm sorry, it's just that we're a little upset. Boris's father died in hospital in the early hours of this morning.'

'I'm sorry to hear it,' Holly said to Boris.

'That's why I was there,' Megan went on quickly. 'To help Boris . . . Boris and his father.'

'It doesn't matter to me why you were there,' Holly said, lightly. 'What exactly do you want to report?'

Boris looked up, then. His large face was a deathly white which picked out clearly the dark circles beneath his eyes. 'On the night of the riot,' he said, his voice a dull monotone, 'we saw Lee Swanson handing out petrol cans to his friends. He was getting them from the back of a white van. That was moments before the old factory caught fire.'

Holly's interest was aroused. 'You're both sure about this? You, too, Miss Rowntree?'

Megan nodded. 'We're positive. We were on the steps outside the flat. We were hoping to get to a phone box so we could call for an ambulance. The others were wearing dark clothes and balaclavas, but Swanson wasn't. Yes, we both saw him very clearly.'

'But the factory was some distance away from where you were, and it was very dark without the street lights,' Holly said, adding hurriedly, 'It's not that I don't believe you, but I want to make sure you're both certain.'

'I told you, Sergeant, we're positive,' Megan bristled. 'I wouldn't say that if it wasn't so.'

'Fine. Okay, would you both be willing to make statements to that effect?'

'Absolutely,' Megan said.

'And you, Mr Cywinski? Would you be willing to sign a statement?'

'It would be a pleasure,' was his firm reply.

* * *

Holly's head was clearing fast, her brain beginning to function along logical lines. Heading back to CID she was already preparing her course of action, excited that she could take full charge of that surprising development. So although she was pleased to see Ashworth standing in reception, a part of her was heavy with disappointment. She hurried towards him, nevertheless.

'Guv, what are you doing here?'

'I was discharged this morning. I went home for a cup of tea and then came straight here.'

'But you shouldn't be on duty,' she lightly chided. 'You need to take some sick leave.'

Ashworth made a face. 'I've heard nothing else from Sarah all morning, Holly, so don't you start.' He nodded towards Sergeant Dutton. 'Martin's just told me that Megan Rowntree and Boris Cywinski came in to report something. Anything we can use?'

'I think you'll be very pleased when you read the statements, guv. They run along the lines of Swanson handing out petrol cans from the back of a white van in the vicinity of the old Curtis shoe factory.'

'What?' His haggard face creased into a smile. 'Well, that's brilliant. We've got him this time.'

'Do you think it'll hold up in court?'

'Why not? Megan Rowntree will make a credible witness. The defence might try to take Boris apart, but he's an intelligent man, and articulate when he wants to be. Plus, I saw the van at the scene of the crime. Yes, Holly, we can get Forensic on to it and hopefully get the fingerprints of the others involved.' He heaved a contented sigh. 'With Swanson

196

and his mob behind bars, our troubles on that estate could be over, once and for all.'

'So, guv, we go for him then?'

'We do, Holly. We'll need uniformed to look after the van and Swanson's house until Forensic get there.' He turned pleading eyes towards Dutton.

'Leave it with me, Jim. It'll give me as much pleasure as you to see that little scumbag inside.'

'Good man, Martin. Come on, Holly, we've got work to do.'

Ashworth hastened to the stairs, taking them two at a time. Holly did notice, however, that he had to slow down after the first flight, his breathing laboured, but she said nothing.

'Have you completed that list, yet?' he asked.

She shot him an indignant look. 'Guv, since you've been off I've hardly had time to time to go to the loo.'

* * *

Holly had supposed they would go in low key, in and out before anyone had time to realise what was happening. But Ashworth had other ideas. On the approach to Kirkstone Crescent he ordered the patrol cars to switch on their sirens. Four cars in all pulled up outside the house and six uni-formed officers piled out on to the pavement.

'Do you think that was wise?' Holly asked, glancing around nervously.

'Yes, I do,' was Ashworth's gruff reply. 'Let them know we're still alive and kicking . . . and ready for the next round, if they want it.'

The street remained deserted as they trooped along the garden path. And when Ashworth rapped on the front door it was opened straight away by Swanson, that cocksure grin on his face.

'Mr Plod. Well, I wonder what you want?'

'You're under arrest,' Ashworth told him. 'Get your coat. We're taking you to the station.'

Swanson remained where he was, merely folded his arms. 'You'll never learn, will you? You can't touch me, Mr Ashworth.'

'Son, you're about to get the shock of your life. Now, come on, get moving.'

'I'll have to phone my brief first, so you'll have to wait a bit.'

Ashworth caught his arm. 'You can do that from the station. Like I said, you're under arrest.'

For a few moments it looked as though Swanson might resist. He peered deep into Ashworth's eyes, a choice swear word not far from his lips, but then he gave a shrug and strode towards the car. Ashworth was installing him in the rear seat when Holly's radio bleeped. She moved a little way from the car and spoke rapidly, glancing now and then towards Swanson.

'Well?' Ashworth said, when she had finished.

'We're in luck, guv. The van hasn't been cleaned inside or out, so Forensic are going to have a field day with it.'

Ashworth glared at Swanson through the car window. 'And with a bit of luck,' he said, quietly, 'they might find evidence that those murdered girls had been in the van.'

'But, guv, I thought you'd come round to thinking that he wasn't our killer?'

Ashworth gave her a knowing look. 'Murder by proxy, Holly.'

'Guv?'

'What better way to evade detection than to get one of your cronies to do your dirty work for you?'

CHAPTER 29

It was another two hours before they were able to interview Lee Swanson. During that time his solicitor, a Ms Forsyth, another of Donald Quinn's colleagues, spent a considerable amount of time with him, too long a time as far as Ashworth was concerned. He paced the corridor, right fist punching left palm, impatient to get things moving. Holly leant against the wall, watching him in silence. Finally, the door of the interview room flew open and Ms Forsyth emerged.

'I'm sorry I had to keep you waiting, Chief Inspector. There were just a few points to be ironed out.'

Ashworth narrowed his eyes at the woman. She was a presentable twenty-five-year-old blonde of immaculate appearance — her navy blue outfit neither too modern nor too frumpy — and there was nothing confrontational about her stature or expression. Nevertheless, Ashworth harboured an instant dislike for her. To his mind the very nature of her visit made Ms Forsyth a natural adversary to the police force and to the whole concept of justice.

'Not at all,' he said, mildly. 'The thought of Mr Swanson not having sufficient time to conjure up an alibi is too awful to contemplate.'

'I'm sorry?' she said, rather taken aback.

'He's ready now, I take it?'

She gave a brisk nod. 'But this interview must be conducted on the strict understanding that Mr Swanson is simply helping you with your enquiries, Chief Inspector. He has yet to be charged with anything, so—'

'Yes, yes,' Ashworth said, striding into the room. Holly followed him in and dealt with the tape recorder.

Swanson was sprawled in a chair, a cigarette between his fingers, a sprinkling of ash around his feet. Ms Forsyth quickly took the seat beside him and shuffled her papers into a neat pile on the table while a uniformed officer closed the door and positioned himself to its left. Ashworth sat down to face the pair, a tiny smile of anticipation tugging at his lips.

'Now, Mr Swanson, I'd like to ask you a few questions about the night of seventh July . . .' He paused, but there was no response from Swanson. 'On the night in question were you in the vicinity of the old Curtis shoe factory that was burnt down on the industrial estate?'

Swanson gave a slow shake of the head, his insolent gaze centred on Ashworth's face. 'Nowhere near it. There was a lot of trouble that night, if I remember, and I stopped in with a mate.' Another half-inch of ash drifted towards the floor.

'Really?' Ashworth said, sliding the ashtray towards him. 'The thing is, I have three witnesses who all put you on that estate around the time the fire started.'

Ms Forsyth shot a startled look towards her client. 'There's no need to say anything at this time,' she said. Swanson merely raised a challenging eyebrow.

'I have to tell you,' Ashworth went on, 'that two of those witnesses claim they saw you handing out fuel cans from the back of your van. They claim you were waving your arms about and pointing, as if issuing orders.'

Swanson idly crushed his cigarette in the ashtray, his confidence still brimming. 'No comment,' was all he said.

'Please yourself, but you can't stay silent for ever,' Ashworth said, dispersing the cigarette smoke with a swift movement of his hand. 'Even as we speak our forensic team is carrying out tests on your van and clothing. If they come up with anything that might support our witness statements, then you'll have a lot of explaining to do.'

'This is an unfair line of questioning,' Ms Forsyth protested. 'You're assuming that—'

'No comment won't be good enough then,' Ashworth interjected.

Swanson leant forward, his leering face only feet away from the chief inspectors'. 'You'll never get your witnesses to court, and you know it.'

'Keep quiet,' Ms Forsyth snapped, with a wary glance at the tape recorder.

'That's a very interesting remark.' Ashworth swung his gaze towards the solicitor. 'Perhaps your client would like to explain what he means by that, Ms Forsyth.'

'Your line of questioning has led to this,' she stammered. 'I request that this interview be postponed for ten minutes while I confer with my client.'

'Oh, shut it,' Swanson suddenly yelled. He levelled a finger at the startled solicitor. 'You tell Don Quinn I want him here to handle this. Now, get out.'

Ms Forsyth leapt to her feet, her demeanour decidedly ruffled. Hurriedly stuffing papers into her briefcase, she said to Swanson, 'I strongly advise you not to answer questions without a solicitor present.'

'Just tell Quinn I want him here.'

Without a backward glance the solicitor hastened to the door which was speedily opened by the constable. In the ensuing silence Ashworth settled back with a contented look.

'Interview terminated at approximately three fifteen p.m.' Holly told the tape recorder. 'Mr Swanson's legal representative, Ms Forsyth, has left the room at his request.'

'Well, Mr Swanson, where do we go from here?' Ashworth asked.

Swanson lit another cigarette. 'I'm sayin' nothin' till Don Quinn's here.'

'You don't have to,' Ashworth replied, quite matter-of-fact. 'You know you're in trouble this time because we'll have forensic evidence. Difficult to get around, that.'

Swanson drew heavily on the cigarette and blew a plume of smoke towards the ceiling. 'You won't get your witnesses to court,' he said again.

'We'll get one of them to court, I'm certain of it.'

'Oh, yeh? And how can you be so sure?'

Ashworth grinned. 'Because it's me, Mr Swanson, and neither you nor anyone of your ilk has got anything that frightens me.'

* * *

Holly was dreading the quiet evening stretching out in front of her, so when Josh and Bobby offered to take her out on the town she jumped at the chance. They were fun to be with, and neither would allow her to brood. After an Indian meal they called in at the Bull and Butcher for a quick drink and then went on to a club where the men took turns in gyrating around Holly on the dance floor. All of that exertion, however, brought on a raging thirst and, rather than pay the exorbitant prices at the club, they stopped for drinks at a quiet country hostelry.

The wine flowed, and they were enjoying a discussion involving a sex aid when Holly felt a presence at her left shoulder. She turned to find Donald Quinn standing beside her. He gave her a broad smile, a smile so open, so friendly, that any bad vibes she might have had were quickly chased away.

'Hi,' he said. 'Can I buy you people a drink?'

'Oh, hi, Don,' Holly said, her smile decidedly fixed. 'Why not? Thanks a lot.'

They ordered, and when Quinn returned with a laden tray, he positioned himself close to Holly.

'I must say, you look very smart,' she said, surreptitiously edging away. 'New coat?'

He glanced down at his knee-length black leather coat, tugged self-consciously at its lapels. 'New phase in life, new image . . . you know how it is.' He changed the subject. 'Anyway, how's tricks?'

'I expected to see you at the nick, today. One of your clients was demanding your presence.'

He made a face. 'From what Liz Forsyth's been telling me, that young man could at last be for the high jump. I'll wait and see what your lot have got before I slip in.'

* * *

Swanson knew he was in all sorts of trouble. He lay on the narrow bed in the police cell cursing himself for his stupidity. He should have worn a balaclava. Christ, he should have pinched a van. What a piss-pot crazy thing to do — usin' his own. He'd got too sure of himself, too certain that nobody would ever dare to give evidence against him. He could at least have cleaned the van, got rid of his clothes.

He tossed about on the uncomfortable bed, searching for a solution, for a way out of his predicament. That ponce Ashworth would have him this time, he was determined to. What would the charge be? Attempted murder? Arson? Riotous assembly? He didn't want to tally up how many years he might get for that little lot.

But perhaps he could get the sentence reduced. Cut it in half, and then half again. Swanson grinned at the ceiling. What if he got some information that Ashworth would be interested in? Yeh, if he played his cards right he could be looking at as little as three years, and with remission it'd come down to two. Two years — hardly worth taking your shoes off for. The thought cheered him.

* * *

Holly had been foolish enough to share a taxi with Donald Quinn and all through the journey he had made a nuisance of himself, pawing her, never leaving her alone. Why couldn't he understand that it was over? Why keep going on and on about getting back together?

Attempting to negotiate a straightish path across her hall, Holly stopped for a moment to consider her reflection in the wall mirror. That was the effect she had on all men . . . except the one that really mattered. No, no, she mustn't slip into that sombre mood again, not tonight. She'd enjoyed herself for the first time in ages and nothing and no one was going to spoil it, not even Mark Hartland.

CHAPTER 30

After pulling a few strings and calling in all the favours owed to her, Megan had managed to secure a one-bedroom council flat for Boris. The accommodation was small — he would probably resemble a giant prowling around the tiny rooms — but it was clean, modern, and all of its fixtures were in good working order. She waited while he put together his belongings and collected the money for his father's funeral which had been hidden under floorboards in the old man's bedroom and then took him to the flat in a car borrowed from a colleague.

Boris almost ran from room to room, his face alive with childlike pleasure, viewing the plain magnolia walls, the second-hand furniture, the modern kitchen units, as though they were the eighth wonder of the world.

'It is so beautiful,' he stammered. 'So . . . so . . . I cannot find the words . . .'

'And it has all mod cons, such as central heating,' Megan said grinning happily.

Boris circled the lounge, his arms spread wide. 'I . . . I cannot believe this is mine.'

'Well, it is.' She watched him, marvelled at the gratitude with which he accepted accommodation that most of her clients would scoff at. 'How do you feel, Boris?'

He gripped the back of the settee and lowered his gaze. 'About my father, you mean? Better when the funeral is over, I think.'

'That's not what I asked you. How do you actually feel, now?'

Boris turned away. 'Relieved . . . I feel relieved. As if some great weight has been lifted from my shoulders.' He gave a heartfelt sigh. 'And I feel guilty, too, because that is how I feel.'

She moved towards him, rested a reassuring hand on his arm. 'It's completely natural to feel like that, you know. I mean, your father was holding you back, but now he's gone. I realise that sounds unkind,' she added quickly, 'but it's not meant to be.' Her hand went to his cheek and she forced him to face her. 'But your father wasn't the only one holding you back, was he, Boris? There are other things, other people from the past . . . They won't let go, will they?'

'I don't know what you mean.' He shrugged off her hand and moved to the window, his back towards her.

Megan sat on the settee and considered him. So many of her clients dragged along emotional baggage, past hurts and injuries that had to be confronted before the healing process could begin. Those clients were usually unwanted results of dysfunctional families — abandoned if they were lucky, abused both physically and sexually if they were not. For an experienced social worker such as Megan those problems were almost run of the mill, sad facts of modern life. But Boris Cywinski was a challenge because he was a victim of psychological abuse, an area in which she was almost a beginner.

In many ways he resembled a retarded child but the real Boris, the true essence of the man which lay hidden beneath so many layers of hurt, was blessed with a rare intelligence that could shine if only it were given the chance. With expert counselling and untiring help Megan guessed that he might achieve much. And she so wanted to help. She watched him running his fingers along the clean white paint on the window sill, touching it as one would a precious relic.

'Boris, will you sit with me for a while? We need to talk.'

'I know.' He went to her, his movements heavy and mechanical.

'You've told me so much about your life, Boris, but you've never mentioned anything about your early childhood, about your mother and your brother—'

'Not now, Megan . . . please.' He turned to her, his eyes dark with misery. 'I cannot talk now; I have the funeral to arrange.'

'Let me do it for you. Let me help.'

'You are so good to me . . . so good. But you bring so much guilt down around my head.'

'Why do you feel guilty?' she gently pressed.

'Because I know what you suggest — that we talk — will help me. But in here . . .' He tapped the side of his forehead. 'In here those thing are locked away and I cannot find the key that will release them.'

'I'll help you find the key.' She took his hands and squeezed them. 'I will, Boris, I will. It'll be painful, but it'll free what you call your demons.'

'I want to . . . so much. But you must promise never to tell a living soul about the things I reveal to you.'

'You have my word.' She sat back, a firm resolve growing in her chest. 'I'll sort out the funeral and tomorrow night, Boris, we'll start delving into your past.'

* * *

Lee Swanson had breakfasted on eggs, bacon and sausage and was picking his teeth when Phil Reynolds, the duty sergeant, came in for the tray.

'Finished?' he asked brusquely.

Swanson pointed to the empty plate. 'What do you reckon?'

Reynolds stiffened. 'You cheeky little bugger. In my day I'd have given you a good clip round the ear.'

'Sorry, pop, but your days have long gone.' He lit a cigarette and tossed the lighted match on the tray. 'You can run an errand for me.'

'Oh, can I?' Reynolds snorted. 'What did your last slave die of?'

Swanson grinned. 'You can tell Ashworth I want him down here. Just him on his own. Nobody else.'

* * *

Fifteen minutes later Sergeant Reynolds was ushering Ashworth towards the cell. 'I can't stand much more of him, Jim. If he carries on the way he is I'll swing for him.'

'The forensic results should be in any time now. I'm geeing them up, so he should be out of your hair before long.'

'And not a minute too soon.' Reynolds pulled back the iron grille of Swanson's cell. Satisfied that all was as it should be, he unlocked and pulled open the door. 'I'll be at my desk, Jim.'

'Thanks, Phil.' Ashworth stepped inside the cell. 'All right, Mr Swanson, what's this all about?'

He was slouched in the wooden chair, his feet on the table. After slowly lighting a cigarette, he said, 'I want to do a deal.'

Ashworth laughed loudly. 'I wouldn't do a deal with you if my life depended on it.'

'No?' Swanson brought his feet to the floor, amusement showing on his face. 'Not even if I've got somethin' important to trade?'

The very arrogance of the man made Ashworth want to explode. 'Listen, son, you nearly killed me and another police officer . . . The only thing of any importance to me is seeing you behind bars for at least twenty years.'

'But what have you got, really?' Swanson scoffed. 'Okay, so I had some cans of diesel in the back of my van. I was deliverin' for a mate, wasn't I? As soon as I knew what they were gonna do with it, I scarpered.' He flicked ash at the chief inspector's feet. 'A good lawyer'll tear your evidence apart in no time.'

'If that's the case, why do you want to do a deal?' Ashworth countered.

Swanson blew smoke towards the ceiling. 'Insurance.'

'I couldn't do a deal with you, even if I wanted to.' He turned to go.

'You've got three murders. Say, I helped you find out who did them . . .'

Ashworth's hand stopped short of the door handle. He smiled briefly, then turned. 'And how would you do that?'

Swanson shrugged. 'Let's just say I've got my spies. They can get into places where your lot'd be sniffed out within a hundred yards.' He sat back, totally confident. 'There's not much that goes on in this town without me knowin' about it, Mr Ashworth. I could find out — easy.'

He shot an amused look at Swanson. 'You're wasting my time, son.'

'Oh, yeh? Listen, I'm lookin' for reduced charges in exchange for the identity of the killer. It's an offer you can't refuse.'

Ashworth opened the door, his gaze still on Swanson's face. 'You've been lucky so far, son, but I've a feeling your luck's about to run out.'

'You don't say.'

'I do say. For a start, we now know that the murdered girls all worked for you—'

'Who the fuck told you that?' Swanson yelled, springing to his feet.

Taking a step forward, Ashworth pushed him back into his seat. 'Let's just say, one of my spies struck gold.' He returned to the door. 'Were those girls ever in the back of your van, Mr Swanson? I do hope so. You see, if the forensic report shows evidence that they were, then the arson charge could be the least of your worries.' He left the cell and quietly closed the door.

'And what if there's another murder while I'm in here?' Swanson yelled at the door. 'What will you do then, you bastard?'

* * *

Ashworth spent his lunch hour sitting in the incident room, staring at the photographs of the dead prostitutes on the blackboard.

'Thought you could do with a cup of tea, guv,' Bobby said, placing a mug on the bench.

'That's good of you. Thanks.' He took a long sip.

'Any joy?' Bobby asked, his own gaze centred on the photographs.

'Lee Swanson says he'll help us find the killer, in exchange for a reduced sentence.'

'And what did you tell him, guv?

'I said once we'd got the forensic evidence *he* could be going inside for the murders — end of story.'

Bobby frowned. 'You look troubled, guv. Anything the matter?'

Ashworth put the mug on the floor beside his feet. 'It's just something he said, it's worrying me. He said, what if somebody else was murdered while he was on remand . . .'

'It could be a load of hot air . . . Swanson just getting panicky.'

'Bobby, I don't think I've ever met anyone half as cunning as that man. If he is getting somebody else to kill for him, it's going to be difficult enough to prove. But if he orchestrates another murder from within his cell, it'll be near impossible to get him for it.'

'Mmm, I see what you mean,' Bobby said, looking again at the blackboard.

'Boris Cywinski,' Ashworth muttered, after a while.

'Guv?'

'I was just thinking . . . I've guessed for a long time that Swanson had some sort of hold over that man — he's always keeping something back. And Mr Cywinski is not all that he seems, Bobby; underneath that gentle giant image, I've a feeling there's a violent streak.'

'We can't pull him in for that,' Bobby said, shrugging.

'No, but we can keep a close eye on him.'

CHAPTER 31

The beard was now gone, the new hairstyle settled into its shape; and should he be clothed in a more conventional out-fit Boris would no longer attract those second glances that had perpetually dogged him on the streets. Megan, sitting opposite Boris in the tiny flat, was enormously pleased with his new appearance. But she was not there to lavish compli-ments; her task tonight was an altogether more serious one.

'I've arranged the date for the funeral,' she said, break-ing their awkward silence. 'They want to know if it's to be a burial or a cremation.'

'Burial,' was his flat response. 'Father saw cremation as sinking into the fires of hell.' He fished a wad of banknotes from his pocket. 'Will this be enough to pay for it?'

Megan gasped. The outer note was a fifty; if the others were too, then Boris was holding a small fortune in the palm of his hand. 'More than enough, but you don't have to pay straight away. They'll send you a bill.' She nodded towards the money. 'You really should put that in a bank where it'll be safe.'

'No banks.' He stuffed the notes back into his pocket. 'I do not trust banks.'

'Let me make you a cup of tea,' she said.

'My father was not always like that . . .' The words filtered through into the kitchen while Megan filled the kettle. 'When he was a young man my father was handsome, dashing. He captured many a woman's heart.' She let him talk, sensing that this was a path he had to take in order to arrive at whatever was troubling him.

'He wanted to be an actor, but everything was run by the state and my people very rarely got what they wanted. He played a few small parts, but because he was a peasant he was always cast as the buffoon, and that did not settle well with my father. He wanted to play the classical parts, characters that had depth and meaning. So, he and my mother left Moscow and went to live in a small village, many miles away. And they attracted a lot of interest, that handsome couple — to the villagers they were city folk, you see.'

'Were you born in that village?' Megan asked, as she came through with the tea tray.

'No.' His eyes took on a faraway look.

'When did you come along?'

'It was three years later.'

Megan poured the tea, added milk, and when Boris fell silent she glanced up quickly. 'Carry on. Why have you stopped?'

'I am sad.'

'Why?'

'Because I know that if I had not been conceived my parents would have lived a happy life together.'

Megan knelt on the floor by the side of his chair and gently took hold of his hand. 'What on earth did you do that was so terrible, Boris?'

He stared down at her for many seconds, his expression grave. 'I killed my mother . . . and my little twin brother.'

* * *

Two nights of heavy drinking had taken their toll, and by 9 p.m. Holly was ready for bed. She would have her bath in the morning — sod it — those cool sheets were too tempting to resist. She undressed slowly, slipped into a short nightdress, and pulled back the duvet and top sheet. But the room was unbearably hot, the air stuffy.

She opened the window and stood there for a while, enjoying what little breeze there was, and she was peering through the net curtain when something moved on the edge of her vision. She glanced that way, but there was nothing to see. A paper bag, caught by a sudden gust, floated into the air and spiralled away; the only movement in a quiet, sleepy street. She shrugged and pulled the curtains shut.

At the very moment that Holly settled into bed, a man was emerging from the front garden of a house a hundred yards along the road. He looked neither left nor right, was oblivious to his surroundings. His steely gaze was fixed on Holly's house, and his determined steps took him ever closer to it.

* * *

Megan almost recoiled in horror; and it took all of her resolve to keep that horror from her features.

'You *killed* your mother and your twin brother?' Boris nodded dully. 'But how? How could you? You were only a small child.'

'You are frightened, Megan. I can see the fear in your eyes. I can almost hear the quickening of your heartbeat.' He gave a tight smile. 'But I am only talking to avoid making the confession.'

'Tell me,' Megan urged. 'However terrible it is, it was a long time ago, in another country.'

Revulsion and relief jostled for a place in his eyes as Boris recalled memories that had lain partially dormant for years.

'My father had gone to visit another woman who lived in the next village,' he began, his voice trembling with emotion. 'She was little more than a prostitute, but he was a ladies' man who could not resist a pretty face.'

'And he left you alone with your mother and brother? How old were you?'

'I had not been born. I was still in my mother's body.' Suddenly Boris buried his head in his hands, an anguished cry escaping through the fingers. 'Much of this I was told by neighbours when I was older. It would seem that my father had been gone for some time when my mother felt the first pains of labour.' He lowered his hands; they were wet with his tears. 'She would have been frantic, Megan, not knowing what to do. She ran out into the snow, knocking on doors to raise the other villagers. A girl took my mother in, but she was young, she knew little about childbirth, only what she had seen when her brothers and sisters were born . . .' A pitiful sigh cut into his words. 'It would seem that my brother and I were in no hurry to leave our warm place. There were . . . complications — is that the correct term?'

Megan nodded. 'So what did your poor mother do?'

'She told the girl to cut the babies out.'

'What?' Megan shuddered. 'Without anaesthetic? Without anything?'

'She was desperate. She begged her to do it. She showed the girl how to sterilise a knife in the flames of her fire and then she bit on a leather strap and waited . . .'

'And?'

Boris gave a helpless shrug. 'Well, you would not expect a young peasant girl to have the knowledge of a surgeon. She cut my mother straight down the middle of her stomach — hacked at it, my neighbours said.'

'Oh, Boris, that's terrible.'

'They said it was a miracle she got me out alive. My mother was bleeding to death and my brother . . . my little brother . . . he could not cope with the trauma. He died instantly.'

'But *you* didn't kill them,' Megan said, shaking his arm. 'Surely you can see that.'

Boris stared down at her. 'My very first memory is of a loveless hovel. And in that hovel I am cowering before my father and covering my ears so that I might not hear the evil words of hatred that tumble from his lips.' He lifted his hands in a helpless gesture. 'Megan, never a day went past without my father reminding me of my awful sin. He could not forgive me for living when they died.'

'No, no . . .' Megan jumped to her feet and stood before him. 'Listen to me, Boris, your father was transferring his guilt on to you. It was probably the only way he could live with what had happened. If he hadn't gone to that other woman, if he'd been there when his wife needed him, then you might all have lived.' She let out a long breath. 'God knows, his life must have been hell with that on his conscience, but he had no right to blame you.'

'I know you are right, but it is so hard to explain. In here . . .' His large hands went to his chest. 'In my heart I know that I was not to blame. But in my head . . .' He gave a despairing shrug. 'There is poison in my head, put there by my father all those years ago. It will not go away.'

Megan returned to her seat, her brow creased in thought. 'Didn't you ever discuss this with your father when you grew up?'

'I told you, it was mentioned every day. My father used to beat me with it, used it to make me do his bidding. There was no room for discussion.'

'Boris, no one can help you with this,' Megan said, shaking her head sadly. 'It's something you have to face alone. Perhaps now that your father has gone you can put it behind you, start afresh in your new flat. And I promise I'll do everything I can to help.'

'Thank you.' He managed a smile. 'There is so much gratitude in my heart for what you have done for me. Already things are clearing in my mind.'

'I'm glad.' She glanced at the window; beyond it all was black. 'I really must be going now. It's getting late.' She grimaced. 'To tell you the truth I'm not relishing the thought of travelling late at night on a bus, but there you go, it can't be helped.'

'Would you like me to travel with you?' Boris asked, getting to his feet.

'No, no, you look tired.'

And he did; the confession had drained him. Sweat glistened on his forehead, and his eyelids were heavy with sleep. Megan shrugged on her coat and headed for the door.

'I'll see you tomorrow,' she said.

* * *

The ring of a bell cut through Holly's sleep. Only half awake she fumbled for the bedside clock and pressed hard on the alarm button. But the ringing continued, and it took a moment for her to realise that someone was leaning on the front doorbell.

'Who the bloody hell can that be?'

A glance at the clock told Holly she had been in bed for less than an hour. Throwing off the quilt, she struggled into her bathrobe and ran down the stairs, muttering well-chosen curses at her unwelcome visitor. But by the time she reached the hall her annoyance was tempered by dread. It was only ten fifteen, but still too late for any casual callers. It must be someone she knew. Could something be wrong?

'Who is it?' she called.

There was no reply; all she could hear was the loud ticking of the wall clock in the kitchen. To the left of the front door was a long glass side panel, and through it the street lights were picking out the dark figure of a man at the end of her driveway. Anger now pushing aside her caution, Holly pulled back the bolts and flung open the door. The drive was empty, but running footsteps could be heard, leather soles pounding the pavement. And then a car door slammed, an engine revved.

She took a step into the storm porch and immediately let out a surprised yelp for a short sharp pain shot across the sole of her right foot. Standing on one leg, with the sounds of a speeding car fading into the distance, Holly felt for the cause of her discomfort and found that a large thorn had embedded itself in the skin. She frowned and scanned the porch step, squinting into the gloom. And then she saw it — a single red rose lying before her.

'Donald bloody Quinn,' she spat, picking up the delicate flower.

CHAPTER 32

Sunlight streamed through the high windows of the tiny church, but little warmth came with it. Megan, sitting beside Boris on the front pew, shivered slightly and forced herself to listen to the vicar. He was short, plump, and he spouted words of praise about a man he had never met in a mechanical monotone. Two mourners and a bored minister. What a pathetic send-off, Megan thought, sadly. She risked a glance at Boris. He was sitting with head bowed, eyes closed, his lips moving in silent prayer.

With the eulogy over, they followed the coffin to its freshly dug grave. For Boris, it was a slow, painful journey along an endless winding path. He tried not to look at the coffin, tried to keep his attention on the ancient gravestones that littered the newly mown grass. But his eyes seemed to stray to the oak casket of their own accord.

So, you have found a whore to tell your troubles to. Does she make you feel better?

Boris faltered. The words, uttered in his father's harsh tone, shot into his mind with the speed of a stray bullet. He looked away, looked to where dozens of wreaths made a colourful covering for the resting place of another. He stumbled and Megan caught his arm.

'It'll all be over soon,' she whispered, reassuringly. 'Just five more minutes.'

Boris looked again at the coffin. Was his father really sitting up, long grey hair billowing in the breeze, insane eyes glaring as he pointed an accusing finger? Pointed at him. Accused him. Boris stared at the ground, concentrated on the difficult task of putting one foot in front of the other until they were standing beside the grave.

He heard nothing, absorbed none of the activities going on around him, was intent only on seeing that wooden box lowered into the ground. Only then would he be free of the old man. Inch by inch the coffin disappeared into the chasm, inch by inch until the pall-bearers let it hit the bottom with a disrespectful thud. Boris stooped down and grabbed a handful of soil.

Tell your whore your troubles. Tell her how you killed your mother, your brother, but it was not your fault.

This time the words could not shock him, could only make him hesitate for a mere fraction of a second. His father could not hurt him now. Bending over the grave Boris spread his fingers a little and let the earth filter through.

Will your whore be so understanding when she finds out about the others you have killed? Will she, Boris?

With a sideways glance at Megan, Boris opened his hand wide and the soil splattered on to the coffin lid.

* * *

It was two days since Holly's late-night caller left the rose on her step, two days in which her off-duty hours were plagued with nuisance telephone calls. They were starting to play on her mind, eat into her sleep. It was time to confide in someone. She was in the police canteen, having chosen Josh and Bobby to hear her troubles concerning Donald Quinn, when Mark strolled across.

'Mind if I join you?' he asked.

'Feel free,' Josh said, pulling out a chair.

'Anyway, it started with the rose on my doorstep,' Holly went on. 'Or rather it started the night before, when we shared a taxi home after our night out. Remember? Since then I've started to get these phone calls and when I pick up the receiver, nobody answers.'

'No trace on the calls?' Bobby asked.

Holly shook her head. 'I try 1471, but all I get is that the caller hasn't left a number. So he must be phoning from a call box or a mobile.'

Josh sipped his tea, frowning worriedly. 'How many of these calls do you reckon you've had?'

'A dozen, at least. I don't really want to make an official complaint, Josh. After all, the guy is crazy about me.' The last sentence was spoken with a sly look at Mark. It wouldn't do any harm to make him jealous, let him know what she'd been going through.

'Poor bastard,' Josh intoned.

Holly made a face at him. 'It's beginning to unnerve me a bit, never knowing when the doorbell or the phone's going to ring.'

'Listen,' Josh said, 'why don't you let me and Bobby have a word with Quinn? That way it'll seem official, but it won't be. See what I mean?'

'Okay — why not? But if that doesn't do the trick, Josh, I'll have to report it before it sends me mental.'

* * *

Donald Quinn's middle-aged secretary offered a warm and efficient welcome as she showed them into his large comfortable office. Quinn looked up from the thick file he was studying and acknowledged them with a friendly smile.

'Hi, guys,' he said. 'I'll be with you in a minute.' They waited while he signed a couple of letters. 'Right, what can I do for you?' he asked, with a final flourish of the pen.

'This is a friendly visit, Don, but the next one could be official,' Josh said. 'It's about Holly.'

Quinn raised a quizzical eyebrow. 'What about Holly?'

'You're pestering her, mate, and it's got to stop. Roses on the doorstep. Phone calls.'

Quinn sat back and gave a bewildered laugh. 'I sent her flowers after we split, yes, and I telephoned her a lot, but that was months ago.'

'What I'm talking about is more recent — like, this week.'

'Josh, I haven't called her in ages,' Quinn protested. 'And as for pestering her—'

'What about the night you shared a cab?' Josh said, lightly.

'Okay, I made a real fool of myself that night, I admit it. I'd had a few drinks — Christ, we all had — but I haven't done any of the things you're talking about.'

Bobby perched on the edge of the desk. 'Look, Don, we know how you feel. God knows, I've been there a few times. Love can make us all do stupid things, but Holly doesn't want any bother and we don't want to embarrass you, but it's got to stop.'

'I swear to God,' he said, his arms raised, 'I haven't the slightest idea what you're talking about.'

'Your clients say that, and we never believe them, either,' Josh said. 'Okay, Don, you win. If it carries on, we'll just have to look elsewhere for the culprit. Sorry to have taken up so much of your time.'

In the car park, Josh said to Bobby, 'I think that should warn him off, don't you?'

'If he's got any sense, it will.'

* * *

Holly had taken her bath and was sipping a gin while she dried her hair. 'There, girl, you'll do on a dark night,' she said to her reflection in the mirror. The glass was once again travelling to her lips when someone rang the doorbell. Holly jumped and half of the gin splashed against the front of her clean nightdress. Grabbing a handful of tissues she mopped at the stain while hot anger blossomed in her chest.

She leapt down the stairs and into the darkened hall. Leaving the light off she peered through the glass panel. Someone was standing in the storm porch.

'Right, Don, you've really got some grief coming your way this time.'

She snatched open the door, and her jaw dropped. Mark Hartland was standing in front of her. He looked sheepish.

'I've left her,' he said, nodding down at the two suitcases by his feet. 'I don't know if I'm welcome, but . . .' He looked so vulnerable, so helpless, and his image blurred as Holly viewed it through a veil of tears.

'Of course you are. Oh, Mark, I didn't dare hope that this would happen.'

'Can I come in, then?'

'Oh, sorry, yes.' She helped him with his luggage. 'Come into the kitchen. I'll get us a drink.'

'I just walked out,' Mark told her later. 'I said it was all over and I packed my bags and left. I've done so much thinking over the last few days, Holly — her mother, the house, there seemed to be so many reasons for putting our future on hold. But they were only excuses to keep putting off the break.'

In the quiet of the kitchen Holly took a sip of gin, and said, 'Does she know about me?'

'No,' he was quick to reply, 'and I don't want her to. You don't know her, Holly, she's so vindictive. If she found out about you, she'd make our lives a misery. No, she can have the house and everything in it, but ideally I'd like her to go back to her mother's so we can both forget her.' He reached across for Holly's hand. 'So, for the moment, can we keep our affair under wraps?'

'Okay, if that's what you want.' She squeezed his fingers. 'I can't believe any of this, Mark. And I can't wait for us to be able to go places together, do ordinary things like shopping in a supermarket.'

He stretched and stifled a yawn. 'Me too, but right now I'm just about ready for bed. How about you?'

'I'm too happy to be tired,' she said, laughing.

He let out a low animal growl. 'You will be when I'm finished with you.'

* * *

Death had not freed Boris from his father — quite the reverse. When the old man was confined to bed, Boris could at least get away from him, could shut the door on his dirty insinuations and raving monologues. But no longer. His father now lived in his mind and Boris could not run away from his own thoughts, any more than he could shut a door on his subconscious.

His dreams were populated with demons far worse than any he had encountered, all of them following his father's ghost as children would the Pied Piper. Every night Boris tried to resist sleep; when his eyelids became heavy and all sounds grew distant he would jerk himself back to full consciousness, so afraid was he of his father's mocking image.

But he could not fight sleep for ever. Eventually he would succumb and the old man would appear, sometimes clawing his way up through the dark earth, dirt clinging to his face and hair, his fingernails full of it. And then that hate-filled voice would start recounting Boris's sins, over and over again until the words became a whining drone that whistled like the wind in and around the gravestones that filled the lonely cemetery.

Tonight was no different and Boris came awake trembling, his sheets damp with perspiration. This could not go on. An end must be found to this hell. He must confess to Megan those final sins. But, dare he? What would follow? The police? Prison? Oh, dear God, he could not face that.

* * *

Holly had accepted from Mark her ticket to heaven and was now fully installed on Cloud Nine. Her green eyes shone with happiness, her whole being radiated contentment. She could hardly keep her hands off him or her clothes on, but she could see his point about keeping their romance under wraps, at least until the divorce proceedings had begun.

With all this new-found happiness in her life Holly just hoped that she would be able to keep her mind on the job. She would hate to make some gigantic mistake that would foul up a case. The guv'nor had already hinted more than once that she wasn't giving the murders her full attention, so she'd better make more of an effort from now on.

Sitting in the police canteen, her mug of tea cold and forgotten, she watched the double doors, waiting for Mark to make an appearance. When he did, a sudden adrenalin surge brought a hot flush to her cheeks. But she kept herself in check, greeted him as she would any other colleague. No one had been told of their new arrangement; not even Josh and Bobby knew they were living together, and that was the way it must stay until Mark's divorce was under way. Her reputation at the station was bad enough without adding more fuel to the fire.

Mark slid into the seat beside her. 'What would you say to a quiet weekend by the sea?' he whispered. 'Just the two of us?'

'I'd say, yes, please,' she whispered back.

'Good, because it's all set for this weekend. And the location's so secret, I can't even tell you.'

'But, Mark, I should let the guv'nor know where I'll be, in case something crops up'

He looked hurt. 'Oh, come on, Holly, it'll spoil the surprise. Anyway, we won't be gone long enough for anything to crop up. What do you say?'

'Okay,' she said, grinning. 'I'm due some quality time off, anyway.'

'We leave on Friday night,' he said, his voice still low, 'and we'll use your car. Holly, I can't tell you what a relief it'll be to get out of the same town as that woman.'

Holly toyed with her mug, the thought of his wife dampening her mood a little. 'Where does she think you're staying?'

'Over at a mate's place.' He glanced around the canteen. 'I'd better be getting back; I don't want Ashworth to find me in here. He's already had a go at me for being too cheerful — I felt like saying, we could all walk around with long faces but it wouldn't bring the dead women back.'

* * *

It seemed to Ashworth that Bobby and Josh were the only ones in his team with any enthusiasm or desire to see the murderer brought to book. Was he being too hard on Holly? Probably. That part of an investigation, when all roads led nowhere, brought out the irritable side of his nature. He knew that any fresh evidence would have them all champing at the bit, all eager to carry the case to its conclusion; so perhaps he should back off a bit, not add to the pressure with his persistent complaints.

The trouble was, Ashworth could not drag his mind away from the murders. Every day they took up more and more of his thoughts, and he worried constantly that another might be imminent.

Bobby now disagreed with Ashworth's presumption that Lee Swanson was involved. It was his theory that the killer was not a local man, and he could already have moved on. But Ashworth would have none of it. The murderer — whoever he was — had too much knowledge of local waterways. Some of them were tucked away in the countryside — Acton pit, for instance — and only a local man would know they were there.

What exactly was the connection with water? Ashworth knew it was deliberate. He knew it was vital. If only he could see it.

CHAPTER 33

It was almost 3 a.m. Saturday morning, when Holly and Mark finally set off. They loaded their suitcases into the car like teenage lovers eloping to Gretna Green, with lots of hushed laughter and furtive glances to neighbouring windows. The roads were quiet at that hour, the atmosphere one of perfect peace, and the air that rushed in through half-open windows was heavy with the perfume of summer. Holly relaxed in the passenger seat and watched Mark's strong hands on the steering wheel, all thoughts of Bridgetown nick, murder, and her duties as a detective sergeant far from her mind.

* * *

Megan was quick to notice the change in Boris. She had expected a difference in him, of course, but one of a more positive nature. After hurrying to his flat with clothes purchased from a charity shop, hardly able to contain her excitement at seeing that final piece in his transformation, she had been met at the door by that old look of persecution in eyes ringed with dark shadows.

'Are you all right, Boris? Are you ill?' she had asked.

He had said nothing, simply shook his head and motioned for her to go through to the living room. It was then that Megan began to worry. She knew that since his father's death Boris had eaten little, existed almost entirely on cups of black coffee. As a result the weight was falling off him; he was tall now, rather than large.

Over the next couple of days she thought long and hard about the new problem. If she could free that last piece of his past then he would be able to live a full and normal life. But first she must get him to open up.

* * *

Mark had told Holly that the location of the holiday cottage was remote and she had in her mind images of lush fields rolling towards craggy cliffs which led in turn to stretches of golden sand and an emerald sea. They were heading east, to the Norfolk coastline, and very soon the landscape became a virtual wilderness, the last large town disappearing behind them. Presently, Mark steered the car left at a crossroads and flashed her a grin.

'We're here,' he said.

They were cruising slowly along a rutted path and Holly caught her breath, for at the end of the path, in a quarter-acre plot, stood a cottage so picturesque that it looked unreal. A honey-coloured thatched roof sloped down to upstairs windows so small they could almost have been painted on for effect. The gable end was thick with dark green ivy, a honeysuckle of vibrant yellow swamped the tiny porch, while the gnarled branches of an ancient wisteria covered the front facade with an abundance of mauve blossoms. And to complete the pretty scene, a deep bed in front of the cottage was packed with annuals and perennials, their reds, yellows, purples and blues almost too bright for the naked eye.

Mark brought the car to a halt and handed Holly a set of keys. 'There you go, have a look inside while I unload the car.'

228

She crossed the threshold, where scent from the honey-suckle mingled with the salty small of the sea, and found the interior of the cottage exactly as she had hoped: low beamed ceilings, large inglenook in the living room, lamps dotted around on the old-fashioned furniture. Taking pride of place in the main bedroom was a four-poster bed enclosed in heavy port-wine velvet curtains. And through the tiny window was a spectacular view of the sea glistening in the lukewarm sunlight of dawn. Holly sat on the bed and hugged herself.

But then a dull thud sounded downstairs, followed by a muttered curse. Making her way on to the landing, and smiling briefly at a brightly painted child's safety gate at the top of the stairs, she made her way down to the hall and found Mark surrounded by their luggage. He was holding his ankle and grimacing.

'What's wrong, lover?'

'I've hurt my ankle, coming up the step.' He hopped towards the lounge and fell into an armchair. 'It'll probably be okay, tomorrow,' he said, gingerly removing his shoe.

Holly knelt in front of him and, placing his foot on her lap, she gently massaged his ankle. 'You'll just have to stay off it as much as you can.' She laughed. 'This means that when I get you in that four-poster, Mark Hartland, there'll be no escape.'

* * *

His father was always with him, now. Everywhere he looked the old man's image was there, that all-too-familiar voice forever in his ear. Was he losing his mind? Had a ghost finally achieved that which the flesh and blood man could never do?

Boris remained in the flat, too frightened to leave it in case he found himself at the lake, at the black stinking water that his father continually urged him to remember. He tried to ignore the voice — but how could he disregard something of his own making? It wheedled and coaxed, challenged him to visit the water. It dared him to kill Megan, too, demanded that he did so.

You must kill your whore now, it said, *choke the life out of her, just as it was choked out of the others.*

Should he? What if the old man was right? Would Megan bring damnation crashing down around him? Would she really let him down when he least expected it? His father sounded so certain.

No one else knows your secret sins . . . not yet. But your whore will keep on digging, probing until she has it all. If you kill her, Boris, there will be no police, no prison. The iron gates will not close behind you, slam shut, never to open again . . .

* * *

CID was in a state of panic. They had received a hesitant call from Mandy, Holly's contact with the prostitutes. She had said that another of the girls had been attacked but had escaped with the identity of her assailant. She would say no more, insisted that she would only deal with the female sergeant. This was not seen as a problem, until, of course, they failed to get in touch with Holly.

'Where is she?' Ashworth demanded to know.

Josh and Bobby exchanged a glance. 'She's not supposed to be on duty, is she, guv?' Josh ventured.

'You know she's not.'

'So, she could be anywhere. I don't see—'

'She may not be on duty,' Ashworth growled, 'but she should have told us where she could be contacted if needs be. She's outside the range of the radio, so that means she's no longer in the area.'

'Don't you think you might be over-reacting?' Bobby was bold enough to ask. 'Any of us can leave the area for a short time. It doesn't mean we've vanished.'

Ashworth calmed himself. 'Yes, I suppose you're right. It's just that I've had the forensic report on Swanson's van. There's plenty to connect him with the arson attack, but nothing at all was found involving the murdered women. Plenty of fingerprints were found, and they'll all have to be matched up with Swanson's gang. Then, as long as Newton is in agreement, we can get warrants to search their homes. But it's all going to take time, and if we're to stop whoever it is from killing again, we need evidence now, today. Josh, keep trying Holly's number. We've got to get that girl Mandy into the station as soon as we can.'

* * *

Megan knew she was taking a chance. If she pushed Boris too far, God alone knew what might rise to the surface. With his background, mental instability must always be a mere steppingstone away. But if only she could exorcise his ghosts, clear the half-truths and lies that had haunted his mind for so many decades. If she could achieve all that, Boris Cywinski would be the kindest, sweetest man she had ever met. It was an unspoken rule that social workers must not get emotionally involved with their cases but how could she fail to feel deeply for Boris? Fate had dealt him a lousy hand; he deserved more out of life, and she was determined to help him get it. He looked haggard and preoccupied when he opened the door in answer to her knock.

'Megan . . .' He ran edgy fingers through his dishevelled hair. 'I did not expect you, today.'

'I was just passing.' She tried to appear casual as she crossed the hall to the living room.

'I will tidy myself up,' he said, vanishing into the bathroom. When he re-emerged, hair neatly combed, face smelling of aftershave, he found Megan pouring fresh tea.

'That took you a long time,' she remarked, handing him a mug.

'I needed a shave.' He settled on the settee and stared across at her.

'Well, I must say, you look very smart. I—'

'Why are you here, Megan?'

'I told you, I was passing so I thought I'd call in.'

'Megan . . .' He faltered, let precious moments pass while he placed his mug on the coffee table. 'I . . . I am most grateful for all that you have done for me, but now I am on my own I have to face my problems by myself.'

'No, Boris, I can't let you be by yourself. Whatever's bothering you will just fester in your mind. You must let it out, tell me about it, like you told me about the deaths of your mother and your twin.'

'But, I cannot,' he said. 'I know what will happen to me if the police find out.'

She took in a long breath. 'You've done something that's against the law?'

Sweat broke out on his forehead; he refused to meet her gaze. 'This is something I do not want to talk about.'

'You must, Boris, you've come too far to stop, now. Everything must come out into the open.'

'I cannot,' he whimpered, his fingers once again pushing through his thick hair. 'Leave me, Megan. Leave he alone.'

'Oh, no, I'm not going to do that.' She slammed her mug on the coffee table, spilling hot tea on the oak veneer. 'Is it something you did in Russia? Is it, Boris?' He shook his head rapidly. 'So, it's something you've done here?'

'Yes.' He cowered on the settee.

'Something you've done recently?'

'Yes . . . no . . . oh, dear God . . .' He was writhing now, his knees brought up to his middle in an attempt to make himself smaller, to make himself disappear.

Megan could feel the blood running cold in her veins, but forced herself to voice the question she was dreading to ask. 'Is it to do with the murders, Boris? Were you involved in the deaths of the three prostitutes?'

'Those whores of Babylon have come back to haunt me,' he yelled.

'Don't try to hide behind that mumbo-jumbo. Tell me, Boris . . . please. I'm your only hope.'

Suddenly he let out a low growl and Megan caught a glimpse of evil in his contorted features. Then she was screaming until her throat hurt, for he had hurled the coffee table across the room. She heard it splinter against the wall at the very moment that his hands closed around her neck.

She prayed, the jumbled words running through her brain, the urgent plea repeated again and again. But his hands had not tightened their grip; the rough skin of his fingers was hardly touching the softness of her neck, his thumb merely rested against her Adam's apple. The realisation took her by surprise, made her drag in a lungful of air while she still had the chance. Through wave upon wave of relief she heard a strangled moan and opened her eyes to find Boris on his knees, staring at his outstretched hands.

'I am sorry, Megan. I am so sorry.' He looked up at her. 'You want the truth, then I will give you the truth. I . . . I am responsible for the deaths of those women.'

Megan sank down on the chair, her legs like jelly, her whole body quaking. The face before her was that of a stranger, now. All that had gone before, all those months of mutual endeavour, disappeared in an instant.

She gave him a wary glance. 'You'd better tell me about it.'

Boris returned to the settee and, still staring at his hands, he told his story. When he had finished he seemed almost relieved to have unburdened himself. A short silence followed, and then Megan cleared her throat.

'I think we'd better go and see Chief Inspector Ashworth, don't you?'

'Yes,' he whispered. 'It is time for me to confess.'

CHAPTER 34

'Here, Mark, soak your foot in this.' Holly placed a bowl of hot water in front of him. 'If we can get it strapped up before it starts to swell, you'll at least be able to get around.'

'Oh, that's so good,' he said, lying back. He laughed. 'A fine weekend this has turned out to be, with me laid up like this.'

'You're not laid up, sweetheart. The rest of you should still be working. And that four-poster upstairs is really gorgeous.'

'Hmm, nice touch, that.' He wriggled his toes in the water. 'But it does mean that we won't be able to get out and about.'

'What? The four-poster?'

He grinned. 'No, stupid — my ankle.'

'That won't matter. Although I might have a wander along the beach a bit later on, if you don't mind.'

'Of course I don't. There's not much to see, though. The nearest village is miles away, and the couple who rent out the cottage said we wouldn't see a living soul for the whole of the weekend.'

'Sea, solitude . . . and you.' She kissed him lightly. 'What more could I ask for?'

* * *

Ashworth was prowling the station. Something was wrong; he knew it. There was nothing specific he could put his finger on, just a gut feeling that refused to go away. He had earlier channelled his frustrations into a burning annoyance towards Holly. It was completely irrational, he knew; there was no written rule that officers should make their off-duty locations known to their superiors. But in all the years they had worked together, Holly had done just that. When her mind was fully on the job Ashworth was hard-pressed to imagine a better, more efficient second-in-command. However, when her thoughts were elsewhere, as in recent weeks, she brought out the worst in him, whipped up his cranky temperament until his usually short fuse became non-existent.

But as the day wore on his annoyance faded, and in its place anxiety flourished. It was so unlike her to go off like that. What could have happened to make her act so out of character?

They had three more calls from Mandy, and each time she refused to speak to anyone but Holly. During the third, though, Josh used his gift of the gab and persuaded her to bring the girl involved in the attack to the station where a WPC would be present during their talk. Meanwhile, Bobby was sent to interview Holly's neighbours; perhaps something could be gleaned from them.

Ashworth sat in CID, drumming his fingers on his blotter. He felt strangely inactive, as if some invisible force was keeping him tied to the station. Unable to quell his restless energy a moment longer he marched along to the incident room. No sooner had he settled in front of the blackboard than Josh walked in, his face a picture of despondency.

'It's not a goer, guv.' He closed the door and sat down. 'The girl was beaten up, all right. She's got a broken cheekbone, cuts and bruises, but it's not the work of our man. He's a lorry driver, apparently makes a habit of attacking prostitutes. He's got a record as long as your arm. But there's no sign of the ritualistic behaviour we're looking for.'

'Pity,' Ashworth sighed. 'What's happened to him?'

'Bridgenorton police have him in custody. So, it's up to the girl to press charges.'

Ashworth exhaled sharply. 'Another dead-end.'

''Fraid so.' Josh hesitated. 'Guv, I don't think it helps all the time sitting and staring at that blackboard, if you don't mind me saying so. It seems to be all you and Bobby do just lately.'

'But the answer's there—' He stopped short and gave Josh a sheepish look. 'Have I said that before?'

'Only a few thousand times.'

Ashworth chuckled, in spite of himself. 'I suppose I have. Any word from Bobby yet?'

'He's not back.'

Just then Sergeant Dutton opened the door. 'Couple of visitors for you, Jim. Megan Rowntree and Boris Cywinski. They wouldn't say what it's about. They'll only talk to you. I've put them in number one interview room.'

'Thanks, Martin.' Ashworth got to his feet. 'You'd better come along, Josh.'

They entered the room to find Boris in a distressed state. Megan was sitting beside him, an arm around his shoulder, whispering words of comfort.

'Hello, again,' Ashworth said, easily. 'Before we go any further, Miss Rowntree, I must know what this is about. Then I can decide if it's to be an official interview or not.'

Without shifting her gaze from Boris, she said, 'It's an official interview, all right. We have something to tell you. *Boris* has something to tell you.'

'Josh, see to the tape recorder,' Ashworth murmured. Then, to Boris, 'So, Mr Cywinski, what can we do for you?'

'I . . . I do not know where to start.' He was in deep shock, staring straight ahead.

'The beginning seems as good a place as any,' Ashworth suggested.

'I . . . I . . .' He gagged. It was as if the words were sticking in his throat.

'Don't be nervous, Mr Cywinski, no one's going to hurt you.'

He looked up at Ashworth's kindly face, and blurted, 'I am responsible for the deaths of the three women.'

'You're confessing to the murders?' Ashworth asked, surprise causing his jaw to slacken. There was a long pause, with much eye contact between Megan and Boris. 'Are you confessing, Mr Cywinski?'

'Tell the chief inspector,' Megan prompted. 'It's too late to turn back, now.'

Boris gave a wretched sigh, then shook his head. 'I did not kill them with my own hands, but I am responsible for their deaths.'

Ashworth frowned. 'You're not making any sense, sir. You'll have to spell it out.'

'I was in the park on the night of the first murder.'

'And what exactly were you doing there?'

'Walking . . . walking in the darkness. I was trying to clear my mind, to sort out my thoughts. It was so cold that night, the frost thick on the ground . . .' Now that he had started the words spilled out, tumbled over themselves to be heard. 'I approached the lake — I had always liked it there . . . so peaceful — and I heard footsteps crunching in the frost. At first I was annoyed, it was so late I thought I would have the place to myself. I looked around to see a couple hugging, or so I thought. I assumed that the woman was drunk and that the man was supporting her, but then I noticed that her feet were not touching the ground. The man carried her to the far corner of the lake, then he stopped, looked around, and he . . . he threw her into the water.' Boris swallowed loudly. 'I could not believe my eyes. I started towards the man but he saw me and ran off. When I reached the spot, I could see the woman floating on the surface. But ice was already forming on the exposed corners and she was being carried towards it. I waded into the water, as far as I could, and I grabbed her ankle. But the water was too strong, the . . .' He turned to Megan. 'What is the word?'

'Undercurrent?'

'Yes, the undercurrent was pulling her from my grasp . . .' He slouched in his seat, his mouth a grim line.

Ashworth remembered the pathologist's report: bruising found on the right ankle was consistent with it being held in a tight grip.

'Go on, Mr Cywinski,' he said.

'I lost her,' he murmured, sadly. 'She slipped away from me, and I saw her vanish under the ice. The water was so cold—'

'Why did you say you were responsible for the deaths of the other women?' Ashworth interjected.

'Because I was.' Boris looked at him. 'If I had reported what had happened, you might have caught the man.'

'And why didn't you report it?'

Boris looked away, flexed his large hands while panic showed on his face.

'Tell him,' Megan coaxed. 'It's nearly all over. Just answer the question.'

'I did not report it, Chief Inspector, because I did not want contact with the police. You see, when I came with my father to your country, we did not pass through official channels.'

Ashworth sighed. 'You were illegal immigrants.'

Boris gave a resigned nod. 'And now you will put me in prison and then send me back to Russia — yes?'

'Never mind all that. Tell me about the man at the lake. What did he look like?'

Boris stared into the middle distance, willing himself to remember. 'He was tall, maybe six foot — not as big as I am, more . . . slim . . . yes? I did not get close enough to see his face, but he was not an old man, I know that from his movements.'

'Twenties? Thirties, perhaps?'

'Perhaps.'

'And what was he wearing?'

'A long coat, for the rain . . . What do you call them?'

'A mackintosh?' Ashworth said.

Boris gave a swift nod. 'A mackintosh. Its colour was very light; it hardly showed against the frost. And he wore dark trousers.' He shrugged. 'That is all I remember.'

'Tell me, Mr Cywinski, could the man have been Lee Swanson?'

Boris paled. 'No.' The word was said immediately, with confidence. 'No, it was not. I would have known if it was he.'

Ashworth considered the man. 'It seems to me, sir, that you become very agitated whenever Swanson's name is mentioned. Why is that?' Boris shook his head, refused to speak. 'Let us help you, Mr Cywinski . . . please. What hold does he have over you?'

Megan grabbed his hand, gave it an encouraging squeeze. 'Tell him, Boris. Whatever it is, it can't be worth tearing yourself apart for.'

'But, I can't,' he whispered. 'I can't.'

'Tell him,' Megan urged.

Very slowly, Boris turned to face Ashworth. 'I used to . . . Oh, Megan I cannot say, I am so ashamed.'

'You used to what?' Ashworth asked. 'Tell me, sir.'

Boris slumped back in his chair, stared at the tabletop. 'Very well. I . . . I used to avail myself of the prostitutes' services. I used to pay for my sin.'

Ashworth frowned. 'But what's that got to do with Swanson?'

'He found out. He said I was breaking the law and he would tell the police if I did not keep quiet.'

'About what?'

'I saw him hurting the girls . . . many times. He said I would be in trouble if I ever said anything.' He looked at Ashworth. 'Am I in trouble?'

'Mr Cywinski, if prostitution were the only crime we had to deal with, I'd be a very happy man.'

'What do you mean?'

'I mean, sir, that we've got far more serious crimes to worry about. And just lately most of them seem to have been committed by Lee Swanson.'

His smile was one of relief. 'I am not in trouble?'

'No, you're not.' Ashworth motioned for Josh to terminate the interview.

'But I will go to prison for entering your country illegally?'

Ashworth flashed him a kindly smile. 'After all these years? I doubt it. England may have its faults, Mr Cywinski, but it's nothing like the Soviet Union that you remember.' He made to go. 'Someone will bring you a cup of tea. Then, we'll take your statement and you can go home.'

'Megan can stay with me?'

'Of course.'

'Could I have a quick word, Chief Inspector?' Megan followed him into the corridor. 'What will happen to Boris, Chief Inspector?'

'Well, he did withhold information, but I don't think we'll be pressing charges. I'm sure the Home Office will be very sympathetic, given the circumstances.' He frowned. 'Miss Rowntree, does he really feel he's responsible for all three deaths?'

'I'll let you read his file. You'll understand, then.'

CHAPTER 35

Although she loved Mark dearly, Holly was nevertheless relieved to get away from the cottage for an hour. The reason? She was desperate for a cigarette. Funny how life always stopped just short of perfect, she mused. Now that Mark was a permanent fixture in her life, would she be all the while sneaking a quick smoke, perfume bottle in hand? She could always try to give up, of course, but it didn't seem like a workable option, right now.

The moment she was out of sight Holly delved into her shoulder bag for the packet, and soon she was gratefully drawing smoke deep into her lungs. Now she could relax. A natural path was before her, no doubt made by past residents of the cottage. She followed it, hoping it would lead her to the beach.

Away from the sea, the day was hot, but where she now stood, mere feet away from the breaking waves, a lively breeze was fast cooling her skin. Sunshine glittered like jewels on the sea's choppy surface, and the world seemed a wonderful place. She strolled along slowly, speculating on the rest of her life. Thinking of a future which included Mark gave her a warm feeling, made her shiver with excitement.

She dropped her cigarette butt and ground it into the sand, already reaching for the packet again. Just one more and then she'd head back. She could suck a peppermint as she walked. Turning her back against the wind, Holly flicked the lighter several times and then it flared into life, the tip of the cigarette glowing red.

She was inhaling the smoke when a grey cloud passed across the face of the sun, almost turning day into dusk. Holly was amazed by this sudden change and she spun round quickly to catch the effect of the neighbouring hills in that unnatural light.

And as she did so she spotted a figure; it was standing on the top of a cliff, some way in the distance. It seemed to be watching her as it stood there, stock still. The figure was tall and slim, and she may never have noticed it but for the way its long white coat stood out against the dark skyline.

* * *

Ashworth made his way back to the incident room and grinned widely when he saw Bobby sitting in front of the blackboard, looking for all the world like an ardent worshipper meditating before the altar.

'How did you get on with Holly's neighbours?' Ashworth asked, settling himself on the bench.

'Sorry, guv, came up with nothing,' he said, moving along to make room. 'Nobody seemed to know anything. Apparently the one guy who might have helped — an old boy who doesn't miss a thing — is in hospital, having a hip replacement. Anyway, afterwards, like you said, I went to Mark Hartland's house to see if he knew where she was, only I couldn't get a reply.' He gave Ashworth a sideways glance. 'It seems to me, guv, we could really stir up some domestic trouble for Mark if his wife finds out.'

'I second that,' Josh said, from the doorway. 'We're over-reacting, guv. Holly's off duty and we can't find her — that's no big deal. She's probably shopping. Anyway, I'll keep trying her number, and I'm certain that by nine or ten tonight she'll turn up after having had a few drinks and a curry.'

'Maybe,' Ashworth grunted.

'It's Saturday,' Josh said. 'You're supposed to be off duty, as well, guv. Why don't you go home? I'll call you as soon as Holly turns up.'

'You're right.' He pointed a finger. 'But phone me the minute you speak to her.'

After one last look at the photographs on the blackboard, he made his reluctant way into the corridor. Josh listened for the sound of the swing doors, and then he said, 'It's the first time I've seen him like this for a couple of years, now.' He glanced at Bobby when no reply was forthcoming, and found him staring, wide-eyed, at the blackboard.

'Jesus Christ, Josh, I think I've got it.'

Ashworth was unlocking the door to his Scorpio when Bobby came hurtling down the station steps.

'Guv . . . guv, I think I've found the link between the three girls.'

Ashworth went hurrying towards him.

* * *

They ate in the dining room, a small intimate area that looked out on to a beautifully landscaped garden at the rear. Holly had kept the lunch simple: ham salad, various cheeses with biscuits, and a variety of fruit. Throughout the meal Mark was most attentive, frequently hobbling around the table to top up her wine glass. They took their time, relishing each other's company, sometimes laughing too loudly at ridiculous jokes, sometimes enjoying a companionable silence. Holly had never felt so happy.

Mark dabbed at his mouth with a serviette and sat back. 'That was a great meal. Now I think I'll go and lie on the bed for a while.' He gave her a broad wink.

She smiled. 'I'll wash up first, and then I'll join you.'

Had they really only been in this paradise for a matter of hours? As Mark made his way to the bedroom, Holly felt she had listened to the creaking floorboards for much of her life. It was a comforting sound; indeed, everything about the place was so homely, so snug. Leaving it would be a terrible wrench — but she wouldn't think about that, not yet.

Soon plates, glasses and cutlery were sparkling clean and dry, and Holly found herself humming a tune while she stacked everything in the cupboard. But, as she glanced out of the tiny window, the tune died on her lips. There, in the distance, no larger than a matchstick, was the figure in the white coat. He seemed agitated, pacing backwards and forwards, his face always turned towards the cottage.

'Holly,' Mark called from the landing, 'are you coming up?'

'Give me a couple of minutes,' she shouted back, not once taking her eyes off the figure.

* * *

Ashworth came bustling into the incident room. Bobby was already there, standing by the blackboard, his eager face flushed.

'It suddenly came to me, guv. I read a book about astrology a while back — God knows why I didn't see it before.'

Ashworth studied the pictures. 'See what?'

'Look at the dates of birth. Julie Stevens was born on twelfth June. Cynthia Labrum, twentieth May. And Helen Palmer, twentieth June. Guv, they were all born under the sign of Gemini . . . the sign of the twins. Those girls weren't picked at random; they were targeted.'

Ashworth looked sceptical. 'It could be a coincidence. Then again, it could explain the symbolic splitting of the bodies. One thing's for sure, though, Bobby, it doesn't take us any nearer to finding the murderer.'

'Oh, shit,' Josh muttered, sinking on to a bench.

Ashworth spun round. 'What's the matter?'

'Holly's a Gemini. Her birthday's twenty-fifth May — remember?'

'My God.' Ashworth paled. 'That settles it. I had a feeling that girl was in trouble, and now I'm sure of it. We have to find her.' He began to pace. 'Now, I can't make this official simply on the grounds that Holly's star sign is Gemini — Newton would laugh me out of his office — so I'm asking for your help.'

'You've got it, guv,' Bobby said.

Josh spread his hands. 'No need to ask. Do you think it'll be worth having another go at Swanson?'

Ashworth gave a firm shake of the head. 'I was wondering that myself but, no, he might just waste our time, he enjoys running rings around us. Anyway, at the end of the day, we don't know for certain that he's involved in the murders. I'm sure Central Control will put out an all-points alert for Holly.'

Josh said, 'Perhaps we should try and find Mark, even if it does risk causing him some bother. Holly could well be with him.'

'Good idea. Keep trying to get him on the phone.'

'Right, guv.'

'And can either of you think of anybody else Holly's been close to in the last few months?'

Josh and Bobby exchanged a knowing glance.

* * *

Holly tried to dismiss the man from her mind. She was letting her imagination get the better of her, she told herself sternly. The guy was probably looking around the area for a holiday home. He could have lost his dog. There were all sorts of reasons why he should be wandering about. Just because she'd seen him twice in a matter of hours didn't mean he was watching them, or the cottage. And it couldn't be anything to do with the divorce; Mark had already told his wife he was willing to admit adultery.

By the time she reached the landing all worries had been banished from Holly's mind, and a broad grin was on her face when she entered the bedroom. All of the bed curtains had been pulled, and Mark was making coaxing sounds from within. Throwing off her clothes, Holly hurried to join him. The velvet brushed her bare skin, and then Mark was pulling her down on to the cool covers.

Their lovemaking was long and slow; sometimes gentle, sometimes passionate. Housed in their dark cocoon, Holly let go of her fears and gave herself gladly. When it was over, when their pinnacle had been reached, she felt herself slipping into a relaxed slumber.

'Hey, I'm the one who's supposed to go to sleep as soon as it's finished,' Mark whispered.

Holly managed a smile. 'That was gorgeous, Mark. I'll give you fifty years to stop doing it.' And then sleep claimed her.

Mark lay back, hands folded behind his head, and listened to her rhythmic breathing. But then his hackles rose. It sounded like someone was knocking at the door.

'Christ . . .'

He had been assured that they would not be disturbed for the whole of the weekend, and already someone was violating their space. He shot a glance at Holly, then threw back the covers and climbed from the bed.

* * *

'There was Don Quinn, guv,' Bobby said. 'He had quite a thing about her, but she broke it off. Anyway, we thought a while back that it might be on again.'

'But he started making a nuisance of himself,' Josh said. 'Phone calls. Flowers turning up in the dead of night. Holly confided in us — she was getting worried about it so we had to give him the friendly hands-off-or-else routine.'

Ashworth pondered for a moment. 'Right, find out where he is. But be very discreet: none of this is official. Use the phones in here. I'll go up to the office and study our files.'

He made his way briskly to CID where he collected together all the information they had on the murders. Next he fished out Holly's file from Personnel, but before he could settle down to study her details, he had to make room on his desk. Mark had once again left an untidy pile of files on top of Ashworth's papers, despite his previous warning.

'How many times have I got to tell that man,' Ashworth muttered, grabbing the pile by its string and letting it drop to the floor.

When no obvious clues to Holly's possible whereabouts hit him in the face, he closed her file and concentrated instead on the meagre amount of information collected regarding the murders. In his mind's eye, Ashworth saw the murky, muddy water of the lake; the silver, dancing rush of the River Thane; and the still, almost sinister air that hung over Acton pit.

'Water, and star signs. That's all we've got.' His telephone buzzed. 'Ashworth.'

'Guv, it's Josh, I finally got a reply from Mark Hartland's number. It must have been his wife who answered. She just said he wasn't there and put the phone down.'

'All right, Josh, thanks for trying.' He replaced the receiver. 'Damn, damn . . . *damn*.'

CHAPTER 36

Holly knew something was wrong the minute she came awake. That warm feeling left by their lovemaking had evaporated; and in its place was an irrational sense of menace. She tried to move, but her arms would not obey. They were stretched out towards the bedhead, heavy, almost leaden, as if something was interfering with their circulation.

What had once been a dark haven inside the thick curtains now resembled a gloomy grave, and Holly found herself longing for light. She moved her foot sideways, feeling for Mark. But he was not beside her; his side of the bed felt cold and uninviting.

Slowly her eyes adapted to their surroundings, and she could see that her wrists were in fact tied to the bedposts with thin grey twine.

Swallowing a sense of rising panic, she called out, 'Mark, I don't think this is very funny. Come and untie me, I'm frightened.'

She listened, but all she could hear was the distant whoosh and hiss of the sea, the slight howl of the wind. But, wait, there was something else — a very faint noise, barely audible. It was the creaking of floorboards.

* * *

Ashworth felt he was himself treading water; his shoes were full of it, dragging him down, pulling him further away from the answer which, he knew, was staring him in the face. He must call Sarah, tell her to expect him when she saw him — literally. This could take hours.

'Very well, dear,' she said, with a resignation born out of thirty years as a policeman's wife. 'Just make sure you eat properly.'

Ashworth replaced the receiver with a heavy heart. If only he knew where to start looking. Where was that gut feeling, that flare of inspiration, when he needed it? This was like putting together a jigsaw puzzle that had no straight edges.

'Star signs,' he muttered.

There was no longer any outwardly plausible motive for murder, as far as he could see. How the hell could he build a list of suspects using star signs as a guide? Maybe it was time to hand over to the computer. He was reaching for the telephone, to call down to Josh, when the man himself walked into the office.

'We've got a sort of trace on Don Quinn, guv, but I don't think it's going to be of much use.'

'Tell me, anyway'

'I managed to get his secretary at home, told her we'd got a prisoner who wanted to see Quinn urgently. She said he was away for the weekend, and she'd got no idea where. But she thought he might be at one of the coastal resorts because he's mad about surfing and sailing.' He shrugged. 'It's not much to go on.'

'It's damn all,' Ashworth snapped. 'I'm thinking of going over Newton's head with this, perhaps put out an all-points alert nationwide. Television coverage, the lot.'

Josh snorted. 'You'd need authorisation for that, guv. As soon as Newton found out — and it wouldn't take him long — he'd pull the rug out from under you.'

Ashworth's already weak resolve shrivelled to nothing. 'You're right. I can't do that just because Holly's a Gemini.' He let out a deep sigh. 'I know I'm just whistling in the dark,

Josh. I suppose all we can do is wait to hear from Central Control.' And wait they did, while the office clock ticked away the minutes.

* * *

Inside the four-poster bed there was little light; the heavy velvet and the tiny window saw to that. There was little sound, either; none that penetrated the curtains, anyway.

For some time now, Holly had been exercising her fingers, bunching them into fists and then stretching. They tingled terribly, but that was better than the numbness which rendered them useless.

She noticed that the corners of the bedposts were badly finished off, the edges jagged. And by hitching herself towards the bedhead a little, she was able to manoeuvre the twine around her right wrist, up and down, against the rough edge. It was tough work; the twine was tied tight and it tore at her flesh with even the slightest movement. The pain was crippling, but Holly guessed that whatever lay ahead would be far worse. She had to get free.

Biting hard on her lip, and employing all of her concentration, she continued to drag the twine across the ragged wood. It was a difficult task, made harder by the fact that she was working blind, but she refused to stop until the twine was cut through.

Her eyes were smarting with unshed tears, and her right arm objected painfully to its unnatural position, but in time her endeavours started to bear fruit. The twine was loosening, its strands breaking, one by one; making the cutting action easier.

But then Holly stopped, her breath held fast, her ears straining. Someone was prowling around the cottage. In the lounge, perhaps? Now and again the sounds came closer — whoever it was would stop at the foot of the stairs but then retreat again.

Holly stepped up her battle with the twine, that lone figure in the long white coat never far from her thoughts.

And then she was whimpering, for the floorboards in the hall were creaking again. Only this time the sounds did not go away, this time they grew louder. While Holly stifled a scream the ancient stairs wailed their protest under a series of heavy footfalls. She counted thirteen — whoever it was had reached the landing. And then the old-fashioned doorknob was turning, the heavy door was sliding over the carpet with a slight shush, the soft padding of feet was heading for the bed. They circled, scuffing the carpet, the bed curtains now and then disturbed by those feline movements.

The man's breathing was heavy, laboured; not from exertion, more from a sense of expectancy. Holly's control was finally threatening to desert her when the curtains were ripped apart. She did a quick double-take, for it was Mark who stood at the foot of the bed. Mark, with that gorgeous grin that Holly loved so much.

'Oh, Mark,' she cried out in relief. 'You bloody fool, you frightened me. I thought . . .'

But the words froze on her lips. Mark was holding a Stanley knife.

CHAPTER 37

'Central Control have come up with nothing,' Bobby told
Ashworth. The chief inspector greeted the news with a grunt.

'They think we're a couple of pence short of a pound,'
Josh said. 'You can see it on their faces, guv.'

'I think we should chase Donald Quinn,' Bobby ventured. 'We could visit his friends, try to find out where he's
gone. Somebody should know.' Ashworth said nothing. 'I
know it's a long shot, guv, but it's all we've got.'

'No, it's not. We've got water and star signs. We've got
to work it out from there.' Ashworth left his desk, almost
tripping over the files he had dumped on the floor. 'Oh,
these bloody . . .'

He fell silent, his heart jumping in his chest as he
stooped to pick up the pile. The string holding it together
was standard issue from the collator's office. It was grey — or
so Ashworth had always thought. Only now, as he studied it
closely for the first time, he found that it was in fact a grey
and white fleck. Grey and white — the colours of the fibres
found embedded in Helen Palmer's wrists.

'Right, you two, come with me,' he said, already hurrying through the door.

* * *

'Mark, what are you doing? Stop it.'

He was running the still-closed Stanley knife over her face and down towards her torso. 'I'm going to cut you,' he said, his tone matter-of-fact.

And then she realised. God, how could she have been so bloody stupid? She had fallen in love, been willing to sacrifice everything — her career, her past bonds — for a killer. But everything had been perfect. *He* had been perfect. Even the enormity of her present situation was pushed to the edge of her mind while Holly struggled to come to terms with such awful reality.

'But I loved you, Mark.' The whine in her voice made her sick to her stomach.

He gazed at her with genuine concern. 'I'm sorry, Holly, I really liked you. But there was never any future for us. You're a Gemini.'

She frowned, searched his face for the merest hint of humour. 'What . . . ? I don't . . .'

'You're a Gemini — the same sign as my wife. Those women I killed . . . I was killing her. I didn't want to hurt them, any more than I want to hurt you . . . I was killing her.'

'Mark, what are you saying?' she yelled, pulling at her bonds.

'When I kill you, Holly, I'll be killing her — it's nothing personal. My wife has got two sides to her — the Gemini twins. There's the nice one who promises everything, paradise . . . And then the other one takes over, the one who makes my life a living hell, takes everything from me. Takes *everything* . . .' He held the Stanley knife like a dagger and aimed it at the pillow, just inches from Holly's face.

'But, Mark, I'm not your wife. It's me . . . Holly. We're so good together. You said yourself we make a great team.' She was pleading for her life.

He frowned, gave her a look which said she was a half-wit. 'I know who you are, Holly. But I couldn't kill my wife, could I? Her disappearance would cause too many questions. Whereas nobody knows I'm here with you, nobody's seen me. Somebody came to the door earlier, but I didn't answer it. So, I can kill you and get away with it because nobody knows I'm here.'

Holly felt it was important to keep him talking. 'You didn't twist your ankle, then?'

'No.' He gave an apologetic shrug. 'Sorry, but I had to have a reason not to go out.'

He sat beside her, facing the foot of the bed. Straight away, Holly went to work on the twine.

'Why couldn't you have been the other twin?'

'What?'

He half-turned towards her. 'Why couldn't you have promised me paradise?'

'But I did, Mark. I still do. I love you.' Her arm was complaining again, the pain creeping into her shoulder, but Holly managed to keep the effort from her voice.

'No, you *didn't*.' He sprang from the bed and wandered across to the window, stood staring out to sea. 'You made my life a misery . . . just like she does. It was all, leave your wife, Mark, or piss off. And when I did — oh, Mark, I'm sorry, please come back . . .' He rushed back to the bed and glared at her. 'Piss off, come back, piss off, come back . . . You call that *paradise*?' He turned away, as if sickened by the sight of her.

The last of the strands was almost apart, and Holly grew bolder. 'You'll never get away with it. They'll work out you were here with me. The other girls — you hardly knew them, you paid them. I bet they didn't even know your name.'

'I'll get away with it, I've worked it all out. They won't break my alibi. I'm sorry, Holly, I really did like you.'

The blade of the Stanley knife flicked out, glinting silver in the light.

And then the twine fell away.

Mark's expression changed so swiftly; in the space of a second his features hardened, his eyes told of anticipated pleasure. He was kneeling on the bed by her side. Suddenly, violently, he grabbed a handful of her hair and yanked her head towards him. The blade was edging ever closer to her scalp when Holly brought up her fist and smashed it into Mark's face. He howled out a protest as she worked her way around the bed and, with a blood-curdling cry, gave him a hefty kick in the chest.

The force of the blow knocked him backwards, his look of surprise almost comical. He dropped the Stanley knife on the bed and went crashing into the wall. While he sank to the floor, his eyes registering shock, Holly made a grab for the knife, her fingers curling around the plastic handle.

* * *

Ashworth showed little regard for the speed limit as he pushed the Scorpio across Bridgetown. Josh was in the passenger seat, watching the needle of the speedometer hovering around fifty in a thirty miles an hour zone.

'Guv, don't you think you should ease off the throttle? We're only going to see some of Donald Quinn's friends.'

Ashworth did not answer, merely pushed the gear lever into third and took a corner at thirty. On the back seat, Bobby frowned.

'Hold on a minute, this is where Mark lives. Guv, you're going to drop him right in it, if you're not careful.'

'Listen, bear with me,' Ashworth growled. 'We may be too late already, but if we're not we haven't got much time.' He brought the car to a halt outside one of the semi-detached houses, blocking the drive where a Volkswagen Estate was parked.

'But what are we doing here?' Bobby protested. 'Mark couldn't have anything to do with the murders.'

Ashworth swivelled round. 'Look, son, you're not the only one who can work things out. We have a serial killer who hates Geminis, which means he's motivated by star signs . . .'

'Yes, but—'

'And he always dumps the bodies in water. Why do you think that is? Could his be one of the water signs? Could he be a Cancerian . . . like Mark Hartland?'

Bobby's eyes widened. 'Are you sure, guv?'

'Of course I am. His birthday's on ninth July — that's Cancer, isn't it?' He shook his head ruefully. 'At first I thought I was getting paranoid. I mean, wondering about one of my own staff . . . But Mark spends much of his day in the collator's office, does he not? So he'd have access to the string they use to tie up the files . . . grey and white string. My God, I just hope I'm right. Tracking a killer by his star sign is too ludicrous, but it all fits. Doesn't it?' He flung open the car door. 'Come on, let's get on with it.'

Ashworth skirted around the Volkswagen and hammered on the front door. It was opened almost immediately by a tall, thin woman, her dark hair closely cropped. The hairstyle and her almost anorexic look gave her a hard, masculine appearance. Ashworth sensed an intense anger within her the moment they locked eyes.

'What do you want?' she demanded, peering past them. 'And you'd better move that car. I'll be wanting to back out of the drive in a few minutes.'

'Mrs Hartland?' Ashworth asked.

She nodded and heaved two bulging suitcases onto the threshold.

'I'm Chief Inspector Ashworth . . .' He produced his warrant card. 'We're looking for your husband. It's imperative that we find him.'

She shot him a scornful glance. 'You'll find him with his latest girlfriend — that little tart from your CID office.'

'Do you know exactly where they are?'

'Yes, I do, as a matter of fact.' She went back into the hall for her coat.

Ashworth bristled at her insolent tone. 'Mrs Hartland, it's important that we don't waste a minute. Now, if you don't give me the information, right now, I'll take you to the station and damn well drag it out of you.'

The woman threw her coat across the suitcases and confronted Ashworth with her teeth bared. 'All right, Chief Inspector, I'll tell you. I followed them — at a safe distance, of course — and I watched that bitch, Holly Bedford, while she walked on the beach. She looked so happy, without a care in the world. But then she would, wouldn't she? — having no doubt spent the previous hour in the arms of my lousy bastard of a husband. I was going to have it out with her, there and then, but I didn't . . . I couldn't.' She paused, tried to calm her emotions. 'I walked around for a while — I was so angry . . . Then, later, I knocked on the cottage door but nobody answered. Too busy screwing, I shouldn't wonder.' She gave a derisive laugh. 'And that's when I made up my mind to leave him for good. Which, as you can see, is what I'm doing now.'

'But where exactly are they?' Ashworth pressed. 'Where's the cottage?'

'My, my, you are keen to find him.' Her expression hardened. 'They're on the east coast. A very remote spot, Chief Inspector, very picturesque. The perfect place for a clandestine affair. I can give you the exact address.'

She pulled on her coat and Ashworth noticed for the first time that it was a white, full-length mackintosh. His heartbeat quickened.

'Are you normally in the habit of wearing a man's rain-coat, Mrs Hartland?'

'It's Mark's,' she said, shrugging. 'I used to borrow it occasionally, but now I'm taking it with me . . . along with a lot of other things. That bastard owes me.'

* * *

Holly took her eyes off him for just a second so she could cut the twine that held her left wrist to the bed. But a second was all Mark needed to leap on to her back, his hands closing quickly around her throat. He squeezed hard, harder, until she could scarcely breathe, but then her hand was free.

To hell with using only the necessary amount of force. She was fighting for her life, and she knew it. Acting swiftly, Holly brought up the Stanley knife and plunged the stout blade into his right side. He uttered a squeal, more from shock than pain, while his grip on her throat lessened. Air rushed into her lungs, but rather than giving her added strength the rush of oxygen caused her head to spin. For a moment her eyes refused to focus and she dropped the knife. Yet Holly was far from beaten. Bringing up both arms she knocked Mark's hands away from her throat then spun round and smashed her forehead into his face, sending him staggering and cursing towards the window.

She needed to get away and, keeping her eyes on him, she rushed to the door, slamming it behind her before skidding to a stop. The child's safety gate was closed and bolted. Mark was obviously taking no chances. Fearful that she would break her neck if she tried to vault over it, Holly veered left, knowing even as she did so that it was a mistake. She was going deeper into the cottage instead of getting away from it.

Too late now. A staircase loomed ahead, leading to the second floor. Without breaking her stride she took the stairs two at a time, her bare feet making little sound. The staircase spiralled round and Holly found herself on a tiny landing, a black door in front of her. It opened on to an attic room filled with a lifetime's junk. An old rocking horse shared space with huge tea chests packed one on top of the other. A child's cot and an old-fashioned pram stood precariously atop an ancient bedstead, its intricate ironwork bent and rusted.

Holly closed the door and threw home the bolts fixed to it at top and bottom. Relieved, she stood stock still, listening for any sounds other than her own breathing. The silence made her flesh crawl. Perhaps Mark would think she had gone over the safety gate and out of the cottage — which is exactly what she should have done, she chided herself. But it was too late for such thoughts. She must concentrate on here and now. He might not search the rest of the cottage. He might even be too injured to search anywhere — she did give him a good bang on the head.

She looked around. There was one tiny window, the light almost completely blocked out by that beautiful wisteria she had marvelled at only hours earlier. If it came to it she would have to smash the glass and climb down the wizened old branches. But not just yet. If Mark thought she'd left the cottage he might be out there searching around. She would lie low for a while. Lie low, and hope for inspiration. Sinking to her haunches, naked and vulnerable, Holly began the long wait.

* * *

Ashworth brought all of his considerable driving skills to bear as he drove at breakneck speed along the labyrinth of narrow lanes that made up that particular part of Norfolk. Josh's lips moved in silent prayer whenever a new bend approached, expecting to see at any time an oncoming vehicle smash into the Scorpio's bonnet. Bobby, however, sat nonplussed in the back, watching the flat golden fields whiz past.

They had done all they could, far more than was within their jurisdiction. They had radioed ahead and reported that one of their officers might be in trouble. Ashworth would give few details, feeling that to witter on about star signs might be counterproductive.

'We're acting on information received,' was all he would say.

The responding officer had listened respectfully, but could only offer to send a beat bobby to call at the cottage and ask if everything was all right. An eye could be kept on the place, but other than that there was little he could do. Ashworth had thanked him grudgingly, and now sat scowling at the windscreen.

'How much further?' he asked.

Josh looked at the map. 'Forty-odd miles, guv.'

* * *

It was impossible for Holly to tell how long she had been crouched in that attic. It could have been thirty minutes, even an hour. What little light there was had dwindled pretty quickly, and the air was a few degrees cooler, but day and dusk were as one in that cluttered dusty room.

There had been not the slightest sound from beyond the door, no creaking floorboards, no footfalls on the narrow stairs, and therefore Holly's confidence was making a tentative return. She knew she would have to move soon; she couldn't stay there for ever. She would freeze to death, for one thing. Not for the first time Holly wished she had grabbed her bathrobe during that sprint from the bedroom.

And where was Mark? If he was still in the cottage, he would make himself heard soon surely? All at once she decided to move. She would take the battle to him — all of this hanging around was doing her no good at all. Taking in a long breath to steady herself, Holly picked a path between the jumble and was pressing an ear to the door when the sturdy wood shook and vibrated, its bolts rattling violently. Holly was thrown backwards; she staggered and collided with the rocking horse, sending it see-sawing on its rickety base. And before she had time to wonder at the cause of the disturbance another heavy blow connected. This time the wood splintered and tiny shards of it flew around the attic.

Holly turned terror-filled eyes to the hole that now dominated the upper left panel. And in that dull half-light she saw clearly every tiny detail of the black metallic axe that poked through it, saw the silver swath of its sharply honed edge in the second or two before it was withdrawn. And when the hulking weapon attacked the door for a third time, removing the panel completely, all control deserted her and Holly started to scream.

CHAPTER 38

One look at the open cottage door had Ashworth clambering from the car, almost pitching forward in his haste. Josh and Bobby followed closely, both silent, neither of them willing to give voice to their fears.

There was no sign of movement within the cottage, and a quick check around the ground floor confirmed that all rooms were empty. Ashworth's size twelve shoes were soon beating a tattoo on the stairs.

'In here,' he called from the master bedroom. 'There's blood on the carpet. And there's some on the bed, as well.' It was then that he spotted the Stanley knife. He pointed it out when they rushed through the door.

'No Holly?' Josh was almost too afraid to ask.

'No Holly,' Ashworth echoed dully, as he stared out of the window to the sea.

'Hi, guys.'

That all-too-familiar voice had them spinning round in an instant. Holly was standing in the doorway. She was cool, relaxed, dressed for a lazy day on the beach.

Ashworth looked as if he had seen a ghost. 'Are you all right?'

'Yeh, fine.' She gave a little shrug. 'No sweat.'

'But . . . what's been happening here?' He pointed to the bloodstains. 'And where's Mark Hartland?'

'In hospital,' she said, her accompanying laugh rather forced. 'First he came at me with a Stanley knife, then he tried to strangle me, and last but by no means least, he had a go at taking my head off with an axe. It was around that time I finally got mad.' She spoke with all her usual verve and sparkle, but they noticed that her eyes were dull and dazed. 'He's not badly hurt, guv: broken arm, cracked ribs, some superficial cuts and bruises . . . Minimum possible force used, as they say.'

'But why are you still here, Holly? Why is nobody looking after you?'

She snorted. 'Things around here aren't quite the same as in Bridgetown. The local copper sent for an ambulance and a police guard for the hospital. Then I was told to wait here till some of the big guns arrived from police headquarters — and that's what I'm doing. He's outside somewhere, having a scout round.'

'You sure you're all right?' Bobby ventured.

'Like I said, no sweat. I just need some space for half an hour.' She handed Ashworth her notebook. 'I've written it all up.'

They were silent while she hurried down the stairs, and when the front door slammed Josh went to follow.

'Leave her,' Ashworth ordered. 'You heard her; she needs some time by herself. Holly's got to sort herself out, now. Nobody else can do it for her.'

But Josh shook his head. 'No way, guv, I'm going after her.'

* * *

From the path Josh watched her run on to the beach. She looked fragile, defenceless; a woman deceived, dressed for a holiday that never was. The light was fading fast, lending a grey tint to the sandy beach, to the gentle incoming tide, and that greyness seemed suddenly apt.

Josh held back. How best to play this? Holly wouldn't appreciate the sympathetic touch; she was too tough for that. She would be filled with pain right now, but like a wounded tiger she would show her claws to anyone who offered her help. For so many years Holly's sole aim in life had been to prove that she could cope, and not even a murder attempt would change that. Even so, she *did* need help. Crying into her pillow wouldn't be enough. Not this time. This time she needed someone to be there for her.

He followed her on to the beach, his soft brogues sinking into the damp sand. Holly heard him coming. Turning, she mouthed a curse and backed away. Josh slowed, oblivious to the frothy tide washing around his ankles.

'You all right, Bedford?'

'What do you want, Abraham? I said I needed time to myself.'

'Just thought I'd keep you company.'

'I don't want any company. Go on, piss off back to the others and have a good laugh about the latest mess I've got myself into.'

'Nobody's laughing, Hol, you know that.' He lifted his shoulders. 'We're worried about you, that's all.'

'Oh, Christ, don't give me that patronising bullshit. I don't need you to nursemaid me.'

'Drop the pride bit, Bedford, it's so bloody boring.'

His words stung her. She strode towards him, a finger pointed aggressively. 'Pride's all I've got left, Josh. All that's holding me together is knowing that every time the bastards knock me down, I'll just get right back up again.'

Josh made a grab for her shoulders, but she backed away. 'Let me through that brick wall you've built around yourself,' he shouted. 'For God's sake, Holly, I care about what happens to you.'

Just then a breaker came rolling in, sending him stumbling on to his knees. Wringing wet and livid, Josh jumped to his feet. Holly laughed.

'You do look a prat, Abraham.'

He grinned. 'You think this is funny? Okay, let's go for a dip.'

Before she could stop him Josh lunged forward and pulled her into the swelling shallows, not stopping until the water had reached their thighs. Holly shrieked; and then another huge breaker reared up and washed over them, the cold water drowning her laughter.

They stood close together, looking deep into each other's eyes. Suddenly, Holly was crying, her tears joining the sea water that ran in rivulets down her face.

She clung to him. 'I hurt, Josh. I just hurt so bloody much.'

He wrapped his arms around her, held her tight. 'Let it out, Holly. Come on, let it out.'

THE END

Thank you for reading this book.

If you enjoyed it please leave feedback on Amazon or Goodreads, and if there is anything we missed or you have a question about, then please get in touch. We appreciate you choosing our book.

Founded in 2014 in Shoreditch, London, we at Joffe Books pride ourselves on our history of innovative publishing. We were thrilled to be shortlisted for Independent Publisher of the Year at the British Book Awards.

www.joffebooks.com

We're very grateful to eagle-eyed readers who take the time to contact us. Please send any errors you find to corrections@joffebooks.com. We'll get them fixed ASAP.

Made in United States
North Haven, CT
11 November 2021

11048991R00157